THE HUSK

THE HUSK

BOB KOOB

abbott press

Abbott Press books may be ordered through booksellers or by contacting:

Abbott Press
1663 Liberty Drive
Bloomington, IN 47403
www.abbottpress.com
Phone: 1-866-697-5310

ISBN: 978-1-4582-1745-5 (sc)
ISBN: 978-1-4582-1747-9 (hc)
ISBN: 978-1-4582-1746-2 (e)

Library of Congress Control Number: 2014913663

Printed in the United States of America.

Abbott Press rev. date: 07/29/2014

To my grandfather,

EDWARD JENNINGS

CHAPTER 1

Alcohol and Coffee

B efore the shadows felt hostile, Nathan found a comfort in them, like a breath of fresh air before a dicey dive. Rotor, New Jersey, wasn't so different from the port town of Silverhill. Looking at it one way, the street sounded like a metallic ocean, and the neon lights imitated boardwalk activities. There was hardly a difference in the sky. Hidden inside, the world sounded like a robotic version of his hometown.

Days went on uneventfully in Rotor for years until Keria called. Nathan answered, assuming it was another recorded message from some cable company.

"Hello?"

"Nathan? God, I haven't heard your voice in a long time."

"Keria? Why are you—"

"I found an opening for that job you've always wanted. As soon as I heard our winery was officially running, you came to mind."

"How was your mother able to afford the land?"

"Not sure. But who cares? Are you coming back? It has to be soon."

Working at a winery was Nathan's dream job. Owning one was really, but he could have the next best thing.

But to return to Silverhill? he thought.

"I...I don't know..."

"It's okay. Just let me know by the end of the week," she said. "How are you by the way?"

Nathan peered at the empty bottles beside him. "Okay."

"Well, that's good. I hope to see you soon."

The conversation was brief. Nathan felt guilty. He stared at the old-fashioned phone, only to return to his recliner. Over the television's yammering, Nathan reheard Keria's voice, as if his mind could not believe the Miles had their own winery. *It's official.*

There was no going back. *No. Not even for a dream.* For now, the closest thing to Keria was a phone number tacked to the kitchen wall. Nathan took a shot of Four Roses and sat his head against the red fabric of his recliner. But even still, with that choice of no return, Keria's voice echoed through the night, past the preaching of late night-programming and city noise, as if it were its own voice.

Two days passed since the phone call, making tomorrow the deadline for an answer. Storm clouds coated the sun, but to waste gas for Net Smart, Nathan's job, a place just down the street, wasn't worth it. He would walk, rain or no rain.

Nathan threw on old work clothes and dragged himself out into the hallway where Doge, the near homeless guy who lived in the room beside the staircase, was lurking.

He hollered, "Hey, Nathan, where ya' goin'!"

"Work!" Nathan replied, irritated.

Outside, two basketball players cavorted in their poorly chalked basketball court. They were too loud and active for the time of day in Nathan's opinion, but the two fools were always there. Being bothered by these junkies had subsided a little. Besides, they sold him painkillers really cheap, and the prescription matched.

"Hey hey! It's warehouse boy!" the taller of these clowns hollered.

Nathan raised one hand. "Yeah, and he's on his way to help make the world a better place."

The taller one, Deon Howard, was also the brighter of the two. Ironically, his sidekick, Klevon Dixon, handled the drugs.

"Nice, dawg. Nice. I like that. You funny!" He laughed.

What Nathan couldn't understand about the two basketball players was how ecstatic they were. From what Nathan knew, Deon's mother was murdered during a home invasion, and though Klevon wasn't nearly as outgoing, he too had a more positive outlook on life than, to Nathan, should exist. A policeman shot and killed Klevon's father during an armed robbery, and his mother's death was never explained, something Nathan could relate to.

It started raining when Nathan made it halfway through the alley. The storm only made the dark atmosphere drearier, soaking the city's unclean materials. Smoke from dryer vents puffed into his face. It smelled good, like sniffing a clean bed. It was better than the alley's actual scents.

As Nathan approached Net Smart, he glared at its neon letters, flashing in the hazy mist not far ahead. A slick red Honda that zoomed down the street nearly hit him. Lights didn't distract the driver. In this city, if a car like that was in sight, odds are, one was a target. The Honda clearly belonged to a rich kid, driving in Rotor to show off.

Net Smart sold computer parts, and Nathan sorted out the shipments. But as usual, the boss, Maxwell, wasn't in today. The guy practically lived on a Caribbean beach.

"Maxwell left for his beach house," said Amber, a curvy young woman with blonde hair who was easy on the eyes.

"Is that why no one's here?" Nathan asked.

"Yeah," said Chris, a large guy who towered over every worker.

At the moment, Chris enjoyed towering over Amber's breasts. The nerdy guy, Donny, was here as well, standing by the coffee machine. Nathan lollygagged to the machine, planning on socializing with the only Maxwell he cared about, Maxwell House, Nathan's favorite coffee brand.

"Mr. Ruiz," Donny said in a proper manner, "you're not looking well."

"Care to explain why?" Nathan pulled out a plastic cup with one hand and the coffee pot with the other.

Donny went quiet.

Working in the back required no uniform, and being alone felt relieving. The usual shift of lifting heavy computer parts carried on for a minor ten minutes before muffled shouting came from the office. At first, Nathan thought nothing of the shouting, but once the gunshots went off, that idea he had about Amber starting fights again migrated to something darker. Nathan hid behind a Dumpster beneath the loading dock, listening to the rain hammer the tin roof above.

The source of the gunshots came into view. Three overly tan, rich Jersey kids wearing black peacoats stood beneath the tin roof.

"I think we got 'em all," said the guy with the golden ring that practically cloaked his pinky finger.

"You think so?" The man wearing black leather gloves gestured like a child hyped up on candy.

All three moved with jittery anticipation.

"Eeeyeah, I think," replied the one nearest to the Dumpster.

Nathan was most concerned with him.

"All right, all right. Let's get back inside. We gotta remove the bodies, burn the place, and get back home."

Burn the place? Nathan thought. *Why even bother coming here?*

The goons reentered Net Smart. Nathan left his hiding place and sneaked around the building to the front. A red Honda was poorly parked by the door, the entrance, done so to show who was in charge. Then a thought hit Nathan like a burst of winter's wind. *That's the same car that nearly killed me.*

Nathan watched as his fellow employees were thrown onto the sidewalk. The guys who weren't tossing bodies poured gasoline over every object and floorboard in the building. *The asshole wasn't kidding. The plan really was to burn the place. And they're smiling about it.*

Making matters worse, one of these clowns held a checklist, and he appeared to be puzzled. "Uh-oh! Hold on! We're missin' someone!"

"Who's that?" One of the men brushed his hands together.

"A Nathan Ruiz."

"Nathan Ruiz? I'll have a group search for 'im."

"Make it quick. We got a pay to collect. Am I right?"

"Yeah, baby, I got things to do!"

"I ain't gonna let this Ruiz dent our pay. We have to find 'im." Someone else walked out of the building with an empty gasoline can.

"All right, you jokers. All of you, look for him," said the man with the list.

The motive for this carnage wasn't clear, but Nathan knew there was nowhere else to go but home. He had to get Keria's number off the kitchen wall and drive his 1992 Audi S4 to Rocky Sky, a motel ten miles away from town. He was most familiar with it, and better yet, he knew the man who owned its shitty beds and outdated televisions.

Water flowed down the barren streets and trashy alleyways of the tiny city, turning it into a strange sort of overgrown fountain. Nathan's luck ran out when another Honda drove by. Of course, he may have blended in if people were walking. *Damn, were the sidewalks empty today.*

The vehicle drove in reverse. The window rolled down, and the passenger asked, "You Nathan?"

"I dunno any Nathan. My name's Nelson."

The goon grinned and turned to face the driver who snickered. "Doesn't matter who you are, pal. I got orders."

"That's cute," Nathan said. "But I got one thing to ask you."

"Yeah, what's that?"

Nathan made a startled gesture and looked at the road in front of the car. He turned his attention back to the thug, who was now looking where Nathan glanced, and slammed his head into the window frame.

The Honda's driver swerved the car in surprise as the goon beside him, with blood now oozing from his nostrils, hollered, "Get that piece of shit! No one fucks with me!"

Nathan ran into the nearest alley, shocked by the success of his last-minute trick. His apartment was only six minutes away. Luck could run both ways with that distance. He had to be fast and remember not to rely on the cops. Any dependence on them in Rotor would put one in a morgue. One's toe would be decorated with a pretty tag, displaying one's name among the others who once depended on something.

He made it inside, again running into Doge. Nathan patted him on his right shoulder. "Come on, Doge. Get up. Go hide in your apartment."

"But I can't, you see, that noise by my window. It wants me out."

5

Nathan shook his head weakly, looking confused. The goons would surely be here. Doge wouldn't make it, and Nathan felt responsible for his safety. After all, he was guiding murderers. Nathan took Doge by the shoulders and dragged him into his room. At least the door was open.

"Stay in here. You got me?"

Doge mumbled something too soft to hear and closed his eyes. Nathan shut the door on his way out.

Nathan's apartment wouldn't be missed. The room sat in a melancholy glow that leaked through the blinds, fueled by the storm. A black bag inside the closet would be enough for the trip. Nathan gathered his supplies, most of it necessary.

The room smelled musty, and hell, there was a good chance the air was hazardous. Nathan treaded through the clutter and entered the kitchen after packing. Time wasn't plentiful. He had to move. He saw the wrinkled piece of paper on the wall and gently removed it. But something caught his eye. Fire was swirling upward into the foggy skyline like dancing fireworks. The pricks didn't simply burn Net Smart. They made a show of it.

Oh, look! something shiny. Maybe they'll let me go and figure not to bother continuing their search and watch the building burn. Wrong!

"All right! I want at least two people around every corner. Nathan is mine. You hear me! You want that fucking money, huh, do ya? Then let's find that motherfucker!"

Whoever this was appeared to be some kind of boss, the leader of the crew responsible for the fall of Net Smart. Or he was the manager. The men willing to perform this job were puppets of the higher power of whatever shameless mob they belonged to. The goons ran up the staircase like a group of children mimicking a SEAL team.

Nathan, among other activities, used to kill time at the shooting range. He had a .40 caliber somewhere. In the nick of time, he spotted the damn thing buried under clothing toward the far left corner of the room.

A flickering fluorescent tube by the left staircase revealed a dying man from the otherwise dark portion of the building. Nathan kept low. His backpack nearly choked him. His hands were nervously glued to his gun.

The man whimpered in the half-cut light. "Hello?"

The man yelped. "Be quiet. Who are you?"

"I'm not saying. Fucking assholes! Shooting and running over people! I don't trust no one!"

"Makes two of us," Nathan replied.

"Please, I'm fine, just…fine. I can't be out there, ya know, man? Too much chaos!"

"I get it." Nathan inched his way down the first few steps. "Go hide somewhere. Expect guests."

On the first floor, rats scampered by the office desk. They discovered the watch guard's misplaced lunch. *How long as he been gone?* The decision to that question came with a cold touch of steel. *Likely not long.*

"Put it up!"

"Wha—"

"I said put 'em up!"

Nathan raised his hands, feeling the muzzle press onto his skin. "Take it easy. Let's talk."

"There's no talking here, wise guy."

"Why are you after me? What the hell did I do?"

"You work for Maxwell, right? That's what's you've done."

"Why does it matter? It's not like I liked the guy."

"It doesn't matter. You worked for 'im. That's enough."

The kid's tan was professional. Skin cancer was well underway for this sorry gyp.

"It's not adding up to me." Nathan tried to keep his cool. "Do you guys realize Maxwell isn't here?"

"Fucker's run off. We know."

"What did he do? He must have known you were coming."

"Fellas, get down here. I got 'im!"

"Just tell me. What the fuck have you got to lose?"

"All right, all right. Your boss killed someone. Yeah, killed someone our boss loved. He and everything he owned must be killed or burned."

"Owned? That piece of shit never owned me."

The goon snickered. "Sure, sure. Don't worry. I'll put you out of your misery."

Bam! The instant the man adjusted his hand, his head was blown off. Who were the guardian angels? It was none other than Deon and Klevon.

"Close call, homie," Deon said.

"Thanks," Nathan replied weakly.

"Know that guy?" Klevon asked.

"No, but he sure knew me." Nathan coughed.

"You okay?" Deon asked.

"I owe ya. Thanks. If shit weren't hitting the fan, I'd buy you both drinks."

"Naw, don't be like that. We neighbors." Deon tapped his chest with his hand curled into a fist.

More like dealers.

"Good luck," said Klevon.

The two were off. Nathan got to thinking the worst was over. His Audi was in sight, and there was still no sign of the others. Then they were everywhere, like a swarm of bees guarding their nest, only they flew into the wrong hive, a city where guns were as common as candy in a candy store.

Their response to gunshots is to come toward the noise without any second-guessing and/or no other agenda but to start shooting whoever they don't recognize. Nathan followed his gut feeling and bided his time in the shadows near the parking lot. However, one guy strayed away from his group. He was too close to the car. Again, Nathan felt his hands stick to his gun. The man waltzed closer, grinning. *Does he know I'm here?*

"Never would I ever," the guy muttered.

He tossed a cigarette to the side and huffed. Faint thunder aroused. The goon looked up at the dreary storm. Heavy raindrops splashed him in the eyes.

"Ah, fuck." He wiped his eyes. "Need a roof."

Thanks to the rain, Nathan got his chance to canter across the lot. He started questioning himself after placing the bag on the passenger seat. *Is ten miles enough? Does Keria really want me back?* He started the engine. *After all this time, she still cares?*

He placed his foot on the pedal. He looked back and drove in reverse.

He shifted gears and drove out onto the street. The windshield wipers kept the rain at bay. The storm worsened. *What about the others? What will they think or do if they see me...when they see me?*

Rocky Sky sat under the afternoon sun. Nathan called Keria and went over his plans for the long trip. By nightfall, he glanced into the bathroom mirror long enough to memorize his face's every flaw. His face nearly imitated his father's, only he had a darker tint to his skin. Still, the Irish look bled through, far more than his German. He had black hair and kept it a tad lengthier than short with hardly a style. And as of now, he had scruffy facial hair.

He got no rest that night.

CHAPTER 2

A Vague Chimera

The scenery during the ride gradually evoked feelings, both sweet and sour. The more familiar places got, the more sour the feelings became, and dread would surely follow. But not entirely. Instead of dread, confusion got its whack. Keria gave Nathan instructions, and as it had been many years since living in Silverhill, Nathan forgot every turn and exit. But this route passed Silverhill. The road led him into a more populated port town that never existed before.

Nathan stepped out of his Audi just outside the new town. The morning light beat on his clean hair and shaven face. He wore casual grey pants and a black, fitted plaid shirt. *A clean look. Are you proud?*

The landscape was naturally haunting with its ocean's dark swirling waters, clasping the rocks of the cliff and shorelines. The ocean breeze was continuous, seasoning Nathan's face with salty air. He admired the view as the lighthouse was still in sight. Its appearance remained the same, skinny and tall with black spiral stripes. Black Bell, the mine, sat obscured on the other end of the cliff.

Footsteps came from behind, and by instinct, Nathan turned around, ready to defend himself. His defensives, however, were soon broken. Keria hugged him tightly and securely.

"Talk about waiting 'til the last minute," she said morbidly.

Nathan took a step back after the hug, allowing Keria to meet him eye to eye. "It's not that I didn't want to come back. I just couldn't."

Keria allowed her eyes to drop before saying, "Well, come on. Let's go get some coffee."

You took the words right out of my mouth, he thought.

Moonlight Diner was located by a tiny beach. Nathan and Keria sat toward the back on a cozy, red sofa-like chair that reminded Nathan of a 1950s restaurant. The window beside them was large, revealing a good chuck of the street and sidewalk, as well as the people who used it.

As Nathan sipped his coffee Keria asked, "What have you been up to all these years?"

"Hard to say," Nathan replied. "You know where I lived."

Keria smiled weakly. "Yeah, but you're not like those people. You can't seriously expect me to think you lived like them."

"Well," Nathan said, allowing an unsettling silence creep in, "you're right about that. I didn't live like them." He then thought, *Can't say that's really much of a lie, depending on how you look at things.*

Nathan took his time, peering back to second-guessing for what he should say and what was better left unspoken. "I found the people like me, stuck with them. Avoiding all the others. It worked out."

"I sure hope so."

Nathan studied Keria's features, the ones he may have missed when first arriving. Her eyes were minty green, and her skin had a little tan. She wore a sun crest flannel over a white T-shirt and tight jeans. She had a cute face, one that was thin but lively, just like the rest of her body. She began playing with the saltshaker, nervously swaying it back and forth between her hands.

"So what about you? I see an entire port town has been built since I've been gone."

"Been okay. Can't complain much. And as for the new town, some new inspiring miners checked out Black Bell and, to everyone's surprise, found gold."

Nathan's eyes widened. He hardly believed or understood. "They did?" Nathan replied loudly.

"Um, yes. They funded the new town with the extra earnings."

"What about now? Are they still mining?"

Keria shook her head. "Nah, it's been closed for two years now."

Someone decided to use the jukebox across the room. The damn thing was louder than a parade full of air horns. Keria began saying something again, but her voice was too soft to hear.

"Why is that fucking thing so loud?" Nathan hollered.

Everyone heard him. Keria only laughed, while the man responsible for turning on the jukebox wandered off to hide up front.

Once the blistering noise was gone, Keria could speak and be heard. "I was trying to say the mine ran out of gold, but we got more than we needed. It's shocking that money went to remodeling. In Rotor, that money would have stayed in somebody's pocket or spent at a strip club." Keria laughed, but her amusement didn't last. Something seemed to be off about her, and Nathan was beginning to worry. "I guess I should start talking about the winery."

"Eh, work can wait." Nathan finished his coffee. "After all, I just got here. I think I need some understanding of this new town, like its name, people, and events."

"Not many events." Keria laughed. "But the name is interesting. It's Hollow Heights."

Hollow Heights? The new Silverhill or simply another piece of it? he thought. "Huh, not a bad name," Nathan finally said.

"Yeah, I like it. One of the miners came up with it. But the people are pretty much the same as anywhere else. If you could deal with Rotor's, you can cope with Hollow Heights."

"I guess, but I'm sure there's more people I should know about before I meet them." Nathan leaned forward, overlapping his hands on the overly textured table. He laughed. "Well, okay. My father isn't a fan of you."

"No?"

"Nope."

"Why is that?"

"As soon as he heard you lived in Rotor, he immediately disregarded you. It's just the way he is."

"Okay. Anyone else?"

Keria placed her right arm on the table and began leaning on it, staring into Nathan almost mockingly. "Yes, there are others."

"Like?"

Keria smiled. "Liz, my friend. I think she likes you. But keep your distance from her. She's known to play around. Believe me. I know her like an open book. Just the other day, she had a one-night stand with some guy she barely knew."

"You showed her my picture, didn't you? All right then," Nathan said. "Who else?"

Keria's pleasant facial expression quickly changed, a common thing of her that Nathan began to understand. "Lots of people like her are here. Just avoid them all." Nathan returned a serious expression, ensuring Keria he was listening. After doing so, her face eased a little. "Good, now let's talk about work."

The planting was finished shortly before Nathan's arrival. Keria began explaining what her family did and where they planted the grapevines. "Right by the beach!" Keria exclaimed.

"Not a bad spot. Though how far is that from our houses?"

"Not far, but you don't really need to worry about picking anything. You said you worked in a warehouse, right? Moving shipments and stuff?"

"Yeah," Nathan replied in a frail tone.

Keria finally took a sip of her coffee and nodded. "I was hoping you'd handle the shipments."

For a while, Nathan could not recall how Keria knew he was a warehouse worker, but he remembered he told her years ago during a late-night chat, like the picture he sent her. *There really was a use for things like Instagram and Facebook. Who knew?*

"Sure thing, not a problem."

Breakfast was nice, actually fantastic. But the Moonlight Diner started welcoming all sorts of people in by ten. And some thought it was okay to use that jukebox. Talking became a struggle for anyone having a conversation.

"Guess we should head out!" Nathan shouted.

Keria smiled before standing up. "I had fun, but I guess you should get to unpacking. I'll guide you to your house and meet you at the winery at two," Keria said as they walked out of the diner.

"Yeah, time to start really settling in." Nathan looked at the Atlantic.

Nathan's house was a quarter mile up the road from the Moonlight Diner, almost in the outer edge of Hollow Heights. After parking in the tiny driveway, Nathan waved Keria good-bye and turned to meet the house. It was a nice place, charming in many ways. The roof wasn't special, but the side paneling was a smooth brown stone one would expect to see used as a walkway for a garden. There was a porch in the back, decorated with chimes and statues of animals, like foxes and dogs. And a few feet away from the porch stood a shed, one past its prime.

There wasn't much in the backyard, so Nathan entered the house through the back door after exploring. It felt like walking into an alien spacecraft with more room, a fancier phone, and better equipped kitchen appliances. The windows reminded Nathan of the Moonlight Diner, as they showcased the outside world in an almost overwhelming fashion. But something was missing, a coffeemaker.

Easy, he thought. *The house is freakin' paid for already! Perks of knowing the big guys!*

Examining the house left Nathan with a few thoughts. *What will happen to it? Will the charming porch remain charming or become a rotted piece of shit? Will the comforting living room's grey floor be littered in stains? And what of the rest of the house? Will I even bother to use it?* The attic, basement, and one room in the very back were extra.

A warm shower every day was possible. Nathan took a long one as the showers in Rocky Sky might have been better than his old apartment, but their warm water was very limited. The bathroom here was also nicer. Whoever decorated seemingly enjoyed lighthouses because miniature lighthouses stood everywhere and the towels were pictures of Silverhill's lighthouse.

Nathan hurried. The time was almost two o'clock. God forbid he was late on the first day. Apparently, Keria's father decided to take a first impression some time ago, so his second had to be a good one. He threw on a new shirt, one that was red and not black like his previous, and gathered his car and house keys. He sprayed on cologne and high-tailed it out of the house, dry as a bone.

Hollow Heights was a busy place. People were always outside, tending to their personal gardens, trying to be like the Miles family. Kids were playing games by the shoreline, similar to the ones Nathan and Keria cavorted in during their childhood, and the sun remained unclouded. But business looked painful.

Nathan took notice of Keria's father, nitpicking at everyone's flaws as if he or she were supplying the safety measurements for astronauts. He was a fat ass with brown hair who wore a black suit despite the heat.

"Ah hell," Nathan murmured. "Who is that?"

Nathan parked beside the winery. An alluring wooden sign hung above the left window by the front door. It read "The Miles Winery."

Keria was waiting outside, as eager as ever to see Nathan. "You're on time."

"Why wouldn't I be?" Nathan asked.

Keria gave an inward smile and nodded toward the fat man niggling at workers on the left field. "My father said you wouldn't get here 'til four."

"Ah, so that's your father." He then thought, *Here we go then.*

"Dad!" Keira waved him over.

After a fair wait, Keria's father made it to where they were standing. "Hey, it's the goon. I'm Neil Miles, Keria's father."

What a fucking asshole. Nathan shook Neil's hand, trying to suppress a sour smile and a loud "Fuck you!" from escaping his throat.

"It's...uh...nice to meet you," Nathan replied.

Neil laughed. "Yeah, well, I'll wait to say the same to you later. Now Keria," Neil said, turning to face his daughter, "have you finished planting all the seeds?"

"Yeah, days ago," she said.

"All right, good. Nathan, I take it you already know how the shipments will go?"

"Dad, he just arrived this morning!" Keria said in a loud, frustrated tone.

Damn was Neil unreasonable, Nathan thought. *How does someone like that become a manager, an owner of a business? This ass whip couldn't make a friend with a single soul, not even with his own daughter. Are good communication skills not required for the job?*

Nathan's mind raced as Keria talked with the bastard. Now was a good chance to examine his style, his annoying gestures. A classic Nathan already picked up on was his tie adjustment. He couldn't stop picking at it. Or maybe it was just the heat?

"Keria, listen. I know how to handle things, and in this step of the process, I have to be stern and to the point, and I cannot allow room for doubt. He must know everything about our shipment polices by tomorrow morning to ensure success. I'm sure Nathan would agree, right?" Neil now held his hands together, wore a smug smile, and met Nathan's eyes.

"Yeah," Nathan replied.

Neil was an easy read.

"I'll be sure to train him properly, Dad," Keria said mockingly.

Neil gave an unsettling stare, like he was unsure or maybe even worried, before walking away, back to the fields to bother more workers. "Come on. Let me show you the winery."

"All right. Lead the way."

Up the smooth stone stairs was the door to the building. Immediately after Keria opened the door, a strong burst of incense hit Nathan's senses.

"What is that?" he asked.

"It's Japanese incense!" Keria said happily. "It's Morning Star, without a doubt my favorite!"

Tia Miles, Keria's mother, walked out of a room beside the first set of wine racks. "Oh, is this Nathan?" she asked.

"Hello," Nathan said. "All grown up and still healthy I see. You got much taller, and your weight looks good! Of course, you were a child when I last laid eyes on you."

"Um, thank you. You're looking very healthy yourself." He then thought, *My health? Nice try.*

"I'm just showing him around," Keria said softly.

Tia's attitude was as sanguine as an angel's could be, but then again, this was only a first impression. The clothes she wore, a brightly colored polo shirt and jeans, helped support her outgoing personality. She was middle-aged, but her skin was quite young in appearance, like she was in her mid-thirties.

"The winery is still new to me." Tia chuckled. "So don't feel bad if you get lost. God knows I do from time to time."

"I'll be sure to keep that in mind," Nathan said.

Keria told her mother, "I'll meet you for dinner around six tonight. Nathan will join us."

Not that I knew this was coming 'til this moment, but hey, got to socialize, right? Nathan thought. To Keria, this was a big event while Nathan didn't feel so hot about the idea. Tia was nice. It was Neil he worried about. Wine wasn't a favorite of Nathan's, but he knew wine carried what he loved. But suddenly, Nathan realized he wasn't here to drink, but to work.

"Up these stairs is the second floor where most of the expensive wine is racked for sale." Keria was almost touching the fake vines that hung off the railing beside her.

"Nice. How expensive are we talking?"

Keria smiled lightly. "Not sure. You're not the only one who didn't complete their homework."

They both laughed before advancing up the stairs. Up here on the second floor, Nathan's red plaid shirt matched the painted walls.

"Bright red walls?" Nathan asked.

"Yup, I feel it sends the whole rich factor to the customers better than any other color...for wine that is."

The creativity was most impressive here. Not only were the walls especially painted and the fake vines most convincing, tiny lighthouses sat properly displayed by every wine rack. Not all these lighthouses were simple decorations.

Nathan picked one off a shelf. "Are these wine bottles?"

"Yes! You like that? I thought, 'Hey, why not make a bottle represent our own lighthouse?'"

"I take it this is the best wine you sell? Since it's so specially designed?" Nathan was still studying the bottle.

Overall, one could tell it was just a wine bottle after a second or third look. But the top was like the Silverhill lighthouse's lantern room. In gold letters on the body of the bottle, it read "Miles Wine."

"Ah, wait. I see. You guys made up your own wine," Nathan said.

"You got it!" Keria replied in glee.

Nathan placed the bottle back on the shelf. "I'll have to try it sometime. Where to next?"

Keria guided Nathan through every room of the winery. Tiny lights that hung from the ceiling on thin wires lit each area. Fake grapevines were tied around the wine racks and staircases, and every so often, Nathan spotted a few brown sofas.

"There's a back porch." Keria aligned her right index finger toward the open door that led to it. "People usually sit there and enjoy the view or free samples we offer."

"Very nice," Nathan replied civilly. "Mind if I have a look?"

"Go right ahead."

The porch was wide, using a sunroof as shelter. A couple sets of tables and plastic chairs were present, inhabiting both corners of the porch. A man was sitting on one of the steps toward the left. Keria had an unusual expression on her face.

"Who's that?" Nathan whispered.

"That's Jeff Jones. He's...how should I put this...a little over the top with his work than most."

"Over the top?"

"Yeah, let me show you. Hey, Jeff! Have you inspected the birdbath yet?"

Jeff spun around faster than the eye could see. "Oh, yes! Yes, I did! All lily pads, rocks, and bulrushes are in their proper place. Oh, I already polished the bath's exterior!"

Keria chuckled. "Okay, Jeff. Let's go, Nathan. Since we're out here, let me show you the grapevines."

Jeff might be good with his work, but he was the outcast, like Donny from Net Smart. Nathan just wanted to get away from the kid. He merely waved him good-bye when passing to the fields.

"What's his job?"

"He just tends to the little things, like the birdbath and the fountain that's up front."

"Well, the birdbath looks nice. Guess I'll check out that fountain sometime."

"Oh, please. It's just a fountain," Keria mumbled.

They made their way to the right field by the ocean. The grapevines were mature enough to grow fruit but were a bit disappointing with their growth. The right field was pretty much the trademark for the Miles Winery. Grapevines by a beach with a memorizing lighthouse not far off in the distance made for a good lure in.

Nathan started wondering if anyone remembered the mine on the other side of the cliff when Keria said, "The left field is less interesting, so I'm not gonna bother you with it." She spoke softly.

"Ah, no problem. I've seen enough."

"Um, about dinner…I'm sorry about that. I just—"

"It's okay. Good actually. I need to show your father what kind of man I really am, and over dinner is a fine try."

"Good," Keria replied heartily.

Nathan gave a quick nod. "Well, I'm going to leave and get ready. I'll see you where?"

"At my house! If that changes, I'll call you, okay?"

"Okay."

They both hugged before departing. Keria felt both fear and pleasure: fear because of her father and pleasure because of Nathan's take on her sudden invitation. But the big question both Nathan and Keria asked themselves was: How will I handle the actual event?

Changing clothes a third time in one day to look convincing seemed ridiculous, and it was. But if Nathan were to show a desire to improve Neil's take on him, then even the smallest things counted. A fresh dose of cologne was applied to Nathan's grey dress shirt and pants. He stared momentarily out the kitchen window and looked at the shed. Why? He didn't have a reason. It was one of those times when thinking gave the eyes no course, no GPS, so to speak. Neil troubled him more than anyone else at the given moment. Sure enough though, there would be others.

Nathan entered his Audi, confident he'd leave a positive impression in at least one way, when a loud thump came from a trash can beside the house. Nothing followed after it, but it was a fruitless search for the source. *Rats in the city, yeah. But here? Really?*

Nathan reached Keria's house in good timing. Only Neil was surprised.

"Welcome," Tia said with a warming smile. "Right this way."

No Morning Star gushed out of this building. Keria's creativity had restrictions.

The dinner was carefully prepared, and this triggered a positive memory in Nathan. He remembered how every so often his mother and father let him stay past dinnertime at Keria's old house. The food was satisfying if one enjoyed overly seasoned seafood. Today's menu was lobster tail and shrimp with a side of oysters. And yes, it was overly seasoned.

"So, Mr. Ruiz," Neil began to say.

Good start, Nathan thought.

"I take it you liked our seafood back in the day? Because unlike everything else, that hasn't changed."

"I do," Nathan replied.

"Well actually, that's not entirely true. We are having our family-made wine tonight."

"Ah, I get the chance to try the Miles Wine?"

"Yes, you do!" Keria said blithely.

The wine was satisfying but also null. The jolt of alcohol was too minor, but the taste was both sweet and original.

"Not bad," Nathan said.

"Not bad?" Neil asked. "Sip it again."

Nathan did as the fat man requested and shrugged his shoulders afterward. "I like it the second time, too."

Neil's reaction was priceless. Neil merely glanced at his family with distrust or dissatisfaction.

Nathan put on a puzzled face. "Something wrong?"

"No, no, just usually people rave about their first taste of our wine," Neil answered with a fake smile.

"Oh, I see. Well, let me be less vague. I've never had the pleasure in drinking such tasteful wine before. I'm just used to the harder stuff, and I haven't had wine in years."

Neil's bogus smile grew in life and suddenly became as real as life's most unmerciful troubles. "Ah, should have guessed that'd be the case with you, Nathan. I'm glad you enjoyed it."

Should keep some things quiet, Nathan thought.

"Well, anyway," Keria proclaimed. "How's your stay going?"

"Great. Only I might be having animal problems. I heard something mess with the trash cans. I need to find a way to keep them closed before I start throwing stuff in there."

"That's not hard. I'll go find some spare lids later tonight for the time being."

"Thanks."

At least Keria's trying to have a good chat, Nathan thought.

Sure, the wine was good, but the lobster and shrimp killed taste buds. Nathan swore the food sizzled in its own seasoning. But he wouldn't dare mention it. Keria was gulping it down. Bothering Neil was one thing, but Keria would take offense with the food. She always liked it for as long as Nathan could remember.

After Keria said she'd find spare trash can lids, Neil began talking about work. At that point, dinner got sluggish.

"All right, I got to head out. I'll see you in the shipment room, Mr. Ruiz. Good night, everyone." Neil dragged his large body out of the dining room.

He left Tia to clean the table and dishes, but Nathan insisted he stayed to help, and he did. Looking at it overall, the dinner improved Nathan's reputation with Keria's mother.

Once finished with the dishes, Tia thanked Nathan for his help. After he hugged Keria good-bye and left, Tia smiled at her daughter.

"What's with that look?" She blushed slightly.

"Good pick." Tia walked away.

Not long after settling in, the cuckoo clock chirped, allowing its little companion to continuously pop in and out of the timbered door above the time. This neat little feature to the house sat by the kitchen entrance, and Nathan never knew it was a cuckoo clock until after he got home from Keria's house. It was an unpleasant startling.

With the welcoming and tours to Hollow Heights finished and the old, disheveled sleeping clothes on, Nathan looked for his unfinished scotch. It was sticking out of the black bag that sat on the dining room table. Just because Keria left a warm feeling in Nathan's chest and he was no longer afraid of being shot through the window in an apartment room, it didn't mean he could stop drinking.

The good malts were short-lived. Nathan's mind wasn't quite lost but rather hazy. Noises came from the trash cans again. But the animal problem would have to wait. There was hardly a bother in chasing a sober raccoon or small animal when half cut.

After returning to the winery the following morning, Nathan noticed a maze off to the right of the store. During his first visit, he assumed this maze was a single hedge. After seeing it wasn't, he decided to check it out. The maze wasn't a challenging puzzle to walk through, but that was the idea. This was a playground for kids to use while their parents were testing wine.

In the center of this tiny maze was the fountain Keria mentioned to Nathan, and Jeff was present, intently working on the fountain.

"Hello," Nathan said.

Jeff, being a spaz, jolted up in a panic. "Shit! Never do that!"

Nathan gave an uncertain look, like a child's stare after he or she had been told that he or she had done something wrong.

Jeff turned back at the fountain. "Ruiz, shouldn't you be checking shipments? Wouldn't want to upset Neil already, hmm?"

"Depends," Nathan replied. "How's the fountain?"

"Top order. All details are polished and examined. Got to pay attention to all the details, Mr. Ruiz, or am I wrong?"

"All right. Well, you have fun with that." Nathan walked out of the childish maze.

The fountain was small, so diminutive that even Jeff's thin body hid a good portion of it.

"Pay attention to all the details, Mr. Ruiz!"

Yeah, sure, he thought. *Why not? It's not like there's an ocean full of them. I got this.*

Nathan entered the winery to see Tia at the cash register. "Hello, Mrs. Miles." He briefly held up his right hand.

"Oh, hello, Nathan! Neil will be here shortly. He's with a customer upstairs."

Nathan nodded and turned to meet the back entrance. The morning light poured in through the open doors, and the lights that hung above were dimmed down, almost off.

"Oh, I should tell you that Keria's away for the week. Neil asked her go to her grandmother's last night. She had to leave two hours ago. I don't want you thinking she just up and left on purpose or anything."

Nathan nodded in disappointment. *A whole week? How often will this happen?*

Once Neil came down, Nathan greeted him.

Neil replied, "Everything's in the backroom. Follow me."

The place where the supposed work he was told to file sat on a desk in a dingy room.

"What happened to the walls?"

"I hope this won't be a problem for you. We haven't had the time to repair everything."

"Right." Nathan did not hide his disbelief.

Neil left without a word.

This isn't the wine cellar. To hell with filing! Where's the wine?

The filing was easy, and when finished, Nathan returned to Neil, got the keys to the cellar, and began checking everything. The day was easy, apart from a few mistakes by whoever first moved the wine barrels. There was hardly a thing to do. The cellar wasn't unkempt or in a poor condition whatsoever. The cellar was a bit small, but nothing could trigger a claustrophobic reaction, more or less. The only problem was the poorly lit cellar.

And after a while, this had a bad effect on the eyes of anyone who spent a fair amount of time there. Nathan left as soon as the shift was over. *Hollow Heights has to have a bar. So why not look for one?*

There was a bar, two actually, but only one good one. The Sleeping Grizzly was its name. The bad bar was Clever Isle. Shortly after Nathan walked into the good bar, Nick Cave & the Bad Seed's "Up Jumped the

Devil" started playing. Grizzly's floor was made of uneven, dark wooden planks. Plenty of neon lights were flashing on the walls, reminding everyone there was enough beer to go around all night.

The long table was nearly empty. Nathan decided to sit on its end by the back and ordered a scotch, Red Label to be exact. Behind the table were rows of fancy shot glasses and a collection of beer steins. One stein was larger than the height of an average five-year-old. After Nathan received his drink, he got a little tap on his shoulder.

"David? Holy shit."

"Nice to see you, too."

David Brakes, an old friend whose thick, black hair was long enough to cover the tip of his ears, showed little change. Nathan envied his lean body, not that Nathan had much of a weight problem.

"I didn't know you were back in town today. Heard you were coming back though. You know Keria was thrilled about you. She started prancing around the whole damn town, telling everyone you were coming back." David wore an inward smile and held a bottle of Coors Light. He looked sleek in his leather jacket. "Sit back at my table. Trust me. The bar stand gets busy. You don't want to be here when it does." David walked back to his seat.

After a few drinks, the long table became a hot spot. The bartender was forced to labor to a group of incoherent fools all baked on drugs. The world of Rotor was returning. Perhaps this was a metamorphosis of some kind. A woman, very skinny but pleasing to the eye, came in with two friends, one guy and a girl.

"That's Liz, Keria's friend," David said after sipping his beer.

"Great. She's exactly how I imagined her," Nathan said.

Apart from Liz's revealing clothing, her personality was surely outgoing, not in the positive way though. It was more of the "I'm aware I'm gorgeous" type. And she advertised herself well to the bartender. Joe was his name. Everyone heard Liz repeat it. He was asking for a hard drink of any kind.

But as a few unrecognizable songs played and the noise mellowed to a mere annoyance, Nathan began to ease and deal with Liz and her two friends who, by the way, were just as revealing and blatant as she was.

Just as Nathan decided to lean back and deal with the stupidity, David stood. "Want me to show you why I still come here and not to the Clever Isle?"

"Sure." The two departed for a backroom hidden beside the bar stand and below a mini rooflike slab.

"This is the heart and soul of the bar, my friend," David said smoothly as they entered the game room.

Nathan's eyes first met with the tiny window straight across from the doorway that faced the docks. The room was small. It could only really fit four people comfortably. There were more neon lights on these walls, too. Beneath one set of these flashing ads stood a table used for catering.

The pool table sat near the window with a light above it, one that had a stained glass covering of a rose over the bulb. The room had a less than appealing brown rug.

"Not bad," Nathan commented.

David examined the wall of pool cues. "Ah, there it is, my lucky cue." David lifted a polished cue out of its black holder. "Pick any. Only this one's mine."

They began gorging themselves in their own party, away from the other drinkers.

As the conversation and drinking carried on, Nathan asked, "How many people use this backroom?"

"Not many. I've seen a few six-people events take place back here, but as you can tell, this room wasn't exactly built for such occasions. But Nathan, I have to ask," David said hesitantly, "why come back?"

Nathan managed to hit a solid ball into a pouch. "I was forced to come back, but between you and me, I wanted to see Keria again."

David released a quick smile. "I knew there were something between you two. But what's this forced nonsense?"

"My boss was an idiot and killed someone from the mob. 'Karma's a bitch' is all I have to say."

David laughed. "It's good to have you back though, whatever the reasons." He attempted to hit a striped ball but nearly hit the eight ball into the pouch closest to Nathan. "As for me, well, I've been busy now.

You know, Keria's a lucky girl. She has her own business. The rest of us are struggling out at sea, fishing, or working on the mill."

"The mill?"

"Yeah, but my point is that Keria must really like you to have saved you work. And a free home? Never heard such a thing. But really, Keria never asked anyone else."

"No?"

"Nope. I'm sure Neil's giving you a hard time. I always hear complaints from the field workers, but you people got lucky. Neil doesn't give out the paychecks. He's really Tia's bitch. And Tia pays good, as you'll soon be finding out."

Nathan examined the pool table. "What about you? What do you do?"

"I help my father fish. You know, the stuff your father used to do."

"Right."

"But hey, I'm not really poor. Hell, this town hasn't been poor since Black Bell's sudden gold rush."

"Yeah, that shocked me. I'll admit it."

"Trust me. It shocked us all. But of course, we want more, more, more."

David won the game of pool, and by the time they left the game room, Liz and her friends had supplied their bodies with enough alcohol to trigger a pass out. And Liz was passed out on one of the tables.

"Should we help her?" Nathan asked.

"Nah, they have this under control. Hey, Joe, here's the tip." David placed a twenty on the long table.

"Have a good night," Joe replied in a mellow tone.

"Come on, Nathan. Let's get out of here."

I thought this place would be quieter, Nathan thought.

The week carried on painfully. Nathan understood the world of Silverhill again. It, outside of Hollow Heights, was still lazy and quiet. Little was known of the new port town, as there were too many new people to get to know in a week's time.

Tia handed Nathan his first paycheck as early as Thursday. Now there was no need to make a trip to the Moonlight Diner every morning for coffee. Nathan got his hands on a neat coffeemaker. *Great! Espresso!*

During his trip to the appliance store, Nathan came across the sheriff who was squinting at him from across the first aisle. He wasn't old or young, a tad overweight though. His tan was awfully pale for being out in the sun all day, or maybe he was always in his office, eating donuts and drinking coffee. *Yeah, too cliché to be true. Or was it?*

Nathan rose his hand up weakly to say hi, unsure if the man were meaning to speak with him.

The sheriff approached. "Are you Nathan Ruiz by chance?"

"Yes, I am."

"Ah. I'm Greg, the town sheriff."

"Sheriff, huh? Nice to meet you."

"Same to you. Listen, I've been looking to meet you. I heard good things about you and wanted to welcome you back. Must have hit you hard. These changes."

"Almost nothing's the same," Nathan said.

"Aye, true, true. I'm honest when I say I'm not accustomed to the new design. The winery's like a Super Walmart, coming in and stealing work. Only the Miles Winery is the most expensive place in town!"

"It's also great quality," Nathan said.

"I wouldn't disagree with you, Mr. Ruiz, but on the contrary, it's been causing a fuss."

"What do you mean?"

"Well, it's making people feel like they need to be just like the Miles. Can't you tell? It's like the place brainwashes people."

"Brainwashes?"

"Aye."

"That's the town's fault, not the Miles," Nathan said sternly.

Greg didn't seem to agree. He peered downward and back up and looked past Nathan to see who might be around. "Well, I just wanted to say hi. I'd like to speak to you again sometime, just as a friend. Don't let the whole sheriff thing make you unconformable."

"I won't, sir."

"Sir?" Greg smirked. "Have a good one, Mr. Ruiz."

Nathan felt bothered. *Is that how people really feel about the Miles? That they have to be like them? Nah, couldn't be. Not possible.* He went to look for a coffeemaker. He killed off any further thought about Greg's viewpoint and bought himself some goods.

Regardless of the peaceful surroundings, the past lingered like a wall, encasing Nathan's awareness in its hollow darkness. He sat against the tiny porch table behind his home after shopping, listening to the chimes overpower the seagulls. Work started late, about two o'clock in the afternoon. So the hours passed. The cuckoo clock chirped, admonishing that time was passing by. There were no windows in the house of sorrow Nathan's mind was matted in, only thin walls that allowed the noises of the outside world to pierce through faintly.

<hr />

David had become Nathan's closest friend, other than Keria, but Liz had it in for him, too. She wanted him in bed, and she was eager to talk to him. It didn't take long for her or anyone else to realize Nathan was lonely and in need of someone. Keria was her roadblock. Word about Nathan's drinking got around fast thanks to Neil. She knew Nathan was due in for food shopping at the local supermarket, so since she worked there, she decided to work every day that week.

Liz was losing hope. Keria would return tomorrow, and she still hadn't seen Nathan. Then Liz spotted Nathan in the seventh aisle. She was stuck at the cash register, but there were only two open today, so odds were fifty/fifty that he'd use her line. Considering how everyone seemed to go to Lillie's, the long wait wouldn't be worth passing up an easy woman, would it?

Ah, please, he's probably drunk as we speak! Why pass me up?

Lillie's line was so long because she was a whore herself. But strangely, not many locals knew. She was the kind of woman who was quiet but kept her legs open and knew how to keep in the shadows. She'd throw in a couple hundred for a charity, too. Liz was aware of Lillie's sex drive, but unlike Lillie, Liz was most outgoing and would surely win.

Nathan entered the battleground and, without any particular reason, chose Liz's line.

"Hello, Nathan."

"Oh, hey. You work here?"

"Yup!" Liz replied cheerily.

"Never knew, but this is only my second time shopping here. Could be why."

Liz laughed, adjusting her already established hair. "Well it's good to see you," she said slyly. "I don't believe we were properly introduced."

"We weren't. David had me go to the game room after you arrived."

"Ah, David, he's nice and all, but don't let him kill off all your parties. We should meet up somewhere. Like…I dunno…the maze outside of Keria's winery?"

"Maybe sometime next week. I'm a bit busy."

"Not a problem," Liz replied.

They exchanged phone numbers, and Liz was satisfied. Her fantasy of banging Nathan behind the Miles fountain would just have to wait a little longer.

Keria stood by the shoreline. Her black hair fluttered in the wind. She was lost in her own world as she gazed out at the lighthouse, waiting for Nathan, who said he'd meet her as soon as he got home. Nathan approached her. His footsteps were soft and quiet in the sand.

Once he was beside her, she turned around and smiled meaningfully. "Hey," she said in the sweetest tone possible. "Remember what we used to call that lighthouse?"

"Spangle, and I'll admit that I still call it that."

"Really? Me, too."

They both stared into each other's eyes, not realizing they were gaping until Keria suddenly glanced down at a wave that dared reach her feet.

"Your friend Liz wants to meet up with me at your winery's maze. What should I do?"

"Don't go."

"Why not?"

"I don't know," she said softly and unsurely.

Keria placed her tiny hand on her left elbow, watching the waves try to reach her again. She soon looked up at him. Her eyes were locked onto his, and the two moved closer, as if they were the planchette on an Ouija broad, giving way to a spirit's demand. They met each other's lips. A feeling of overwhelming alleviation and happiness came over them, consuming them. It was a physical answer to the question, and it was the best of its kind.

CHAPTER 3

Outgrown Playground

Nightmares became fluent and similar, like a reply button was broken. Nathan's remembrance of the past, both recent and old, showed vivid images relating to the events of Rotor and childhood tragedies. Nathan wanted to hug Keria, kiss her tender lips, and talk the night away. It would be the great bubble of safety, the guard that kept all the darkness away. But he couldn't. She was at her grandmother's (Noreen's) house again. He felt like the fates held his salvation above his head, one he hadn't noticed in years.

It's been taken away again, so I can forget, Nathan thought. *But I never forgot her. It's just…just…*

Keria told him the details of what was happening. Jake Miles, her grandfather, had passed away from lung cancer two months ago, leaving his sweet wife behind with mild Alzheimer's disease. The scary thing was that the Alzheimer's disease ran heavily on Keria's mother's side, as Jake too had a case of it before he passed away. And the disease wasn't happy where it ranked. The illness was advancing fast.

There was little to do but explore Hollow Heights or the less desirable location of Silverhill. David was out on a boat half the time, but the nights were good. The game room became the ideal place to go every other night. Liz was only there on weekends, but she and her two friends weren't the only hard-core dipsomaniacs in town. Every night, someone was at the bar stand, demanding poor Joe to hurry and provide his or her libation.

"Come on, man. Hustle!" yelled a customer.

"Yeah, it's what? Fucking Saturday night! Tomorrow's a work night!" hollered another.

Nathan leaned back on a chair by the catering table, shaking his head in disappointment. "You sure the other place doesn't have a room like this?"

"Positive. The Clever Isle's only got one thing going for it, and that's cheap business. You think this place is bad?" David chuckled. "Don't bother yourself with the other."

"I'll take your word for it."

"You should," David said cheerily, toasting to Nathan before finishing off his bottle of Coors Light.

Of course, the night wasn't without its bullshit. The loudest asshole came into the game room, asking for respect. But this whole issue turned into a memorable moment. David handled the drunken hypocrite in a humorous convention. Once the fool spotted David sitting calmly across from Nathan, he shut up and left, as if he suddenly recalled David's face.

Nathan asked, "Why?"

David replied, "Oh, him? Ah, we got in a fight before. I kicked his ass."

"Impressive."

David snickered. "Sure, if you say so. If I don't get wasted in public places, I have the advantage. Secret's out." David leaned forward after a brief phase of silence. "On another note. What have you been doing with yourself lately? Like with Keria and your spare time besides coming here."

"I say things are good with Keria. My spare time is relieving."

"Ah, well, I hope you're not sitting around all day. Have you met up with Howard Huggs yet?"

"No."

"You should. He hasn't been the same since you left."

"Why since me? What did I do?"

"Beats me, but you should visit him."

Nathan did not like where this was going and sure as hell did not want to revisit the past more than he already had. "Where is he?"

"Up where we used to live when we were kids. Before Hollow Heights was built."

"People still use that town?"

"No, another reason you should go visit him." David leaned back again.

David was wrong, but the only people who stayed behind were damaged in some way, more on the mental side. Like David's house, the residents of Silverhill got their newly built homes free in a sense. They had to keep paying their old mortgage, but it was for a better home. It was such a steal. There was hardly a reason to stay.

"I'll think about it."

"Good to hear. Maybe you can talk some sense into him. God knows I've tried."

They left before happy hour arrived, though it appeared it already had prematurely.

The shitty, archaic TV by one of the windows in Nathan's house babbled on about a converging thunderstorm. *Whatever,* Nathan thought, *I'll still go.*

David had convinced Nathan to go back. Or perhaps it was the buildup of curiosity that had been held back for so many years.

The trip to Silverhill was basically a morning stroll on the beach at first. Nathan left the next day, wearing a blue plaid shirt and jeans, as early as eight in the morning. Getting to Howard's house would be quick, but there were ghosts to face along the way and not the kind one could just walk through.

The sand was cool, and the air was warm. A tiny fishing boat sat just beyond the forming of waves, and the sun was beaming with strong, eye-wrenching light. And then there it was, the old town, practically dead. Nathan stood in a weird state of limbo, nearly balanced by the distance between the new and old towns.

Just what was the reason for coming here? Was it to conquer the past? Or was it to reshape the future of an old man? He didn't know. He only continued by the water's edge.

As Nathan approached the wooden stairway that would lead him to the town's main pathway, a noise came from the water. He peered over and saw a mummer suit, something people used to attract the eye during a parade, almost mimicking a peacock. It was submerged and weighed down by sand under shallow water. The white mask had red lines that stretched from the eyeholes to the bottom of the mask and faced him. The body portion was tugged in one direction, and the mask slowly turned to meet Nathan, as if it were denying the current. *Because it wants to look at me.*

He walked up the wooden stairs, the first two bounded in weeds, and made it to the top, entering his past more physically than he had in a long time. The air felt heavier as he approached the first house, one that looked more like a shed, and took a deep breath. Beside him stood the road to the beach where he used to sit and watch the storms roll in. Nathan merely glanced over before advancing, seeing the town for what it had become, an empty, outgrown playground.

Like most of the houses, Keria's was empty, abandoned, and giving way to the elements. Mother Nature had some serious high blood pressure issues in this part of the world. To his own surprise, Nathan never went inside. There was nothing about Keria's past he felt needed attention, and he had things to do.

Broken furniture and indoor objects sat outside. Who placed them out here? In a house near Keria's, someone was staring out the window at Nathan, wide-eyed and dressed in raggedy old clothing. *Guess showers didn't work here either.*

With little consideration, Nathan returned a crude look, and the old woman crept away.

Raising his eyebrows, Nathan said softly, "Howard's not the only crazy one."

And neither was the woman in the window. There were others, poking around for something to do in their time-beat homes. One would think they would keep their houses nice since they treasured the place so much.

Instead of advancing toward the Huggs' house, Nathan approached the beach. It was littered with beach grass, and much of the sand was missing, but the view was the same and probably (hopefully) always would be. The lighthouse (often called Spangle by the neighborhood kids) sat on a rocky cliff. If someone were to jump off its edge, the individual would find himself or herself submerged twenty feet below the ocean's surface.

An abandoned mine was sculpted below Spangle. Even on the sunniest days, the mine remained a black spot with the average townsperson rarely seeing its interior. All the kids spread rumors about the mine, like how it was haunted or how the miners who used to work in it died within its deepest, most isolated core. The miners named the mine Black Bell because it was often reported that, depending on how deep someone traveled, a faint bell would be heard, throbbing as if it were a human pulse.

Nathan daydreamed. He pictured the childhood version of David looking for a golden seashell his mother claimed was lost on this beach. He never found it, of course, as his mother was lying. David was the kind of kid who saw the world for what it was, and his mother did her best to blind him of that. She filled his maturity with childish tales, trying to turn him back into a happy kid. David suffered no losses, but something happened to him and caused him to turn into a quiet, collective, and meditative type person.

"I will find it! I swear!" he always said back in those shady days. "It's right here under our feet!"

This little trick David's mother played was flawed, as in the end, it killed her son's belief in anything not proven. It was like telling a kid at the age of six that Santa isn't real and the Easter bunny is some sweaty guy who may or may not enjoy having children sit on him. *Guess David just really liked shells*, Nathan thought.

The shoreline, if one could really call it that, sat behind the Ruiz house. He went inside and saw what changed and what remained the same. Light was creeping into the hollow interior, nurturing the plants that flourished in all the rooms.

The first memory that surfaced was when Nathan first caught a fish.

He ran home from the docks, trying to balance the trout in his right hand. Eve turned to see her little boy enter the kitchen with a warming smile.

Finally though, completely out of breath from having to run, Alan came in. "Look at this. Our boy is catching fish at the age of five."

Eve wore a smile that, when looking at it now, worried Nathan. It was a smirk, not a smile. And shit, she was in the kitchen again. Her hands were soggy like plums. Alan guided his son into the living room after taking a picture of him with his first catch, a four-pound flounder, quite the size for a five-year-old.

The first thing he heard after handing Alan the fish was, "How are you going to cook it?" Alan's tone of voice changed to a craggy demand.

"I don't know," Eve replied.

Little Nathan walked away, still lost in a lie, the one where his father was proud of him. *Or maybe he was? Perhaps, but who can say?* Nathan wondered if his daddy even remembered the event the following morning.

In present day, the house was a mess: dusty floors, mangled weeds, oxidized household commodities, and junk. Upstairs in Nathan's old bedroom, nothing was touched. A fish tank sat dry. The shipwreck and chest were still inside. Nathan turned on the green light for self-amusement, surprised power was still fed into the building. He sat on his old bed, looking back and listening to the commotions of the past.

"What keeps you motivated?" Nathan's grandfather often asked. He would wait for an answer, too, even if it were complete bullshit.

"My family," young Nathan would say.

The grandfather's name was Albert, and he was the happiest Ruiz in the family. His face was often unshaven, but the look suited him. His hair was a thinning brown. He never wore suits, but rather T-shirts that promoted Silverhill's fishing team. At the moment, the two of them were on the ocean, past where waves formed, fishing.

"Why can't you go?" Nathan tried to keep his red and white bobber from floating toward the boat's turbine.

"I have something to do." He smiled.

"Can't you do it later?"

"It's not one of those jobs that can wait, bud. I'm sorry."

Albert grabbed a can of Busch and relaxed. His senses were dulled. "I have something to give you," he said cheerily. "It's under your seat."

A poorly wrapped box sat in a plastic container.

"It's for your sister," Albert said. It meant the world to him. Little did Nathan know.

"Okay, I'll make sure she gets it."

"Hey, the fishing tournament is comin' up. We need to go. Can't have them guests take the crown, ya know."

"Who's involved?"

"Same guys from last tournament. Those assholes who took the win. They've come for more, but we got 'em this time. Right?"

"Right!"

Nope, not quite.

Nathan returned home from Albert's house on Sophia's eighth birthday, a year before the haunting events of her ninth. It started with a knock on the door. Howard begged Alan for help as a storm arrived. His wife Maria was out on the Atlantic. Alan left and never came back. There was hardly a mystery to that, right? Later, as everyone hopelessly waited for Alan's return, Sophia got up and walked through the hallway, looking dazed, taken by blind ambition.

"Sophia? What are you doing?" Nathan asked in a childish voice.

"Come with me," she said, not halting her walk to the stairs. "I found Daddy."

The light hanging from the hallway ceiling was bright, and Sophia's shadow was cast in an unnatural way for a brief period of time.

Nathan rubbed his eyelids and followed his avid sister to the living room. "Now what?"

"Just follow. I know."

"Can't you just tell me?"

"Ocean."

"Ocean?"

"Follow."

"Stop. We can't go out. It's pouring." Nathan insisted.

"That's where Daddy is."

"Mom! Mom! Sophia's trying to go outside!"

Eve never replied. Nathan wasn't the only one in the family to use painkillers and alcohol.

As Sophia made it outside, Nathan expected tree branches, wild winds, and a wall of water to come flying at them, but none of that occurred. Aside from wetness and dark clouds, the world was calming.

"This way," Sophia said, so damn sure of herself.

Nathan couldn't get over how harmonious the sea looked. *That can be tricky. That sea. You never know what it looks like beneath those waves! My father taught me that.*

"Let's ride that boat," she said keenly, pointing her finger with pure demand at the boat that nested in the sand by the pulsing water.

It almost looks like it's pulsing, they both thought.

Nathan decided to follow his sister and ride the boat out, but he felt like he left his mind on the beach. It was one of those moments when sense wasn't useful, and trust was the only way. Or so young Nathan thought as the boat hit the large body of water, and their search for Daddy got serious.

"So where in the ocean is he?" Nathan then stopped and thought, *Dare I ask?*

There was no reply.

Nathan looked down at the water and suddenly felt his premature leadership kick in. "When we reach as far as Spangle, we go back." He turned his eyes to Sophia, whose attention was fixed upon the dark horizon.

The boat stopped moving as though an anchor had been dropped, and Sophia smiled.

"What's funny?" Nathan asked.

"Daddy found us," she whispered.

"Now what do we do? Where is Dad?"

"I'm listening. Wait."

"To what? The waves? Waves can't talk, Sophia!"

"Yes, they can!" Sophia peered down at the shifting water. "At this moment they can."

Trying to make this seem logical led Nathan to believe the absence of their father triggered something in Sophia, a defensive train of thought that would help her cope with the possible (and definitely likely) loss of her father. But her defenses sucked. They'd dragged her out here into the fucking ocean.

"Enough. Let's go back." Nathan took over or tried to.

The boat was stuck.

"If waves could talk, I'd know where to go. Daddy isn't talking anymore."

"I haven't heard him yet. Let's just go."

Sophia looked up at her big brother with no resistance to leave, but the boat wouldn't move.

"Eh, I think it's stuck." Nathan put all his force into the paddle. The water around the boat began sinking and refilling. "What's under us?"

The area was too dark. Lights from the town and lighthouse were only present, aside from a tiny flashlight Nathan kept in the boat, tucked away inside a fishing box he never used. He examined the water with it after hearing movement that sounded like a bathtub drain sucking up what was left of its murky water.

"See anything?" Sophia asked.

"No."

The water shifted beneath the boat. Nathan and Sophia looked at each other, both feeling the same emotions at equal measures.

"Maybe we hit a whirlpool," Nathan said, not really knowing what a whirlpool was.

Something hit the boat, and it nearly tipped over, causing Sophia to topple over the edge and land into the unearthly current.

"Sophia!"

This memory was too vivid. The pain never tapered. Nathan felt like a spirit in its death state, reliving the horrors in which it endured before death. The last thing he remembered was the fading aura that harbored Sophia's blue eyes. They seemed to have glowed in the dark water as she declined. *But how did this happen? Could the currents have really been so strong?*

Eve was awake when Nathan returned. The boat was pushed out of the strange current, and it drifted almost perfectly toward the beach behind Nathan's house. He was in shock, not caring where the current took him. When he got home, tears, the kind both disheartening and terrifying, drenched Eve's face. He couldn't remember how he told his mother what happened. It just came out, and those tears, already consuming and controlling, grew.

The empty fish tank sat still in dust, but the past was far from dishabille. And Howard seemed to be fishing in the same boat. Nathan had nightmares of his childhood, and here they fled throughout the remains of the house as echoes with the oncoming storm, creeping out of the horizon at an unbelievable pace. He let out a heavy, almost relieving, sigh before pushing himself up from the dreggy bed.

The wind picked up, hitting every side of the aging house like an angry baseball player slamming his bat against a fence. Weeds made the living room look like a bedraggled porch, and now, drafts were roving their way in the house, feeding the rust that formed wherever rust could form. *Another serving of real food was about to flood in here soon.* Mother Nature was about to add some cholesterol to this lovely establishment.

Howard's house was across from the high school. This might sound close, but one shouldn't be fooled. A piece of the sea that sat between the residential homes isolated the high school, Silverhill High. These high school kids were bothersome. If they weren't fucking each other behind bushes, they were cursing each other out about their mothers and sisters, boyfriends and girlfriends, and something about their uncles.

Blank tombstones sat around the Huggs' porch, and the front door held a bouquet of dead flowers that were nailed to the door's ugly surface with a nasty object that looked like a crooked piercing a hard-core emo kid would wear.

Howard answered the door. He sure took his time, too. He looked terrible. The worst eye shadows ever seen on a man appeared painted beneath his dark blue, bloodshot eyes, and he grew a beard, one that didn't only save flavor but stored the remains of what missed the man's mouth. He dressed almost like Albert had. Only Albert stuck to a certain style. Howard just hid his birthday suit under a thin, white T-shirt and a baggy pair of jeans.

"Howard?" Nathan asked, not sure how to start a conversation.

"Yeah?"

"How've you been? It's been years since I've seen you."

"Ah, you know...this."

Nathan studied the house as Howard walked into another room. "What exactly is this?"

One could picture walking into an old retirement home and having all but a set few items flipped or broken. The only stuff kept nice was featured in a shrine consisting of a mummer suit and a hearty collection of family photos.

"My stuff," said Howard. "Heh, what else?"

"Everything's flipped," Nathan replied. "Why is that?"

Howard entered the living room holding a silver tray containing sparkling cider.

Nathan took his eyes off the shrine. "I haven't touched that thing since you've left. God knows I've wanted to."

"So why haven't you?"

"Remember what you used to do with my mummer mask? You used to throw it into the water."

"Yeah, I remember, back when I was nine or so."

"I remember so clearly how you ran to the edge of the street and cheered us on. You were always so happy to leave town for the parade. Maybe it was just because you got out of town for a while."

"I've had my share of that. What about you?"

Howard studied Nathan's appearance, not accepting what time had done. "You look too much like your father," he said in a low tone. "I wish—"

"Stop." Nathan demanded.

Howard chuckled. "Why stay here, you wonder? Well, this is my home."

"How should I put this without sounding like a terrible person? This town is dead. You have tombstones on your lawn! You need help, and I can get it for you."

"No!" Howard burst. "I'm never going there. It's a trick. Can't you tell?"

"A trick?"

"There's something in the sky, killing everything! Gnawing at minds like a pack of hungry, baby sharks." Howard shot up from his seat.

"Relax," Nathan replied.

"Look! I'll show you!"

The fool tumbled out into the drizzling rain and pointed at the clouds that fled through the sky. Howard's pale face grew whiter, and his eye shadows darkened.

"Howard? Are you okay?"

"No, I have to sit down."

"Please do."

Nathan took Howard by the hand and guided him into his house. The poor man felt heavy, like death. His hands, arms, and entire body briefly jittered.

He mumbled something so soft that the wind outside nearly hid it. "Black pollen."

Howard sat on his lumpy chair and gulped down his cider, causing his Adam's apple to move up and down like a piston. He sighed heavily. "Why did you come here?"

"I was asked to visit you."

"By who?"

"David."

"Ah," the old man uttered. "Wonder why."

"Hardly. Everyone, well, almost everyone moved to Hollow Heights. He doesn't understand why you haven't. None of us do. It's hard for me to come back to this place. You have to understand that. I wouldn't have come here unless I thought it'd be worth bringing you back. What happened to you since I've been gone?"

"Is that really why you've come? To drag me to the Miles' playing field? You think everyone's holly jolly there, don't ya? Well, nothing works like that, you hear? Nothing!"

Nathan crossed his arms and glanced at the mummer suit, reimagining the one he thought he saw swimming in the sea during his walk here.

"You see me as outlandish. I get it," the old man said. "I have this vibe...this ambition to continue what I am doing. It's not harming anyone.

Not you. Not I. My mind's more at rest because of it! Everyone here with me is fine." Howard took what was supposed to be Nathan's cider and chugged it down. "I never wanted this, Nathan. Never! I wanted to come home that night and bring my wife and Alan home. But they were gone, taken from me, you, and everyone who ever cared. But it was fate, can't you see? Eve hated that man!"

"How could you say that?" Nathan hollered.

"Because it's true! He abused her. You were young, but not that young! You noticed! You had to have noticed!"

"Fuck this! You want to stay here and mumble bullshit lies all night for the rest of your sorry excuse for a life. Then fine. Stay here and play with your tombstones." Nathan turned to face the door, hearing the wind beat against it. "You killed her. You had her go out and do your damn job," Nathan said roughly. He turned to meet Howard again, feeling a horrible pain in his stomach. "If you did your own job, she wouldn't have died. My father wouldn't have been lost. You talk about fate? It sure served you. Maria drowned in water. You drown in grief."

Howard's voice shifted to a daunting somber, and the greatest of human grief bled through every word he spoke. "I'd never harm my wife."

As Howard's eye shadows darkened mysteriously, a faint thunder aroused from the arranging storm. Nathan was guilty of throwing his near uncle into the pit of self-pity or, at the very least, further down. He was sobbing now in his little corner. All the cider was gone.

Ya did great helping the poor guy. Yes, you did!

Now it was time to run away.

CHAPTER 4

Shadows of Emotion

H e felt groggy leaving the house, stumbling over objects as if he were drunk. Not far ahead was the high school, isolated by a gap filled with salty, wild water. But it wasn't just wild. It was anxious and moved unnaturally. *Just like the dreams.*

Each burst of wind grew more forceful as the rain fell harder until objects even as heavy as a lamp became Maine's tumbleweeds. As Nathan ran home, being pushed forward by the strange winds, he continued to glance at the waters. They seemed to sink and rise, sink, and rise.

The wind's momentum was a terse way of guiding Nathan home, leaving behind an imprint as it settled to a normal speed. The waves remained anomalistic to an average summer thunderstorm, reminding Nathan that this storm was still at work. *I'd never harm my wife.*

Through the rain, Nathan could see four figures standing on the cliff around Black Bell. They appeared to be holding pickaxes. *But who were these people? Miners? Tourists? Why would there be tourists holding pickaxes? But also, why would miners stand outside a useless mine during a wild storm?* It was eerie how they seemed to stare back.

A clash of thunder ended this sighting, as the four figures were gone and the storm slowly began to pick up again. Tall, thick waves clasped against the rocks. The mist from the impacts brushed the bottom of the lighthouse. The glimpse of his house ministered a cozy feeling. The chimes rung eerily in the back, and the front screen door was off a hinge. Nathan kept his keys by his chest as he unlocked the door. The groggy, heavy feeling he endured put on weight.

Sand drizzled off Nathan's clothing as he stumbled to his dresser. The idea of a warm bed and eight hours of sleep sounded magical. Neil planned a nice early shift for Nathan tomorrow. Just the thought of being stuck checking wine bottles all day from six in the morning until seven at night was vexing his mind. But something else was bothering him, a feeling of numbness, like a snake cut off blood to his arms and legs.

Nathan changed into dry clothing and crawled into bed. The storm rang in his ears as the numbness he felt shifted to an agonizing feeling of pins and needles. Slowly but surely, the loud tapping of rain and clashes of thunder faded, but not the visuals of lighting. Those flashes transpired to the beam of Spangle's light passing through the starry sky. The water below an empty, imaginary boat was utterly silent, but there was a noise, a weird murmuring. He was asleep now within a blink of his eyes.

The air was brisk. Waves crashed onto the shoreline. Heavy clouds painted black, blue, and grey embarked toward the little town of Silverhill, Maine. Young Nathan, age twelve, sat on the edge of grass and sand. An incoming storm regularly caught his wild imagination.

His mother, Eve, spotted him. "Honey, get inside. It's gonna rain!"

"Not yet, Mom!"

Eve was a beautiful woman. Her eyes were a dark blue, and her skin color had the perfect tan. Her fashion was simple, a tank top and short pants. She was the woman in town who was envied by appearance alone.

The storm did its best to make the area completely gloomy, but to Nathan, all it really did was hide the caliginous nature of Black Bell. The sun might have been shaded grey, but Spangle remained visible, or at least its beam did.

In the kitchen, Eve prepared a special dinner for her loving daughter

Sophia. It was Sophia's ninth birthday. She sat in her nearly prismatic-shaped bedroom, playing with her favorite dolls. Sophia had a vivid imagination of her own. She used her rosette pink walls as an escape from stormy days such as today, pretending she and her dolls were in a hair salon. She also had what her parents said was an imaginary friend.

Like her dolls, Sophia was well kept and always in style. Of all her friends, Sophia was the most outgoing and optimistic, always looking for the positive in the worst of times her eight- and nine-year-old friends got themselves into. She usually listened to her parents, far more than Nathan had.

"Your father should be home soon." Eve looked out the window.

The wind had picked up, causing the chimes outside to sway and hum a natural melody giving by the storm.

Little Sophia came down the stairs. "Where's Daddy? I want to party!"

"Should be here soon, dear."

Should be here soon. Sure enough, Alan, Nathan and Sophia's father, arrived home before the rain poured. His family hugged him, a true tender moment.

"So when can I open my presents?" Sophia's eyes were shimmering in their own aura.

"Let Daddy get changed first, okay?" Alan insisted.

Alan was a fisherman, so to speak. He didn't look like one. Usually when people first saw him, they thought of a miner. He had a thin, unshaven face and dark hair. He always wore jeans and a sweater unless the day was unbearably hot.

The dream skipped events, as dreams tend to. Nathan blinked and found himself in his bedroom, and his logic decided to act as a messaging system. He was checking his fish tank, which restrained three clown fish, a few yellow anglerfish, and a couple sea horses in thirty gallons of salt water directly from the Atlantic. He fed them, turned on the green light inside the tank, and, for a moment, watched the moving chest cough up bubbles by the shipwreck where the sea horses often hid.

Nathan's window rattled with the wind, so he glanced outside. A terrible foreshadowing of what was yet to come occurred as he peered out at the storm.

"Come on, Nathan. Your sister wants to open her gifts!" shouted Eve.
"Okay, Mom!"

Nathan had to tell his father what had happened outside, but Alan wasn't around. The party downstairs had become more festive, so Nathan forgot.

The grandfather clock clanged, showcasing that the time was eight. Sophia had two friends, Lilly and April, over. Nathan sat in the dining room as the three girls played Twister in the living room, laughing and shouting childish things.

"You girls ready for cake?" Eve was carrying a large homemade cake on a silver tray.

All three girls came running in, attending to any seat they could find. By eight thirty, the cake was eaten, and the presents were opened. Little Sophia got everything she wanted, which were solely remakes of what she already had. But did that really matter?

The happiness ended with a vigorous knock on the door, which soon flew open.

"Alan, we need your help!" exclaimed Howard. One could almost take the image of a stereotypical fisherman and say it was him. "The storm blew away the dock, and my wife never came back!"

Funny how Howard made his wife go fishing for him, Nathan thought.

"Okay, just give me a minute."

No one knew what to think of it, the sudden interruption. This event wasn't anything supernatural, just life reminding that forgetful joy was temporary. Alan kissed his daughter good-bye, apologizing as if it were his fault. Howard was in a hurry, urging Alan to make haste.

"Where's your boat?" Howard asked.

Oh, yeah. It kinda drifted away, Nathan thought.

"We'll just use mine. Come on."

"Oh no! You're not going out now." Eve crossed her arms.

"I won't. Don't worry."

Howard glared at him but remained quiet. He knew Alan would go out, and so did Eve.

"I'm coming with you!" Nathan yammered.

"No."

"But—"

"No buts. I need you here."

Alan retrieved his gear and left with Howard to deal with the storm.

Too bad you can't deal with a storm, Nathan thought. The dream shifted again. The sand had sunk beneath their boots as the two fishermen ran across the shore to the ports. Out in the wild waters was Mariel Huggs, Howard's wife. That was where they were going. The dock that had been detached not long ago lay fastened in the sand of the shallowest water.

"This is one hell of a storm!" Alan yelled.

"Yeah, it is."

They left for Mariel, holding onto every ounce of faith they still had that she was alive.

"There she is!" cried Howard intently. "Mariel! Mariel!"

Mariel Huggs was still afloat on the boat.

"Relax." Alan steered toward Mariel's possible gravesite.

Just because she was okay now did not mean much, as the waves were reaching their climax, elevating higher than the horizon, and breaking onto the tiny shelter of the wheel Alan handled.

"Mindless storm!" Howard shouted.

Who's to say it's mindless, Howard? Nathan thought. The waves made the air misty and enigmatic, nourishing the storm with its matter. Sure, the two fishermen could see the outline of Mariel. But then again, was it Mariel? Something caught Alan's eye. Mariel's outline had broken down somehow, like water taking the form of a human being and then suddenly collapsing in only a way water could.

"I don't see her!" Howard yammered.

Assuming Howard hadn't seen what happened, Alan said, "Just keep your eyes on the deck. The fog's getting bad."

Nathan's dream returned to what he knew. After all, little Nathan was with his mother and sister. What happened to Alan remained unknown to him. Eve had left to wash dishes, often peeking through the window above the sink and examining the pouring rain and untamed winds. There was a bizarre smell in the air, like the storm carried a bundle of freshly picked roses within its basin.

"Lisa loves the air here." Sophia giggled. "She loves it and sells it."

"Sells it?" Nathan asked.

"Sells it!"

Lilly and April left with their fathers, who were, like everyone else, eager to receive any news about Alan's and Howard's rescue plan. Eve did not want her children up any later, as it was past their bedtime.

"Okay, you two, it's time for bed." Eve began to collect the wrapping paper left behind from the party.

Nathan and Sophia climbed up the wooden staircase and made their way into their bedrooms.

The fish tank lit Nathan's bedroom green, casting more eerie feelings and thoughts. Sophia began talking to herself. Nathan placed his ear against the wall to listen.

"Why would I go there? It's wet and dangerous."

Was she talking to Lisa? Nathan thought.

"My daddy? Why? Because he likes shells? When is he coming back? Okay, I'll go, too."

Nathan only got half the conversation. What was unspoken ate at him like a crow feasting on a corpse. Nathan followed his sister. This was the part where dream logic blended with the facts again. Little Sophia dragged her feet to the staircase. If a human being were to walk in the style of "Dream Sophia," they'd break their toes and feet bones.

The lights above flickered strangely, as if they weren't lights at all but rather pulsating orbs. Once Sophia turned the corner where the staircase stood, she was outside again, the logic of a dream. Nathan burst through the front door of the now-empty house of the Ruiz family. Little Sophia was drifting away on the boat that had been lost about an hour ago.

"Sophia!" Nathan shouted.

Once Sophia faded into the night, another boat crept into view and hit the shore. It was empty. Nathan approached it. He even entered it, feeling the shaky, unstable balance it maintained as it moved itself into the fog-covered water.

As the dream boat made its way through the night, growing further away from the lighthouse, out toward the voluminous open sea, a murmuring intensified. A mere foot away, another boat lingered. In it was Dream Sophia.

"Sophia?" Nathan asked.

"No, not quite," she replied.

"Then spill it. Who the hell are you?"

"Logically speaking, I am you," she said. "I'm only a messenger telling your subconscious where to go."

There were no strict traits to this girl, none that belonged to the original Sophia Ruiz. This replica or dream agency sat perfectly still in the perfectly smooth boat. Her hair was straight. Her eyebrows were curved with no imperfections whatsoever. Her skin was paler than Alan Ruiz's, and her clothing was all white.

"What's your real name then? Or what should I call you?" Nathan asked.

"That organization doesn't matter here," she replied. "I have no name, no different from your own."

Nathan looked to the side. "All right. What am I doing out here in a boat talking to you?"

"You're in a boat because you'd be otherwise forced to swim, and chances are, this being your head, you'd be drowning."

"Right then."

Dream Sophia closed her eyes, smiled, and said yes, showing a trait of the person Nathan knew for the first time.

"So what do you want to show me?"

"I'd like to simply warn you with depictions, little clips of what may occur. A great stressor has taken effect. Whatever it is, I don't even know. It's all a fireworks display on your part."

"I only have to watch?"

"Yes." This time around, there was no smile. No emotion of any kind lit her face.

A thickening fog crept in from afar, as if it weren't foggy enough, nearly blanketing Dream Sophia and her perfect boat.

Just as Nathan was about to say something, Sophia said, "Just watch."

Nathan closed his lips and relaxed as the fog covered every detail but the lighthouse's beam. What occurred was a shift, the fog being the great leap to the next showing. In the ocean, bags, the very kind Nathan carried from New Jersey to Maine, drifted. As they floated along, they began to fade out, as they had faded in.

Keria's tender voice was forged in the air. "Talk about waiting 'til last minute."

Nathan thought of his long trip to Silverhill and the comfort of Keria's welcome. But why was this charming memory being shown? The next images focused less on the whole "traveling on a boat" feeling and came up like a movie in a drive-in theater.

It was Howard's house in the present time. This image came so clear that looking into a mirror with no faults or smudges on its surface wouldn't even be as vivid as Howard when he left his house to the front yard.

"What is he doing?" Nathan asked aloud.

What was he doing? He was hammering in those blank tombstones. Behind him was a looming mist that not only lingered behind Howard but could be seen stretched out across the entire scene like a jet cloud in the sky.

"I miss you both, my dreaded and most profound anchors of this world," Howard spoke. "Why am I left behind to wait?"

He had buried people on his lawn. But who? Mariel? Who else? There were quite a few tombstones, blank but clear as day around him. But Nathan got this feeling that they weren't really there at all, but rather images he created both in and outside this dream. Unstable thoughts and feelings of his mind flowed out of his personal reality. No, the images were being forced out.

In a strange, crazed way, it almost felt like Nathan was Howard, like their minds were now connected through the logic of a dream. *Is Howard dreaming the same thing?*

Howard eerily looked up at him, causing Nathan to flinch back. And like Sophia, Howard showed no traits of either the normal man he was in the past or the crazy man he had become in reality, outside of this nightmare.

As Howard began to fade away like the traveling bags had, Nathan stared into the fishermen's empty eyes, and all the feelings of connection to his whereabouts, though empty of emotion, had gone away with the image of Mr. Huggs.

Howard's empty house sat still in the cloudy night, under a full moon that scarcely exuded light. As thunder clashed and lightning lit the horizon and as rain began to fall, small, black dots formed in the sky and slowly drifted ahead, toward the direction Nathan's boat was going, only slightly faster.

"What the hell?" Nathan murmured. Then a thought occurred to him. *Black pollen.* That was what his mind wanted to call it.

The feeling of dampness came over Nathan, and he swore he'd wake up in a puddle of sweat or rainwater. But despite knowing that this was in fact a dream, his mind wouldn't let him wake up. There was more to be shown. Never once in his life had he felt his willpower and brain so separate from one another. And a voice in what Nathan assumed to be his mind's eye kept pursuing the term, "black pollen."

It was the supposed stressor that infiltrated Nathan's body, the one that wasn't known. He watched Howard's house decolorize in fog. This whole dream had become crazy, the kind of senseless that was only sane in a dream.

"Is that the illness?" Nathan hollered. All that remained visually were the dots, fog, and Spangle's beam. "What should I do about it? What's the cure?"

There was no reply or other thought to answer the question, only the few images. The silent ocean gave way to the sounds of the open sea. The dots remained, but Spangle's light was now beginning to fade. Nathan peered back at it until the beam was a tiny star, the only star in the sky.

Something began hitting the sides of the boat. Nathan looked down and saw Busch beer cans floating in the water. Considering the obvious fact these beer cans weren't a natural sea expectation, he knew these cans were of a great importance.

The boat continued up the current the beer cans traveled through until it hit a hollow object. Just beyond a thick portion of the fog was another boat carrying a distorted map on one of its wooden seats. Nathan thought about grabbing it and stood up to do it; however, his boat rocked wildly. He sat down on his seat and stared at the map, trying to get a hardy glimpse of its depictions. His desire to hold it in his hands only grew.

He stood up a second time. Again, the boat rocked, almost throwing Nathan out into the utopian waters. He held his ground and inched toward the boat's edge, trying to balance the shifts of his boat's strange physics. The sea was lulling, for the boat to react so intensely was an odd result of simply standing up or moving normally.

Nathan kneeled by the edge of the boat and leaned over, stretching out his right hand for the map, nearly blindsided of where the hell it was. When he reached it, the map nearly shred apart. As wet as the map was, the ink appeared to be dry. As Nathan carefully placed it on the seat beside him, still kneeling, the boat was fairly idle on the water's surface. Something flipped him over in an instant. The rush of cold water hit his skin and filled his nerves with a chill. His vision was now burry. *Still can't wake up!* A feeling of overwhelming power adopted him. *No trace of the real world.* And he felt like the current was dragging him deeper into the unknown. *Is this a dream?*

During the drowning phase, there was nothing except a feeling of weakness and a sense of having no options to escape. It turned out that this current dragged Nathan to the shore behind his old house. Right as his body hit the sand, all those feelings stayed behind with the water. *You can feel pain in a dream. But you usually wake up!*

Unless running back home was a part of this nightmare, Nathan knew he wasn't awake. He peered up, taking notice of four tiny shadows aligned in a circle around one large figure on the beach. He squinted his eyes, but no new details emerged. Then suddenly, all the little figures began to laugh among themselves. They were children. There was one little shadow with long hair.

This little figure turned and said in a soft, childish voice, "We want to share our babysitter's favorite nursery rhyme with you."

This was a little girl. She turned to face the larger shadow, and it nodded slowly. The little girl stood. The others watched as she approached Nathan and stopped not far away. This person wasn't Dream Sophia or anyone Nathan knew. *But I had to have seen her. This is a dream, and in a dream, your mind only shows people you've seen in real life. It doesn't make up new faces.*

This little girl had a ponytail, very fair skin, and a pink tank top with a white undershirt. She also wore Hello Kitty sneakers. All details could be seen once the child walked closer.

"Are you ready?" she asked.

"Uh, sure," Nathan uttered, just loud enough to hear.

The little girl let out a heavy breath. "The Dark Place. Drifting minds without their senses. An endless pit of growing trenches. The place where none of us belong. Where our misfortunes tag along. It holds the world's darkest creatures while giving us its darkest preachers. Ruthless sounds fill our ears, reminding us of our greatest fears. Anxiety flows through the cracks, giving the mind no time to relax. Its existence revealed in the night, while the mind travels not so light."

The girl smiled and turned away, now facing her group, and returned to her seat. The largest of these figures patted the child's head, and as she sat down, all details of her being faded into a shadow. Her only difference from the others was now the outline of her long hair.

Our babysitter's favorite nursery rhyme? What was it about? Nathan couldn't understand what the group was exactly. *The large figure in the middle was a babysitter? And the others? Were they the kids she was watching?*

"Anyone else have something to say to me?"

One of the other kids shouted, "No, the presentation's over!"

That voice distinguished a boy, one whose age must be two or four. The girl looked like she was seven.

"All right. I'll just…leave…now."

"Where are you going?" the boy asked.

And then they faded. The dream ended with the sound of the alarm and annoying cuckoo clock. *If this shit weren't enough to question one's own sanity, then what was?*

CHAPTER 5

Abstract Insanity

Keria placed a heavy load of laundry by the living room sofa. She pressed into her back with both hands to relieve some pressure, alarmed by the sharp pain that shot up her body. Her grandmother nested on a worn-down red recliner beneath the summer morning light, blissfully unaware of her problems for the time being. Noreen was asleep in an ugly flower nightgown that still needed to be washed or burned. Noreen wouldn't allow Keria to remove it.

"No never, you witch!" she would say. Or "How dare you take this away from me, hag!" Her mild Alzheimer's disease had heightened to an advanced state.

Keria was about to cry but held herself together, like a leader guiding cancer victims through a ten-mile maze. Her anxiety was caving in. Perhaps the colors of the house caused this feeling of sickness—light blue chalky rugs, pink wallpaper, an old knob television, aged furniture, and ill-kept rooms. No, what really caused it was the treatment given to her by her grandmother. Keria imagined Nathan caring for her in the same way, forgotten, ridiculed, hated on, and hopeless.

Yup, runs in the family, she thought, rehearing Tia's words as if they were on replay.

"Have to be careful, Keria. It's in our blood."

For a minute, Keria believed her. By the stairway to the front door was a table display of old family photos. Among the morning glare, Keria could see these images and escape the present time. They were windows into sanity. Noreen set them before her illness took effect years ago.

The first picture was framed in bronze, nearly obscured by the sun's reflection. Keria wanted to move it but feared there was an order that shouldn't be disturbed. She did her best to see it where it shined. It was Noreen as a baby, bundled up in a blanket, being cradled by her mother. Keria smiled thinking of her Great-Grandmother Christina. The smile didn't last. *Do I dare turn my head and compare this photo with the present?*

Noreen snorted, nearly waking herself up. So that "comparing photos idea" ended up happening when Keria turned to notice. She moved on to the next, another picture framed in bronze. Only this one was a whopping time leap. Noreen, age eight, was at what appeared to be her own birthday party. It took a moment, but Keria realized why this picture was so important. Noreen's eighth birthday party was where she met her husband. That felt weird thinking about, but it was true, and Noreen framed that day proudly on her brief timeline. *Now how did he die? A car crash. That's right. Come on, Keria. Stop thinking so damn morbidly!*

There was a lot left to do chore wise, aside from finishing the laundry. Dust was making its home upstairs, the most unused portion of the house. *Whatever. In a minute.*

The middle picture was framed in a dark blue casing and staged Keria being cradled as a baby by Noreen. There was a much smaller picture framed in black of Keria being held by Tia beside it and a fake dark red rose lying on the left side of the larger frame. The beauty of a photograph is that someone can see what he or she feels outside of his or her mind, out where other people move about. It was almost like reliving the event again.

There were several other tiny pictures in black frames, also brown and silver, of Keria as a child. The only picture not harboring the morning light was a snapshot of Keria making cookies at a family kid's reunion.

The idea was to get all of the closest cousins on Keria's mother's side together to bake cookies, all different kinds really. In this particular photo, young Keria was smiling, very much so. But was it truthful? Yes, it was an almost apathetic smile.

The kitchen was, in fact, a disaster. But Noreen didn't care. Charlie, the son of Tia's sister Mona, was the messiest of all and responsible for nearly two thirds of the kitchen's condition. He held the silver spoon to his mouth, waiting for Noreen to yell at him to set it back down on the table.

Don't be fooled by the present time. Noreen's bad fashion sense didn't exist ever, not even now really. That ugly nightgown reminded Noreen of her own mother. Perhaps she was the one with the bad taste. Noreen was a prisoner, caught in the olden days of someone else's youth, one who she missed very much.

In this particular photo, Noreen wore a green T-shirt and black pants, nothing ugly or special. Stacy, Mona's daughter, was the quiet one of the group. Like David, she knew too much of both life and her daddy, who, by the way, often thought it was okay to sleep with other women on weekends while off on travel or other nightly chores, as he often put it when questioned. Despite being so concealed to oneself, Stacy had the most to say, and when in the right mood, she expressed herself well. She dressed cleanly and was the most mature out of the group. She was only seven years of age.

Chris, Tia's bother, had only one kid at the time, and his name was Kevin. (Chris was now the father of three.) Kevin looked the most like his father. Stacy could very well be the child of another man. She sure didn't look like her daddy, but since Charlie hardly looked like either one of his parents, nobody bothered to think of it any differently than the usual "You were adopted" joke.

If someone were to order the maturity of the kids in a line, there'd be a weak irony to it, young Keria thought. *The most mature is the smallest; the least mature is the tallest. The smaller they are, the more mature they must be!*

When everyone was in the living room, Keria lingered in the kitchen, still messing with her cookies, excessively decorating their still-cooling surface with more frosting and candy.

Noreen began placing dishes in the dishwasher when Keria asked, "Do you think Nathan would have come if he were still here?"

Noreen was surprised Keria asked such a question. Stacy usually dug deeper. It almost seemed like even Stacy forgot about Nathan or was trying to.

"I'm sure he would have," Noreen replied.

"Will he come back?"

Noreen placed one last dish in the washer before approaching Keria and saying, "Not if you don't talk to him."

"Really?"

"Yes really. Nobody else will. Everyone's trying to forget about him or…just has."

"What should I do?"

Noreen smiled. "Have you ever used the telephone yet?"

"Yes, a lot."

"Figured. You're getting so much older now. Why don't you call him? Hold on a second."

Noreen walked out of the kitchen and came back with a piece of paper. "Here's his number. I set him up, you know. Got him a good mother and father figure. The sooner you call him, the better. All is lost if he changes his number. I haven't talked to him in about a month."

Keria took the paper. "I'll call him tonight."

Noreen was to thank for Nathan's being here. Tia was, too, for supplying Nathan with a house and job. But it sure felt like fate. Only one more week, and all would have been lost. Nathan was about to change cell phone providers in a week's time since that chat with Noreen in the kitchen.

All good things come in time, Keria thought happily. *All good things come in time.*

Sad to say, Noreen's time was about to come to a close. In two weeks, she had to move into a nursery home. From there, nobody knew how long she had left in this motley arranged world. But like always there was a balance to Keria's fortune, one she could take notice of fully. This allowed her to return to Nathan much sooner in Hollow Heights.

Keria sighed, embraced all negative feelings to adjust, took back control of the happy thoughts she had just recently recalled, and went upstairs to clean.

News reporter Brian Herman stood by the shoreline beside Nathan's house, waiting for the cameraman to arrive. The news van was parked on the grass. Ryan was inside of it, tweaking the needs for a perfect signal. It was morning. The sun was not far above the horizon. Once Ryan leaped out from the van with his camera, Brian shifted his weight and adjusted his red tie. He was sinking in sand, which messed up his slick shoes, but if Ryan were as good as his boss claimed, that wouldn't be an issue the public would ever know.

"In three...two...one." Ryan signaled Brian with his hand. "That's right, Casey. Yet another strange wash-up here in Hollow Heights, Maine."

Ryan followed Brain closer to the water and angled the camera to show the viewers a cluster of dead jellyfish and squids. But there wasn't just a few. Down the water's edge, countless sea creatures lay in the sand.

"As you can see here, more of the Atlantic's sea life has washed up onto several beaches. We were called here to show that only after thunderstorms does this happen. Now researchers have been occupying this site for further studies as to what exactly is causing this mysterious Moving Graveyard phenomenon many are calling it. But the thunderstorms may be the wrong idea."

A clip was now being shown on Fox News about motorboats and how they were the likely cause for the Moving Graveyard. Brian smiled, thinking the same thing as Ryan. *Bullshit! It's the boats!*

When the clip ended, Brian got his moment to shine again. "Whether or not this issue is caused by nature or the actions of Hollow Heights remains unknown; however, this isn't the first time early morning beach walkers came upon the dead, and chances are, it won't be the last. Casey, back to you."

"Dumb shit, why bother with this report? It's just nature being nature." Ryan smirked a good twenty seconds after the shot finished. "You didn't show my shoes, right?"

"No."

Brian nodded. "Fuck, I don't care about the stupidity of this. Look at it this way. We're at the beach and already done for the day, well, on the air. After talking to a few more people, we can call this off and enjoy ourselves. We could hit the bar tonight. I heard they have the finest pie and coffee combo in Maine."

Ryan rolled his eyes, thinking of how rich he'd be if given a dime for every time Brian made a reference to Special Agent Dale Cooper from *Twin Peaks*.

Right on cue, Nathan came out of his house. Mr. Herman spotted him locking the front door as he and his camera buddy drove onto the road.

"Found someone! Let's make this short and sweet," Brian said.

The two newsboys waltzed up to the house.

Brian shouted, "Hey, buddy! Mind if I ask you a question?"

Ryan held up the camera and ensured the blinking red light was flashing to encourage the beach boy to reply.

"Sure, but be quick."

"What are your takes on the dead sea creatures behind your house?"

Nathan looked confused. "Um, what?"

Ryan lowered the camera as Brian opened his mouth to speak but sealed it shut.

After the silence the news crew endured, Nathan said, "You guys are out of time. Bye."

"Hold on there, speedboat. We're talking about the washed-up sea creatures on the beach behind your house. Apparently, this is a fairly common event here."

"I wouldn't know, considering I just moved here."

The two news reporters glanced at each other briefly until Brian pulled out a card. "Well, here's my number. If you come across anything—and I mean anything about the Moving Graveyard—please let me know. Good day."

Nathan peered down at the card as the two news reporters left thinking, *Moving Graveyard? What the hell are these people talking about?* Then the thought of black pollen came to mind. *Just another crazy story.*

At the Miles Winery, kids were playing hide-and-seek in the maze. Jeff wasn't thrilled about it. He hated Jacob, the leader of the hide-and-seek game they were playing. Most of all, he loathed how high-pitched the kid's voice was when he screamed and shouted. Jeff wiped the sweat from his face, only to have it replenish. The temperature was already ninety degrees and muggy. The afternoon was still far off. Anger was easily triggered in hot and humid weather, and Jeff wasn't a saint with his temper.

After Jacob knocked over a pot of flowers, Jeff hollered, "Get the fuck out of this maze!" His face was never redder and more deluged in sweat than it was now. It felt like his head was burning from a fever, and his voice was only making his throat drier. "Kids," he mumbled. "Can never work in peace around here."

"Got that right, sweetie. Or should I say sweaty?"

Jeff turned to find Liz standing beside one of the kids toward the left. Jeff launched up onto his feet. "Liz, how are you?"

"Doing better than you, it appears. I hope Mike hasn't been too bad. It's usually Jacob who—"

"I know. Believe me. I know, and it wasn't Mike exactly. Are you babysitting?"

"Yuuuup. Been at this all week, but today's my last day. Mike here—" Liz patted the boy's badly cut hair. "Can see his busy parents again soon."

"That's great." Jeff squeezed and shuffled his overly used cloth between his filthy hands.

"Have you by any chance seen Nathan around?" Liz gave a stare made of pure seduction.

"He's at work. Won't get out 'til later tonight sometime. I don't know when."

Jeff couldn't stop staring at Liz's revealing breasts. Her white tank top was slipping down on the right with her right breast nearly displayed. She wasn't wearing a bra.

Oh no! It's much too hot for that. She knows it's slipping, Jeff thought. *She has to know, and she's giving me that stare. And really could her pants be any shorter?*

Liz leaned toward the right. "I have to admit that I'm pretty impressed. You out here in the heat like this? I'd never be able to do it."

"It's just dedication, I suppose. I love this maze. Well, maybe only because I've spent so much time on it. It kind of just grew on me."

Liz was looking irritated in the heat. Jeff wouldn't lead her to the city boy, and though Jeff knew she was quite done with his consistent stuttering, he wanted to continue this pointless rambling. Though deep down, he thought she enjoyed men who stuttered when speaking to her. The reason behind it was pleasurable, a confidence booster.

"Well, honey, it's a shame you can't get Nathan for me. I've been meaning to talk to him." She shifted her weight back to neutral. And for kicks, she gave Jeff another one of those stares. "I'll be seeing ya," she said shyly.

Jeff turned his attention back to the flowers and then toward Liz who was purposely rocking her ass back and forth almost wildly. *Really though? She wants to see Nathan of all people? I guess she likes it bad. The city life is probably where she's always belonged,* Jeff thought angrily and unsurely. *Well, fuck him. Ruiz needs to burn in hell.*

Too bad for poor Jeff, if anyone were burning in hell, it sure wasn't the city boy sitting in the air-conditioning, checking off shipment orders.

In the Miles Winery building, Neil was the only manager present—if one could even really call him much of a manager—and he was eager to take advantage of that. He got up, finished his coffee, and traveled down to the basement. The steps creaked like someone adjusting wrist or nose bones, successfully snapping it back into its proper position. Nathan knew damn well who it was.

Aside from a young couple and an employee, Jimmy, who were up in the fine wine section, nobody else was in the building. It was funny how easily it was to pick up on noises when down in the basement. It was Nathan's own security system.

"Hello, Neil." Nathan did not look up to make sure it was the big bastard.

"Just coming down to see how things are going. Jimmy's got his hands full. That couple's always been picky."

"You personally know them?"

"I wouldn't exactly say personal, Mr. Ruiz. After a while, we learn about the customers who shop here more than once a month is all. I know Jimmy can handle himself. It's you I don't know anything about."

This was one of those moments when the employee is working, but the boss finds it okay to stop the work and insult the worker, Nathan thought. *Believe it, asshole.* Neil staggered over in his suit. *Had he ever changed it?* He adjusted his red tie and leaned against the stone wall by the desk.

"You do a lot of sitting around, huh?" Neil asked. "You do check the barrels, right?"

"Yeah. Why wouldn't I?"

"And you clean the tops of them, correct?"

"Clean the tops?"

"Yes, every barrel." Neil smirked.

"I would have done such a tedious task…if I were ever told to do it."

"Nobody's said—"

"I was never told to dust anything Mr. Miles. Never."

Neil straightened his standing posture. "Well, you will be cleaning the tops of every barrel today."

"Sure thing," Nathan remarked. "Then I'll go ask the real boss what I should really be doing and what the janitor is really doing during his shift." *Oh, that face is priceless*, Nathan thought, watching Neil hold back a wiseass comment.

His face showed it all. "I'm your boss, Nathan."

"More like a lower form of one. I know how this place works. The person who pays me, the one who supplies me with the work I do need to complete, is your wife." Nathan got his right to smile and displayed one but kept it brief. "I'd like to hear sudden job requests from my boss first. That's all I'm saying. I will clean the tops of every barrel today, but if I find out, I never had to…" Nathan waited to hear a response. This was where and when Nathan touched on Neil's nostalgic personality.

"I'm sure she'd think it's a great thing to do, Nathan. It would help Chris so much, don't you think?"

"It would lessen my time to check and move shipments."

"If I were in your position, I would gladly help my fellow peers."

"Oh, that's great then," Nathan replied. "You can help Chris now as I'm too busy. See, you'd be helping the two of us by doing one thing. Feels good to help, huh? I'll let ya know if I can't get it done or not, but I'm doubtful."

Nathan one. Neil zero. Sorry, pal, but you're doing this to yourself, Nathan thought, putting his attention back at the shipping lists.

Neil only smirked. The insult came through almost unnoticed.

"You know something, Mr. Ruiz, the day I met my wife was quite something." Neil smiled a little embarrassed as he began saying, "A bit cheesy, too."

Neil's eyes didn't match his own posture. He appeared to be holding something back, and as he spoke, he let that something slip out little by little.

"The sky was a mix of violet and a hazy, dusky orange as I stood by a ring toss booth. I was watching people enjoy themselves, waiting for my friends to finish stocking up on more tickets. I just wanted to leave. The carny at the ring toss was taunting me, trying to get me to play his stupid game. I was sick to death of watching every couple in the neighborhood walk by holding each other's hands, in their mouths, faces, and, shit, even in their pants."

Neil sighed, stared down at the grainy floor of the cellar, and gave Nathan a look that reminded him of his ex-boss Maxwell.

"It was hot and muggy. My friends all had their girlfriends leeched upon them. And there I was standing alone like some creep at high school lingering around another couple, hoping to see some action. That's how I felt anyway. You get me?"

Nathan nodded, not sure where this chat was going, so he played along with crazy old Neil.

"Good. But I'd be lying if I said the air wasn't gratifying," he said with a hardy laugh. "That cotton candy and funnel cake couldn't be matched. I thought to myself, 'Hey, at least I'm here and not in my apartment.' That's when she must have spotted me. I was in shape back then, you know, in my senior year."

"And that was a problem?" Nathan asked.

"For someone single it was. Now hear me out. This story may inspire you. She came up to me and gave a smile. She didn't need to say anything to grasp my attention. You know that kind of feeling, right? Well, she began asking me how I was and what I was up to. I thought I made the wrong decision in telling her the truth, about me being so single."

"Sure."

"True stuff, so we ended up buying tickets and leaving on our own. Didn't bother to tell my friends where I was going. I just left. And from that moment on, that night was enriched. The already pleasant smells of the carnival enhanced it, and damn, was I eager to throw her behind one of those absurd booths and give the place a new attraction, one that'd make the paper."

Nathan pictured a headline that read "Crazy Sex behind Game Booth in Annual Carnival Lacks Secrecy!" He laughed at the thought of it. "Why are you telling me this?"

"Hold on. I'm getting there," Neil replied. "We were ambitious teenagers who hadn't the slightest idea of what we wanted ourselves. I studied her eyes as she studied mine, and our faces drew nearer, just like you and Keria, only younger and wiser."

"How did you know about that?" Nathan shouted without hesitation.

"I have my ways, Mr. Ruiz."

"You better start explaining yourself."

"Huh, what? Listen to me. I don't want no city trash fucking my daughter, and I sure as hell aren't allowing it. That's it. Nothing complicated. I may not control your paychecks or your orders, but don't think I can't make your life a living hell."

"You and Keria get along, right?"

Neil gave Nathan a look of disgust. "Of course we do."

"What makes you think I can't tamper with that? Keria wouldn't let this slide. She'll notice what you're doing."

Neil held on to a brief silence, chuckled, and took in a dose of air. "I'd like to see you try," he muttered. "I won't have to. Keria would become distant with you. That'd be enough for me, making things a little awkward with you and Tia, too."

"Good day, Mr. Ruiz." Neil held a face that screamed, "What's wrong with you?"

Nathan watched the fat man leave the cellar. But he paused midway to the top of the staircase. "You know something, Nathan. The only reason why she wants you the way she does is because you're a mystery to her. That's all. The man she really wants is David. Poor guy's just being what every women needs. Then you come along." Neil finished his climb and shut the heavy wooden door slowly so the squeak would linger.

He's throwing more bullshit at me, Nathan thought. *He has to be. What was more wrong? The way Neil discussed his wife or the fact he knew about the kiss? Keria likely mentioned it.*

Even so, Neil gave unwanted questions. *Was—or is—David a possible lover of Keria's? Is Neil stalking her and Nathan? And is Neil planning on ruining the newborn relationship?* That last one seemed obvious.

The work shift dragged on longer than usual. Nathan thought it best to take a stroll on the beach and maybe see what the news reporters were going on about earlier. When he arrived, the place was near empty with a few couples here and there. Nathan chucked off his shoes and stepped into the blistering sand, only to jump back out. The burning sensation was incredible, like he had just placed his foot on a four hundred-degree oven rack. He yelped, not expecting the shock. Someone looked over. Nathan ignored it.

With his house paid off, new shoes weren't hard to buy. Hell, he could purchase half the store's stock of dress shoes if he wanted. Nathan slipped into his shoes and tread through the unforgiving sand, feeling like a child complaining about the water being too cold. Everyone else was taking a walk barefooted. Up by the water's edge, where the tiny tiki torch pier stood, laid a dead crab. Beside it were two dead jellyfish. *Oh, please don't let this be the big news! Of course a storm would do this.*

But Nathan failed to realize that a thousand dead sea creatures laid a half-mile away. His personal shoreline wasn't the only one littered. The sun's rays, even now at the beginning stages of evening, made things hard to see.

Nathan sat on the pier for a half hour, thinking of how he'd have to explain his reasoning behind making Neil's life a living hell if he were to go through with it to Keria. As opposed to Neil's thoughtless activities with his wife at that carnival, he had a bigger heart and starting point in his relationship, so Nathan thought. He then realized he'd set up lunch by the grape fields, all the perks of a great picnic included. He thought of the Miles trademark and the special wine they sold. This left an empty feeling somehow. *What have I done lately? I've been giving what I needed and more, yet I'm always in some cellar getting overpaid or wasting away in my mortgage-free home.*

A few speedboats zipped by, pushing tiny waves into the pier's legs. A group of kids, around ages seven to nine, was playing catch on the green grass.

"Hey, don't throw it over there!" the kid in red hollered. "You'll risk hitting the Wilkerson's shed!"

"Then move over!"

"To where? The ocean? Let's move to the sandbox!"

"There's no room there!"

Hollow Heights turned out to be a noisy place. No matter where Nathan fled to be alone, someone was always around, but there were no complaints from his mouth. During the trip, he wondered if he should record the city's nightly pandemonium. Moving from a location of hostility to a quiet, humble small town on Maine's oceanside felt like living in a cabin with a tiny trailer complex just down the road and nothing else for a hundred miles. Also small towns had their drama. If Liz and Neil were good for something, it was that mental sticky note. Drama lingered in the air.

"Rick! What did I tell you?" yelled the only girl in the group. "You get it. It's your fault it's in there."

Nathan glanced at the eerie home the kids feared. The smartass kid managed to throw the football though one of its windows, one that, to their fortune, had no glass to begin with.

"First of all, I can't even fit in there, and second, I'm not asking to open the door."

"It's your ball, Rick," said the girl. "Nobody cares to get it but you, so get it or leave it."

"Fine," Rick replied harshly.

Rick stumped toward the shed and peeked in, not aware the big, bad owner had already spotted him. His friends sure noticed. Mr. Wilkerson was a beefy man coated in a red flannel. He wore huge black boots and a yellow bandana tied to his brown ponytail.

"Hey, you," he said in one of those thick Southern accents. "Why you here?"

"Uh, to get my ball, sir."

"Why you throwing it in my home again?"

"It was an honest mistake."

Mr. Wilkerson got a kick out of Rick's shaken body. He stared at him almost like a stalker would his prey or maybe, to the locals, a molester. These thoughts sent a chill through Nathan's spine.

"Let me tell ya somethin'. My momma whipped my ass for doing such a thang. Never once had I gotten away either. I was always—" Mr. Wilkerson raised his hands and made brutal beating gestures with them. His large palm made an unsettling slapping sound on impact, like they were floppy beef patties smacking each other. "I always got hit!" he exclaimed. "How 'bout this? We make a deal. You don't get smacked. I keep the ball. Our secret. Like that?"

Rick stared at the hillbilly unsurely. He began stepping back, turning his tiny body around to face his friends when the creep shouted, "Hey, I ain't joking 'bout this. Watch your ass, or I'll beat it like a peach."

Rick ran back to regroup with his friends. Despite Nathan being a good distance away, Mr. Wilkerson turned to face him and smirked before returning to his trashy home. The kids looked terrified as if they'd spotted Godzilla walking up from the Atlantic's darkest depths.

Never heard of that freak, Nathan thought, looking out at the open sea. *Too far away to get a good look at him, but something tells me he's as ugly as Nanny McPhee.*

***

Back in the house, Nathan brewed coffee and sat on the sofa, thinking about David's involvement with Keria in the past years of his absence. When the coffeemaker's beeper went off, he got up and poured a cup into his favorite mug, the one that had the words "City Junk" written in brown letters. He kept his coffee black and sat on the sofa. He remembered something that might keep him away from the booze. *Something other than coffee.* He wanted to draw out his thoughts literally.

Two years ago, he had taken drawing lessons from a lady named Mariel Hopkins, a women who was artwork herself. Nathan reimagined her appearance, a twenty-one-year-old blonde whose body curved perfectly and wore the skin of a design only a born model had. She was, in fact, a model. She only enjoyed teaching people how to draw on the side.

"I hate being up on stage like that. It's horrible, but I need the money, and it does boost my confidence," she said during the first class session.

She only had a group of six men, all in their forties with tongues hanging loose, nearly all ugly. No wonder she gave Nathan special treatment and most of her time in class. She felt comfortable in his presence, and she secretly fancied him, too, but he'd never know. He was of a fitting age at the time, a young nineteen-year-old.

Nathan stopped going because Miss Hopkins left. She finally had the money to leave Rotor. Nathan remembered the gentle kiss on the cheek she contributed to him on her last day. She publicly gave it and later ignored the demands of the other men.

"Bye, Nathan. I'll see you on the news. World famous artist." She hurried out, leaving the creeps mumbling in depression.

Nathan rushed out as well.

Placing the memory aside, drawing was a skill Nathan had but never used. Back on the pier, he wondered what good he could do, merely drinking heavily in a free house and working in a cool cellar filled with wine. Others, like Jeff, worked outside in the scalding sun. It didn't feel so good. It felt raunchy. In a sense, Neil could be understood. A city boy mooching off his wife's money came to take his daughter.

Draw her something. Write her a poem if you dare. Show her you care, you stupid, stupid fool. He went to take a sip of his coffee, but as he did, an unexpected coldness hit his tongue. Hardly a minute had passed after pouring the steaming hot liquid into his mug with no sugar or milk added. *How is it cold?* The sensation hit him like a hot shower turning brisk cold in an instant. He placed the mug down and felt the cup. It was also slightly below room temperature.

As bizarre as the change in temperature was, it gave Nathan an idea for a poem. He wasn't a writer so he took that idea and simply made it a list of words: cold, warm, bitter, sweet, anxious, solitude. And he thought of how he could draw them out. It didn't take a long time to continue the production. He got right to sketching.

The night ended admirably. Depending on one's take on such a claim, Nathan thought it perfect. The outlining, an almost complete first draft, went well. The only alcohol he drank was cupcake wine, just to mellow the mood and reduce the anxiousness given off by the caffeine (as much as he could manage). He knew he wasn't a world famous artist, but after having drawn something again with a passion for the first time in years, he felt like the kind of artist that stood out from the rest of his class, that type of famous.

He tucked away his art in a drawer beside the bed, not realizing how late it was. *One in the morning? Can't be.* But it was. Keria never called, but neither had Nathan, so the guilt trip tied itself with the both of them equally. However, calling her now was almost a must. No, it was a must, a moonstruck kind of desire. But he didn't. Not this late he couldn't. Keria was probably asleep.

Nathan held his phone, looking down at its screen like a medium peering into another world. He felt alone, not really understanding his place in her life. Neil's words had installed a nagging recall system in his head. *Poor guy's just being what every women needs. Then you come along.*

***

The next six days of the week flew by for most. Nathan and Keria began a nightly routine of calling and talking until after midnight, but to them, the week dragged.

"Only a week left, and I'll see you again!" she exclaimed gleefully.

"Yeah, and I've got something planned," Nathan replied slyly.

"Oh, really?" she said, letting the "really" really drag out.

"You bet."

"Can I get a hint?"

"Hmmm, I suppose."

"Oh, come on. It doesn't have to be that revealing. Just throw something at me here. I'm dying."

Nathan laughed. "Okay, it has something to do with outdoors. Happy now?"

"Satisfied."

He last spoke to her on the phone an hour before calling it a night, an early hang-up at eleven o'clock, when he heard a steady *Klonk!* on the door. All the noise did was raise an imaginary eyebrow in Nathan's mind, but when it happened again, he decided to check the door. Hefty gusts of wind hit the door and windows. As this occurred, that *Klonk!* made a return.

Nathan slowly opened the front door, allowing the screeching wind to travel through his living room. Nothing was outside. The phone rang, and Nathan went back inside to answer it, unnerved by how unexpected the call was.

"Hey, Nathan? It's David."

"Is there a problem?"

"Oh no. I just wanted to ask a favor. Could you help me fish this Monday morning? My dad's away on travel soon. He says he wants to refresh his mind."

"Um, sorry, I can't. I work unless you can change that day to tomorrow morning somehow."

"My dad will be with me tomorrow. No point there."

"I'll see what I can do. Neil's been trying his damn hardest to make my life a living hell. If Tia's not there, I won't be able to."

"Ah, shit."

"What?"

"Nothing. Just I know how he can be. Don't listen to him. He's responsible for so much shit around here. The things he says put people in awkward positions."

"Like how?" Nathan asked.

"Shit, where do I even begin? That fucker's been stirring up trouble like a teenage girl. Hollow Heights is a small town as you know. It makes it easy for people like him to be crowned king...at least when it comes to drama. Anything—and I mean anything he doesn't agree with—he'll let ya know and do something about it."

"Yeah, I got that much."

"Shit. What did he do?"

"Well…" Nathan pondered for a steady moment of whether he should mention what Neil said or not. "He mentioned you."

"Me? How so?"

"He said Keria was after you but found me mysterious so she…I dunno…drifted away from you to me for a sense of mystery. Thrills. Some shit like that."

"Aw, hell. Sounds like old Neil."

"So he's throwing bullshit at me, right? Like I didn't come and interfere with anything?" Nathan's tone of voice was antsy and flustered.

"Just as much as any teenage whore," David replied.

There was a feeling of relief with those words but also an unnerving sensation of distrust.

"Good," he replied. "I'll try to talk to Mrs. Miles tomorrow."

"Actually, I think I should. Maybe I can convince her. It is my idea. I should push it on her. Not you. And if bad old Neil comes in, I'll deal with him so you won't have to."

"Sounds like a plan," Nathan said, waiting for another *Klonk!*

About an hour later, David called back. Tia answered David's call and made it possible for Nathan to take off the day despite the short notice. It was almost like the woman could just snap her fingers and make things work.

Here's a new house free of charge, and here's the job you've always wanted! And I got specially made paychecks just for you! And well, extremely flexible hours! Nathan thought, imagining Tia speaking the words. So that was it, a nice fishing trip with childhood friend David out on the Atlantic. *Out beneath the black pollen, listening to the otherworldly children chant their creepy nursery rhyme, all huddled together by the tall, skinny, silent entity. The water as black and quiet as deep space. All is an uncharted realm that will never be understood by the living.*

The cuckoo clock chirped at five o'clock in the morning, but the talking fish, the Big Mouth Billy Bass, on the wall woke Nathan.

"Here's a little song I wrote!" the bass sang and sang.

Nathan couldn't find the thing at first. One of the three rooms that were little explored held it. It was the small bedroom in the very back. Nathan entered the room, saw the moving bass on its wooden plank, and smirked. There was a tiny mattress by a dirty window, and a white rug cloaked the floor. Finally after the bass finished its song for God knows how many times, it stopped. This room was eerie. And damn, was it small and nearly useless, but also interesting.

What made it so odd was the shelf above a white door. It held five dolls no taller than a pinky finger and no wider than a thumb. They were all made with thick brown fabric, similar to the characters from the game *Little Big Planet*.

All the fishing gear was with David, or at least that was what Nathan expected. He slipped on a grey T-shirt that had a little trout on the top right corner, an old pair of jeans, and sneakers. He combed back his hair and brushed his teeth. Suddenly, the bass began singing again.

"Don't worry. Be happy!"

He left it alone, seeing no use in caring. *Let the batteries wear out while I'm not here. Doubt it'll take long, seeing as it's been there for years. Unless Keria placed it there.*

He left the house, got his fishing license from a fishing store (the one he was technically working for today), and left to meet David. The docks were packed like always with both people and boats. David stood by his, wearing his favorite fishing hat, the one with the golden hook. *His golden seashell.*

"Good. You passed the first part, getting here on time."

"Funny. I don't usually sleep in."

"Well good. We gotta get going, so hop onboard." David leaned on a large green bag.

"Only if you got the equipment."

"You mean fishing rods? I got bobbers just for ya because I'm sure you can't fish without those yet, city rat."

Nathan rolled his eyes and climbed onboard. He bent over the edge to help David carry in his fishing gear. "Gave a name for the boat?"

"I call it the *Golden Shell*."

"Saw that coming." Nathan chuckled. "You should paint it gold."

"You think you're wise?"

"I'm just messing."

The sun was hardly above the horizon. It was already hazy. Two miles from shore, they dropped two crab cages.

"Best time to fish and catch a few crabs. There's nothing quite like it." David sat on one of the benches, wet and sandy, soon-to-be coated in fish guts. David pulled out a bucket of bait, dead fish heads, bodies, and tails. "I find the heads the most annoying, but the tails can be a bitch to hook up to. I'll use them." David picked up a fish head and stuck it onto his hook.

Blood and gut dripped from the scaly, evenly sliced cuts. It made a nice, little plop and splashed on Nathan's sneakers.

"That's gonna happen a lot," David said in a low tone.

***

"Ah, no more bodies, all heads and tails," David spoke a good three hours into the trip. "I thought I carried enough of those."

"You probably did. I've been losing bait like there's no tomorrow. My grandfather would be busting on me for this." Nathan laughed.

He peered out at the cliff and Spangle. He was looking for the miners he had seen in his dream and felt foolish for doing so. The sky was clear of all clouds, but the weathermen had mentioned another thunderstorm for later tonight.

"Hey, have you heard about the dead sea creatures before?" Nathan still looked out at the cliff's rocky features.

"Yeah, why?"

"I ran into reporters who asked about it. I didn't know it was a common thing here."

"It happens during intense thunderstorms. You know how the media is, always making shit seem like it's linked to other shit. I know in a lot of cases that things aren't what they seem, but this? Come on now."

"Yeah."

"You live by a beach, right?"

"Right in front of one."

"Then that's why they're bothering you. Don't—and I mean it—never let them make a habit of asking you about that. Believe me. They won't stop."

"I think they got the hint this morning."

David laughed. "For your sake I hope."

After helping David for the day, when Nathan rested at home, the TV flashed on, and a terribly loud buzzing hollered out of its speakers. *White noise doesn't sound like that, but there's only snow on the screen.*

He felt cold again, but as his skin reacted to the sudden change in temperature, his head began to burn, like a fever just occurred. The pain beat on him. It was odd to feel all cold in his body but overheated in the head. His body reacted to the sensation with violent chills. Soon, noises came from the hallway. They were soft thumps. *Footsteps?* No the noises sounded like someone bumping into the walls.

Nathan poured icy water onto a rag and placed it over his head, still feeling like he had a fever, and sat on his sofa. The TV stayed off, but Nathan eyed it, expecting it to flash on again and pierce his head with that terrible noise. *The thing's worse than that jukebox back at the diner.*

Thump thump! The noise in the hallway retuned. The sofa Nathan lay on stood near the hallway. Nathan listened closely. The noise did not stop. Nathan pushed himself up and placed his feet on the floor, trying to urge himself up off the couch, but felt the pressure in his head delay his every attempt to stand.

What? Are you already old? Get up! Blue fuzz rushed into his eyes, temporarily blinding him. He saw something glide across his fuzzy vision. It was a shadow, very human-like but small.

The hallway was empty. The cause of that noise wasn't a person or a loose object outside the wall, but on the bottom of the left wall was a vent.

Bingo! It was the air coming through the vent! Duh! Relieved, Nathan sluggishly approached the sofa, holding his right hand on his head. He didn't want another head rush. Despite his effort, another rush of blue fuzz blinded him, and the loud buzzing returned. When he could see properly, Nathan turned to face the TV. It wasn't on, yet the buzzing continued. And it grew louder and louder.

He got up to leave the room, only to fall onto the floor. He stood up and saw that he had tripped over nothing, maybe his own shadow.

With the aid of ibuprofen and the decision to sleep in another room, the cold chill and fever went away. But the coldness lingered around. So for now, after that lovely nap, Nathan turned off the air-conditioner. It got that bad.

Jeff sat in his house, feeling every bit as lonely as a hateful, single, old man in a nursery home. "TV sucks, hobbies that aren't boring cost too much money, and people fucking suck," he mumbled to himself. He was on his second Budweiser, sitting on his sofa, ready to fall asleep, when his phone rang.

"Hello?"

"Jeff?

"Mr. Miles, how are you?"

"Interested in what you have to tell me."

"Of course you are. Well, Nathan's doing the usual, nothing different from a typical alcoholic, I presume."

"Just continue watching him for me. I fear for my daughter. Really, I do."

"I personally, Mr. Miles, don't trust that man as far as I can throw him."

"Doesn't prove much, but I know his type, crafty and horny, drunk, and armed. Remember where he came from. Have you set up a day with Liz yet?"

"Yeah," Jeff said, rolling his eyes, "it's been discussed in the fashion you've asked of me."

"Don't think you're doing anything wrong. This is just a precaution. I want to know what Mr. Ruiz will do if given an opportunity, if you get me."

"Of course." Jeff's voice got more irritated.

"Great. See you at work tomorrow."

Jeff hung up, almost unable to resist slamming the phone into the wall. *I don't give a fuck. Let Neil suffer. Who gives a shit about Nathan and Keria? Rumor has it that Neil can't fire a soul. I should be the manager. I shouldn't do anything for that asshole.*

Anger rooted in his every thought. No woman really wanted poor Jeff. Oh no. And he knew it. But Liz wasn't picky. He knew her secret, that little cashier trick she played. But he didn't want it like that. He felt awkward, like that day when he bought condoms from that 7-Eleven clerk who looked at him funny. He didn't even want them. His damn friend told him to get them for him.

But now, Jeff got his chance to be the big guy, thanks to Neil, the kind of man who didn't care about people's judgments and understandings or, best yet, get pushed over to the side.

Oh, whatever, Jeff thought. *I'm not that shy or weak. I'd break the ice for Liz. If she were passed out, he sure would. Oh shit! That's right! There's a party coming up!*

Anger again fissured his mind-set. Thinking of Nathan triggered the emotion he buried so deeply. He could bring that city boy down, teaming up with Neil. Then he'd rank up from being the caretaker and boss Nathan around, too.

But Jeff Jones was a pushover and always would be. He was a scared, helpless, thirty-year-old caretaker. He was book smart but would die in a day if left alone in the city unless he happened to become someone's goon, likely a quiet bookworm planning out the thefts and deals. He wanted Neil's job badly and would sucker him in so he'd become the next co-manager. But his thirst to start up trouble was growing, and Neil's little plan was the beginning of a long-winded series of questions he'd have to answer to in the near future.

CHAPTER 6

Balance

He first saw an angel in his dreams the day Keria returned home from Noreen's. It wasn't an angelic being, but rather a stone depiction of one, a piece of a very expensive tombstone. Under a sun so dim, it could be mistaken for the moon it stood, shimmering in what appeared to be an otherworldly gleam of green light. This terrified him, and it was a recurring image, both animated and still.

David managed to collect enough fish, lobster, and clams the day Nathan assisted. Progress came later that day when David's nerves screamed, "I'm gonna get fired for this!" He showed his anxiousness unwillingly. For a guy who was calm, cool, and collected, he sure wasn't in character in the heat of the moment, so Nathan thought.

The following day was an important one for Nathan. After the bills were paid off, he made a list of supplies and orders for the surprise picnic, so far able to afford every damn thing without having to remove a single item. *Kind of a shocker. Or maybe I'm still living in the past.*

Before he left for work, Nathan gathered his second draft of the art he'd been working on and decided he would begin his final draft tonight after running those few errands. An unsettling concern was Neil. *Just how far would the man be willing to go to ruin my relationship? What insanity lives in his brain?*

By the Miles fountain, another game of hide-and-seek was taking place. Kids were out way past their bedtime. Jeff wasn't there to holler. He was with Liz and Lillie.

"No. I would never do that with you!" Lillie slammed the table with both her palms.

"Sorry, bud." Liz held up her hands.

"What's the deal with this guy anyway?" Jeff asked. "I mean, he's trash."

"That's all Neil talking." Liz reminded him. "The fact that Keria of all people is his girlfriend says something. He must be a sweetheart."

"Fuck that! Nobody gave me a chance. Nathan shows up out of nowhere, and everyone thinks he's great!"

"That's because he is," Lillie replied. "Maybe you need to lay off the Miller. You get angry when you drink."

They were sitting in the Miles Winey during after hours. Neil was about to join them and discuss his concerns. However, Lillie carried in Miller's Light. The whole thing was turning into a party, something Neil would preferably like to avoid. After all, this was supposed to be a secret.

"When's that geezer getting here?" Lillie spoke loudly.

"He's actually not that old," Jeff said.

"Whatever! Hey, Liz! When ya gonna fuck Nathan?"

Liz chuckled. "So why does Neil want to talk to me?"

"You'll see. He's worried about Nathan."

"Oh, really?"

"Yea, really. And could you tell your friend to settle down? We're supposed to be quiet about this. She shouldn't even be here."

Lillie snorted as she laughed at Jeff.

"Um, Lillie," Liz said. "How much did you drink before we met up?"

"Truckloads!"

"Good God," Jeff muttered.

"Lillie, maybe you should wait outside."

"Aw come on. Not you, too!"

"Hey, Lillie, you got a little something on your face." Jeff tapped his left cheek.

"Oh no. Get it off."

"I can't. Go check it out in the bathroom mirror. It looks like hair dye."

Lillie began stumbling up and entered the hallway that led to the restrooms.

"Nice one," Liz said.

"Just trying to keep things quiet."

"Heh, so what is it you do? I see a bit of a smartass in you, not some mindless yard worker."

"I work on computers as a hobby. I'm not expecting to hit big with it."

Jeff was nervous, tapping his index finger on the table like a woodpecker beating bark. The heat from the lights above suddenly became noticeable, and he was worried if he looked sweaty or not.

Liz leaned back in her chair and smiled. "I think that's neat. You know, I just bought a new computer about a week ago. I can't figure the damn thing out. I had someone build me one for a good discount. It's kinda just sitting up in my room."

"What operating system is it running on?"

"What's that?"

"Do you have a Mac or PC?"

"Windows 8. I can't find the damn Start icon anywhere." She laughed.

"Is that the only thing you don't understand?"

"Nah, there's a lot I don't get." Liz slipped another one of those stares Jeff always looked forward to and smiled. "If I need any help, I know who to call."

"Any time," Jeff replied nervously.

A door flew open in the hallway, and in came Lillie. She wasn't looking so well. "Don't go in there!" she hollered, nearly falling headfirst into the floorboards.

"You gotta do something about her," Jeff mumbled, "If Neil—"

"Neil? Neil? Oh, please! What's that fat bastard got to say to me, huh?" Lillie bellowed.

The front door of the winery opened, and in came Neil. He stood quite still, staring at Lillie who was allowing her weight to lean more on the left, causing her to trip on herself every so often in a stuttering sort of fashion.

"Who's this, Brittany O'Neil?"

Jeff smirked and gave into a quick chuckle.

"Fuck you, half-pipe," Lillie said.

Neil rolled his eyes. "Jeff, do us all a favor and take Miss Hot Stuff outside so I can talk with Liz."

"My honor, sir."

"Thank you."

Lille sluggishly walked herself out, but Jeff followed her through the front door to ensure she remained outside or left for home. If she were to leave, he'd have to guide her.

"Sorry about that," Liz said. "She's my follower, like a puppy dog. I can't leave anywhere without her. Kind of like...you and Jeff, right?"

"Afraid so," Neil replied as he sat down.

Liz placed both her elbows on the table and leaned her head into her hands. She spoke softly, "So what's this about? Why are we being so secretive?"

"I don't trust Nathan and can't have him dating my daughter. He came from a city with crime rates off the charts. Of all the places in the world, he chooses to live there? Why? The only reason I can think of is he enjoys a crime-filled agenda. Worst of all, some people think he killed Sophia. Nathan's running-away-from-the-past act that Keria keeps throwing at me is nonsense. You get me?"

Liz nodded. "Okay, but why get me involved?"

Neil leaned toward the center of the table. "I want you to shed his true nature. Have Keria see this man for who he really is."

"You want him to cheat on her with me?"

"Yes."

"That's a bit much, don't you think?"

"It is, something the wrong kind of man would do. You follow?"

"I follow." She smirked. "But what if it doesn't work? He seems like a decent guy."

"It will. He's got a talent for hiding. Something we all know, right? I'm sure he's playing that card here, too. To trick Keria's the only reason he came back."

Liz wasn't convinced. Neil was that type, the kind of person whose confidence ruled over thought, especially common sense.

"You can count me in, but it was all your idea. I'm not a fall girl."

"Understood. I'm glad you can help."

"Sure, if you say so. I'd better get going. Poor Jeff's dealing with my drunken puppy."

"Just remember what you're doing isn't bad. You're uncovering the truth," Neil stated. "There's nothing wrong with that. If he chooses to cheat, it's his doing."

"Sure." Liz was starting to feel a little guilty. The more Neil spoke, the more wrong the idea felt. She left the building and saw Jeff holding onto Lillie.

"Oh God! I hope she didn't do anything too stupid."

"She scared the kids, but that can be forgiven." Jeff was struggling to keep Lillie on her feet.

"Run or the witch'll get ya!" she hollered.

Jeff swiveled his eyes at Liz. "You owe me."

Rich Mount's bus stop was swarming with flies, shit eaters who felt too comfortable placing their sorry excuse for legs on April, while she was waiting for the bus to arrive. She was also being watched. The follower was admiring April's purple hairlines. She sat under the black hood of the bus stop booth, feeling the heat beat on her skin like a hot sand bag was smacking her.

Maine wasn't a far drive, but the bus would be easier, or so she thought. She felt disgusted with herself for consistently wiping the top of her forehead to remove sweat. She often had to place a chunk of hair that fell out of place over her left ear, too, for added annoyance. She had a black case sitting beside her. It was carrying her prize possession, a violin. And she had a green backpack.

She continually glanced at her iPhone. The bus was twenty minutes late. She felt edgy in the heat, shifting her weight the best she could without standing up to stretch. The bench was awful, thick, hard metal shaded with black paint. All of the sun's rays were drawn right to the fucking thing. The hood above kept the worst of it out, but that was hardly an help. It was like roasting in an oven. *Just because you're not touching the flames doesn't mean you're not being cooked.*

"You okay?" said a voice by the street.

April looked over. It was a man in his early twenties wearing a muscle shirt and white Nike sports shorts. "Yeah, I'm fine." She quickly looked back down at her phone.

"The heat sure is something, huh? What's the manner? Can't drive?"

"I chose not to, and don't ask why. I'm not even sure I know the answer."

The man laughed a bit much, showing April he was all on her like the flies.

"Yeah," she replied almost sarcastically. "You know, I've been waiting for the same bus. I left to get a drink about ten minutes ago. I hate the heat and got antsy. It looks like this bus ain't showing up. Want an iced tea?"

"Didn't you just drink something?"

"Yeah, but it didn't help much. Come on. It'll be on me."

"Sorry. I really can't miss this bus."

"It's right there." The man pointed at a little corner shop.

Couples were eating ice cream beneath some shade cast by large umbrellas that sprouted out from the center of a few tables. She quickly peered up at the store and let her eyes drop back to her phone.

"Yeah, I know," she muttered.

"Ight. I see. I see. Well, if you change your mind, you know where to find me." The man jammed his finger at the shop one last time.

Still, even after the moron left, April didn't feel safe. The guy was watching her, more or less. April decided to call Keria and see how things were going. Keria picked up on the second ring.

"Hello?"

"Hi, Keria?"

"Aw, hey, sweetie. How's it going? On your way yet?"

"I wish. I'm waiting at the bus stop and—" April glanced over as discreetly as she could and saw the guy talking to other girl, a blonde with a little dog, but not the kind from *Legally Blonde*. She was like the trashy type whose face was drained of youth, courtesy of drugs.

"There's some guy hitting on me. Not in a good way. He was like really straightforward," she said in a soft voice.

"Men," Keria said mockingly. "Luckily I found a special one."

"You sure about that?"

"Of course I'm sure," Keria replied defensively.

"Okay, okay. Can't wait to meet him then. That is if I don't get raped and murdered first."

April was overacting. The stalker was merely another prick looking for a one-night stand who already found another candidate, the blonde in the yoga pants with stale-looking skin. She wore a white T-shirt that screamed, "Look at my hard nipples!"

April wore shorts that weren't modest herself and a shirt a size below her actual size. Her hair was also an eye-catcher. Her purse looked as if it were made of purple duct tape. It wasn't though. The whole duct tape-making shit bothered her.

"Oh, please. And relax. I'm not even in Hollow Heights yet myself. I'm still with my grandmother."

"Aw, I hope that all works out."

"Same. It's been rough lately. Her illness is getting worse."

"She has Alzheimer's, right?"

"Yeah, and I hate saying it, but she can't stay in her house. She's always asking me, 'Where am I? How'd I get here?' It's hard for me to handle, you know?"

"Sounds like you need a girl's night out, hon."

"More than you know. We should go out to the boardwalk. Still with Chris? We could double date."

"Meh." April sighed.

"Aw, sorry. I know somebody I can hook you up with. He's a great guy."

"What? Is every guy great up in Hollow Heights? Look, I just broke up with Chris. I'll think about it. I have to see how he is myself."

"You will. He and Nathan are best friends, even after all this time. Well, I better get going. I still need to set up everything for Noreen before her move-in date. I'll see you at my house when you get there. And just avoid that other guy, okay?"

"I was planning on it." She glanced over again. "Bye, baby. Best of luck to ya."

"You, too, hon. You need it more."

Finally, the bus arrived, four minutes after the conversation with Keria. April leaped up off the bench, took her violin case and backpack, and waited impatiently for the driver to open the door. When he did, April launched herself in and said, "You're late."

The overweight bus driver merely rolled his eyes and huffed. Surprisingly, no one else joined in during her stop. As the bus drove past the corner store, she spotted the guy who she thought was a stalker. His face was a mere inch away from the blonde's breasts.

"Creep," she muttered. But a microscopic feeling of jealousy was in her, one she couldn't avoid.

The scenery stayed the same, no matter how many miles she traveled, with trees and small towns here and some there. April hated it. She had her headphones glued into her ears, tapped her foot on the metal leg of the seat she sat behind, and glared out the thick window of the bus. She wasn't in the best mood; however, the thought of seeing Keria again kept her somewhat upbeat. The man across from her gawked. He liked April's sense of fashion, like the other guy from the bus stop had.

The bus was muggy. "Sorry. The AC is busted" read a label pasted above the driver's seat.

"Ugh," April whispered.

The bus was gross, inside and out. Below her feet, the metal floor was sticky and foul. Every seat was overdue for replacement, and the ceiling looked rusted. *If it rained, the water would likely sink through and flood the bus*, she thought.

The walls, especially around the window she sat beside, reeked of old toothpaste but looked as if it had been used to hold someone's used gum. The heat turned the chewed pieces' hard surfaces into an odd flexible-stiff sort of string if pulled on, something April never thought of doing. There was a name written under a nest of softening gum that was carved into the metal. Tim Joyce. It didn't mean anything, but April automatically blamed that person for the gum housing.

After a while, April removed her earphones. The ambience of the bus came tunneling through. *Clung! Sniffle! Cough! Clung! Rattle! Clung!* Shit like that. April's ears were sore from her loud music, but no way would she listen to the public. She placed the plugs back into her ears.

Afterward, the driver stopped the bus and hollered, "Hollow Heights stop!"

April heard it, but barely. She leaped up, took her belongings, and jolted through the narrow hallway and out the door.

A steady breeze was outside. The ocean stretched out on the beach, leaving pieces of its life in the sand. April felt tempted to look for seashells but figured it'd be best to settle in first and vacation later. Just venturing though the town was interesting enough. Everything was bones and veins, wooden planks and machinery, the last time she'd seen this place. Now it was almost like a resort town, but the port town showed when she came across the docks and its lively stock of fishermen. Business was booming. Miles Winery was inspiring people to grow their own gardens, and the lighthouse stood just the way it had for a hundred years.

A girl could get used to this, she thought. *The sun is bright; the ocean is alive. A postcard everywhere you turn.* As she walked the dirt path, a wooden sign stood where a split began, and it was saying that the docks were to the left and the fields were to the right. The fields were empty of anything but grass. Keria said to follow the beach nearest and look for the lighthouse and the field of grapes. That was how'd she find Tia and the store.

It was an easy find. The winery stood nearly as noticeable as the black and white-striped lighthouse when one got close enough. April knocked on the door of the Miles Winery, but nobody answered. She decided to let herself in.

"Oh my God! This place…" she said softly. "It's gorgeous."

April explored the winery, all but the cellar. She studied the placement of the décor. All Keria's doing, that she was sure of.

As April made her way back to the first floor, Tia came up from the cellar and surprised her. She was wearing a purple polo shirt and white shorts that had a fuzzy look where they were cut.

"Oh my goodness! You scared the shit out of me."

"So did you. I heard someone walking around up here and wasn't sure if I should come up to see who it was."

"Sorry about that. I've been out in the heat all day. My brain is fried."

"Oh, please, it's no problem. Come sit down."

Tia walked toward the wooden table across from the host's desk and pulled out a chair for April to sit in. "Make yourself at home. I'm sure Keria will be here by tomorrow morning."

April sat down and placed her violin case and backpack on the table. "Lovely place you have here. The whole town is."

"Thank you. We've been working so hard to keep it that way. The town isn't exactly crowded, it's just...it's a port town, plenty of fishermen. I can't say they're the cleanest of all people, you know?" she said with a brief laugh.

"Oh, I'm sure." April laughed. "Is Nathan working?"

"No, I was just down there to make sure everything was done correctly. He's still new. But he hasn't made one mistake yet. I believe Keria told me he was a warehouse worker and has already done this kind of work before."

"That would explain why he's so good at it."

"Would you like anything to drink?"

"Yes, please. Water above all else, but I've been dying to try your homemade wine, the one with the lighthouse bottle."

"Oh, the Miles Wine? It'll be my honor. And you said you wanted water, right?"

"Yeah, I ran out during the bus ride."

"I'll be right back." Tia left the room in an antsy manner.

April sat comfortably in the chair. It sure beat the bus' seat. The place smelled like Morning Star and was so well kept that it felt like being in a palace.

When Tia returned, she held a glass of water and the Miles Wine bottle. "I'll be right back with the glass." She placed the bottle and water on the table.

"Great."

The bottle had Keria written all over it. April thought it was sweet of Tia to allow her daughter to design their best homemade wine. It was also very impressive work on Keria's part.

"So what've you been up to all this time?" Tia asked.

"Oh, not much. I've been practicing on the violin."

"Really? What songs?"

"All my own," she said cheerfully.

"You'll have to perform then. I hope you expected, too."

"Keria made that pretty clear." April laughed.

"Well, it's good to have you back. I'm sure Keria's anxious to see you."

"Yeah, she's dealing with a lot I heard with your mother. I hope everything's going okay."

"I suppose it is." Tia did not sound quite as lively.

"I think you'll be happy to hear that I've written a song about you guys. But I'm not revealing anything else until I play it," April said while Tia poured a glass of wine.

"Well, secrets up with this." She handed April the glass.

April smiled, took the glass of specially made wine, and sipped it. Her eyes widened as she said, "Amazing."

"You sure?"

"Sure I'm sure! I'm promoting this when I get home." After April finished her wine, she said, "I hope I'm not holding you up or anything."

"Oh, not at all. Do you know where your place is?"

"Nope, all I know is Keria said she'd see me at her house."

"I have a place for you right next to Keria's. The owner, Mike Ribbons, has it up for rent during the summer. He treats the place like a vacation house. I'll write the address for you."

"Awesome."

April wanted to learn more about Mike Ribbons when she arrived at his house. *This place was eaten by acid*. She looked beside it. Keria's house was well crafted, the outside as charming as Busch Gardens. But here, the world had made an unpleasant shift. No wonder why the guy hardly lived here. She walked closer. Stepping on the property's lawn felt remote, like ambulating from the mountains to a lone desert.

April sat her violin case beside her when she reached the door. The key Tia gave her struggled to unlock the house's aged lock, but when it did, a horrible metal screech followed, coming from somewhere in the house.

"Hello?" She picked up her violin and entered the home, not sure whether it was safe or not.

The inside wasn't well kept. Judging by the outside, that wasn't much of a surprise. The sofa looked okay, so April placed her backpack and violin case on it to have a look around. The house, first off, smelled like rotting cheese. Second, it was dusty. And third—and the most unsettling—was how the living room walls looked punched into, and some of the floor was badly damaged in the dining room. It appeared like somebody had purposely destroyed this place.

"Hello?" April said, hearing footsteps. "Mike?"

The sun leaked in, but dimly. Large white curtains cloaked every window, and the wind blew them wildly every so often. The house also felt damp. Considering it stood near several beaches, this was understandable, but this understanding didn't make up for the damage the air seemed to imply to certain features of the house. A lot of rusty metal was lying around.

"Mike, are you still here?" she asked.

April placed her soft fingers onto the dusty railing of the second-floor staircase and began walking up when a metal screech squealed. April flung her hand back and stopped herself from getting any closer to the top because that sound wasn't coming from upstairs. She traveled into the dining room, finding more holes and other damages, and entered the kitchen.

Not that it was outdated, but some of the appliances were old school. On top of a modern electric stove stood an old teapot from the 1800s, and above the entrance April had just walked through was suspended a very old, rusty apple peeler that, to her, looked more like a torture device of some kind. *This place is torture*, she thought, nearing the basement door. The kitchen also smelled like rotten eggs. There was a plate of eggs and bacon on a tiny wooden table across from the stove.

The knob of the sickly door was made of real diamond, a trait of some older homes. But Hollow Heights wasn't an old town. In fact, it was one of newest in the world. When she placed her hand on the diamond knob, the screech made its revealing call. April freaked out and backed into the table with the soiled breakfast. She gathered her balance back, swung the door open with little hesitation, and took a few steps back. The basement had a flickering light on by the bottom stair. April was breathing heavily but felt a strong urge to peek and did. The floor of the basement was made of damaged, uneven stone. *Stepping on that barefooted would be like running down a rocky street in bare feet.*

Just past the flickering lightbulb on the wall was a knitting machine. It was rusted and active. Something was jammed inside. As April glared at it, the jam momentarily let loose and gave out that metallic screech. It was almost like walking into a room and seeing a broken record player in motion. The only thing now that felt unnatural was the loudness of the sound, but April thought little of this and went to shut off the thing, not thinking twice about who or what may be in the darkness that surrounded the dying light and the aging machine. When the knitting machine was off, April noticed the darkness, felt uneasy, and left the cellar.

On July 21, as early as four in the morning, Nathan set foot in his made-up adaptation of the Miles Winery. The only difference was the lighting at first. The winery looked the same as it did in the real world; however, Nathan felt like he was in Net Smart.

He slowly walked along, examining everything, not sure what he was looking for. Then he spotted Keria sitting on the back porch with another man. He was fairly lean but didn't look inviting, like the kind of person you'd expect to hit on a woman who already had a man and does so blindly. The man's tongue grew and slithered among her face, proving too much for Keria to handle as it escaped her mouth and tasted whatever else it could reach.

Nathan turned to face the interior wry-eyed. The green glow was brighter down the hall that led to the restrooms, as if the waypoint of the dream had changed. When he set foot in the hallway, gunshots went off. Nathan held up his arms to cover his face as bullet holes appeared on the walls and floor around him.

When they stopped, Nathan lowered his arms and ran for the men's restroom. He made sure no one was occupying the stools and sighed heavily. The green glow was most colorful here.

Nathan washed his face, hoping he'd wake up, but like his previous nightmare, it could not be done. In the filthy mirror, he looked into himself and saw his father. He saw him deep inside, yet still alien.

"What were you really like?" Nathan asked. "The child's mind is so blind to reality. I could never find out myself."

"Take a look. What do you see in me?" said a voice.

It came from a stool behind Nathan. "I see a man washed up, worse off than me. Prove me wrong or say nothing at all."

"You'd like that. Your mother was a sketchy woman, Nathan, like those people in Rotor, only skilled at hiding it. You know that feeling. It's brutal, huh?"

"Depends, Father, whether you're telling the truth or not."

"You got lucky with that city. You flushed them out before they emptied your brains. I had it worse off than you."

"What?" Nathan turned to face the stools.

"My lovely marriage with Eve. Come on. You're an adult now. No excuses! You know how Eve acted. How she was always talking to other men while I was away working! She sure knew how to get around."

"For someone who was always home, that's a pretty wild thing to accuse her of, especially for a man who never was."

Alan said nothing. Nathan shook his head, realizing he was either a step closer to understanding his father or perhaps farther than ever before. The color faded to a mild light green mist so he left the restroom. He began thinking that maybe something nearly forgotten was trying to reach out in order to be remembered. So wherever the color was strongest, Nathan followed.

It was luring him deeper, yet still he was in the Miles Winery. *That organization doesn't matter here.* And still, the green-colored air remained mild. *Was it time to wake up?* A cold chill sunk into the winery like water on a sponge. The air felt like winter. The green mist faded entirely as a blue, frosty, almost white color one would see when finishing a blue raspberry Slurpee, the point when all that remains is the ice. Nathan followed the frost as it covered the floors and walls.

The feeling of Net Smart's presence was gone. Now it was pure Nathan and the Miles Winery. The frost trailed out of the building, leaving Nathan thinking the worst. *Was it going for Keria?* However, it stopped by the maze. He glanced outward, around, and then finally up at the winery. The green glow again surrounded the building. It always had been on the outside. On the roof stood a tombstone, an angel leaning over the inscription of the person it was made for with her arms overlapping her head.

There was no hope of seeing the person's name; however, the angel was clearly a tombstone. The thought of the Miles Winery ending up like Net Smart was too much to handle. But that was what Nathan got from it.

The frost moved again out toward the shore. It zigzagged through the town, teasing Nathan. It was going for Keria's home before stopping at the main beach, which was called the Golden Seashell. Whether that was its real name or not fit. Keria likely named it for David, if not Nathan's psyche, courtesy of this very dream.

The air was chilly here. A heavy, frosty fog lingered. Nathan advanced toward the water's edge and saw an empty fishing boat caught in the sand. It had the same shape and design as Albert's. A familiar odor came from all around. The fog was so thick that Nathan had to kneel to find the sand, so he did and saw dead sea creatures.

"What the hell?" he murmured.

Off the corner of his eye, Nathan saw a hand nearly white in the fog, lying still in the sand. Unsure of himself, he went closer to it, soon revealing not only one body, but several. He jumped up and felt something cold touch his shoulder. He glanced at it, seeing a black mass shaped to be a hand.

Nathan tugged himself away, feeling like a puppeteer tied in his puppet's own strings, and turned to face the same dark mass that appeared with the children during his previous dream. It jolted at him, and Nathan fell hard.

When he next opened his eyes, the fog was gone. An empty boat was still there, only it looked nothing like Albert's.

"You okay?" asked a fisherman carrying a box of bait and a fishing rod held between the box and his waist.

Nathan stumbled up and placed his right hand on his head. "I think so."

"Aye, best you get home then before you screw that up."

"Yeah, I'll manage. Thanks."

The old fisherman trailed off for his boat as Nathan brushed sand off his shirt and pants, feeling the beat of the sun's rays on his skin and eyes as if he were sun gazing. The morning's muggy air was as cumbersome as the afternoon's. *Feels almost as heavy as the green fog.*

Kids were throwing a large beach ball around and flying kites. This was his first time ever seeing the main beach, let alone stepping foot on it. There was one thing Nathan had to see before leaving. He slowly plowed his way through the warming sand, stepping on rigid seashells and tangled beach grass. The cement road and walkways weren't far. Nathan could see the welcome sign.

From on the beach, he could only make out the back, a bunch of wooden planks nailed together with a dusty coating of sand. He walked in front of it and held his right hand above his eyes to battle the sun's light as he read: "Welcome to the Golden Seashell!"

The sign was vague in the dream, as the thickness of the looming fog covered the décor above, beside, and below the wood. Above the sign was a thick cardboard cutout of a blonde beach babe wearing a bikini with large sunglasses over her eyes. There was a picture of a beach ball beside her toward the left. On the right side, a cartoon crab smiled and held out his right claw. Its shell color was a glossy orange. Below were thin ropes holding tiny anchors. All these things reminded Nathan of a pop-out picture book. He stared at the name, written in gold letters, but the sun was turning his headache into a migraine. He turned to face the road. He thought about tying his hands to something—anything—that would keep him from walking back here. Somewhere far in the back of his head, he always wondered what sleepwalking would be like.

Both embarrassing and scary, he thought. *That's enough touring for one day.*

<hr />

"Wait? What?" Keria said, giggling. "I have something planned for you. Think of it as a welcome back present."

"Aw, Nathan, you didn't have to."

"Of course I didn't. That's what makes it so necessary. When are you stopping by?"

"Well, I have to meet up with April. I don't think I ever told you she was staying at Hollow Heights yet. She surprised me with it a few days ago."

"Not a problem. She should join us. I'll bring David along, too."

"Sounds great. I can't wait to see you again. Feels like it's been so long."

"It has been for the both of us."

Keria smiled intensely, holding the phone tightly to her ear, sinking in every word Nathan spoke. "I'll call you before I leave, okay?"

"Okay, see you soon."

Finally, the day arrived. The drawing Nathan worked so hard on was perfected in the nick of time. The picnic would be prefect, too. Originally, it was planned for Nathan and Keria but could easily be applied for four people, a friendly get-together by the winery.

Nathan sat comfortably on his sofa, trying to forget his nightly tour of the Golden Seashell. Today made that possible. Too much good awaited him in the coming hours. A murder could slip right by him, and he wouldn't even notice. He kept imagining Keria's warming smile, her giggle, and her desire to be with him. He dialed David's number and told him to meet him at his house at noon. David said he'd go but didn't sound convincing.

The weather was shown on a five-day forecast, claiming there would be no rain for the next three days and possibly for the whole week. The newsboy and girl sat at their desk, going on about a potential drought. Nathan shut them up by turning off the power, got a quick bite to eat, and changed into a blue plaid buttoned shirt and khaki shorts.

The talking bass hadn't spoken a word since its little concert the other day. But damn, were the raccoons bad. Constant movement by the trash cans continued. Nathan bought mint-scented trash bags. They claimed to keep animals away with the overwhelming scent of mint, which were too much for an animal's sensitivity or something an old lady said, but yet they didn't seem bothered.

Around one in the afternoon, Keria called. "Hey, April's with me. I'm ready to come over."

"Great. David's already here, so when you're ready, head on over so I can start the surprise."

She laughed. "Can't you just tell me now?"

"Nope."

"Ugh! I hate suspense!"

"Then hurry up and get over here!"

"Okay okay!"

After Nathan hung up, he turned to notice David staring at him, smiling. He was dressed in white striped shorts and a Hawaii T-shirt with a large toucan sitting on a leafy tree. "I see all is well with you two."

"Yeah, I guess absence really does make the heart grow fonder."

"Only for the lucky ones," David replied.

"Of all people to say that too. Luck was never on my side."

"Says the guy who's been giving a free house next to a beach, a beautiful woman, and a job at the best winery known to man."

Nathan didn't say a word until David asked, "Can I have a bottle of water?"

"Sure. Hold on."

"Thanks. I'll stick to this over the wine today. So where's the stuff, Ruiz?"

Keria and April arrived a half hour after the call.

"Finally, you two show up," David said.

"Well a hi to you, too," Keria replied. "Now where's Nathan? He owes me an explanation!"

David had to study Keria for a moment. He had never seen her so happy before. Not that she was a miserable person, a mellow shade often tainted her mood. Now she was happy, purely so.

"He went upstairs to get something. You girls ready to go?"

"I've been ready," April said. "Keria here was touching up her makeup."

"Oh, please. So were you."

"Ladies, relax," David said.

They both stared at him intensely, shutting him up with demanding eyes.

Nathan came into the room. "Ready?"

April replied, "Just waiting on you."

"All right. Everything's ready to go. David and I got the stuff packed already."

"You're killing me, you know that?" Keria had a stern expression on her face.

"You'll figure it out on our way there. It's nothing out of the box," Nathan said.

"Well good. Let's get going. This case is murder." April was trying to relocate her violin case on her back.

"Okay, girls, just follow my lead." Nathan allowed Keria and April to leave first.

As they rode through the town, April noticed things she would have normally overlooked. Keria's creativity was the skin of Hollow Heights. Vines covered at least half the lampposts, miniature lighthouses sat outside people's homes, and grapes could be found everywhere.

"Wow, Keria, the whole town looks like your winery," April said.

It was only the two of them in the car. Nathan and David were in their own car in front.

"Yeah, but I don't really like that. To me, it takes the originality out of our place. The town as a whole too. I see too much of the same thing."

"Yeah, but all these people look up to you. That counts for something. I wish I had that."

"You do. Me."

"Really?"

"Yeah."

"So then technically, I'm responsible for all this greatness then," April said in a friendly but cocky tone.

"You would say that." Keria smiled.

April grinned, looking out the window at the lively town.

Nathan parked his Audi beside a large hill just past the winery's grape fields. David left the car first to begin unpacking. He was a bit antsy today. Everyone noticed. He seemed to act this way after Nathan said April would be joining them. As David opened the trunk, Keria approached Nathan.

THE HUSK

"Have you guessed it yet?" he asked. "It's a picnic!"

"Yup!" Keria hugged Nathan tightly and jumped a little.

No one knew about the picnic expect Nathan and David; however, the two girls were dressed for it. Keria wore short yellow pants and a thin, light peachy shirt. Her hair was smooth and smelled like conditioner, and it reflected brightly in the sun. April kept her purple hairlines. She wore thin white shorts and a light grey shirt. Her natural hair color was as dark as Black Bell. After Keria let go of Nathan, she went to help unpack.

"Is all this necessary?" April asked.

"Says the girl who brings along a heavy case," David remarked.

"It's a violin," April said.

"You play the violin?" Nathan asked, surprised.

"Yeah, Keria insisted I played a song. She told me you'd want to hear it." She felt slightly embarrassed.

"Of course."

April smiled, guilty of falling for Nathan's pleasant charm. David kept to himself as the crew finished moving the supplies up to the large trees.

They all felt the beat of late July, and most people were inside, watering their gardens or shopping in air-conditioned stores.

"Looks like the hill's ours for the day." Keria leaned on Nathan as they sat against a tree their blankets lay near.

David had his tiny grill with him. "Yeah, but when it cools down, I'm sure they'll be a comin'."

"I wouldn't put it past them." April chuckled. "I guess the heat's the only thing keeping the town from bothering you, Keria."

Keria rolled her eyes. "So Nathan, what possessed you to do this?"

Keria looked up into his eyes with determination and innocence. The two traits appeared to be weaved into her flesh, deep within her own green leafy eyes as if she were those two things. *A source of what every doubtful man needed*, he thought, peering into them.

There was no excuse. It was what drove Nathan. He felt overtaken by her perpetual stares, those inspired eyes. Each time they gazed into him, he felt alive, and all pain became neutralized, balanced within his own soul.

"This port town has become my home again. All I've been doing is checking wine bottles since I've gotten here. I needed to do something else."

"Aw, that's sweet," April said.

"Good thinking," David said.

"Yeah, so let's enjoy ourselves. Try to forget the heat and party." Nathan insisted.

"Ah, please, I'm a summer baby," April said.

"Same," said David in a mellow tone.

April quickly glanced at him.

"We need to start cooking. Who's up for it?" Keria asked.

David stood up and stretched his arms and legs. "I got it."

"Cool. Just make sure you cook over there, away from us." April pointed toward the empty field behind them.

"It's too hot for more heat." David gave her a tiresome stare.

April chuckled. "I'm only joking. Here, let me help you."

April stood. "Where's the food being stored?"

"Looks like they're getting along," Keria said. "What to do while they cook...hmm."

"Let's explore. Like the good old times. Hey, David, April, we'll be right back."

"Where are you two going?" David spotted both Nathan and Keria standing up at the same time.

"Out to explore the fields. I don't believe Nathan's gotten a full tour. Am I right?"

"Yup. See you two in a bit. Don't burn anything Dav—"

The fields were lush with green, healthy grass. Several dragonflies were zooming along like traffic during rush hour.

"I hate to spoil your tour, but let's be quick. I'll make up for it later tonight when things cool down," Keria said.

The field's grass wasn't long. Otherwise, Keria wouldn't have gone. But even still, she wasn't a fan of treading through wild grass. Nathan didn't mind.

"Not much here. Just nature and open sky," Keria said.

"A lot of bugs, too." Nathan heard a few crickets sing.

"Yeah, imagine walking here at night. Gross."

"Don't worry. We'll be home then or up on the hill."

"Good to know. So I have something to ask you, and don't take it in any wrong way. You don't feel like you're mooching off us, do you?"

Nathan paused and fell completely silent longer than Keria expected. "I do a little. Like I said, all I've been doing is checking wine bottles since I've come here. I own a free house and work at the place everyone wants to. I can't really help feeling like that, you know?"

"Yeah, but understand, Nathan. Sometimes it may feel like you're not doing anything, but just being here is enough. When you left, all I ever did was wonder why. I know. I know. People spread rumors about you and Sophia that you...you know...but I wanted to go with you. Most people agree it wasn't you. I mean, come on. You were a freakin' child at the time."

"I just couldn't handle being here anymore. That's it. No other reasons. It's hard to explain. I missed you too. You were the only reason I ever had to go back."

Keria let her face draw near Nathan's and hovered there as she gently spoke. "That's all I needed to know." She dropped her position onto his lips and, with much passion, pressed against his mouth with her own. It was a long, meaningful kiss.

On the field, their souls touched physically, the final mingle before full affection took place. It was the profound event that almost shaped what a relationship would become in the future or maybe what stabbed and shredded it. It cut the heart and soul into pieces and watched it go dry.

On their return to the picnic, black smoke was spiraling out from the grill.

"David!" Keria hollered.

Both David and April turned around, looking as guilty as a dog using the floor as its restroom.

"Don't give us that face," Keria said, not resisting a laugh.

"Don't you laugh, Miss Miles. I don't see you cooking." April quarreled. But she began laughing, too. They all did.

From on top of the hill, the haze seemed thicker, hovering above the grape fields like it were the usual clouds. The ocean moved serenely, appearing most tranquil with the lighthouse sitting in the hazy fog and the boats gliding along the simmering water of the Atlantic. And today, just to annoy, it seemed the cicadas were at their loudest.

"So what are we eating?" Keria asked.

"We could always head down to the fields and take a few grapes." David was still trying to rein in the smoke.

Nathan took over. Thankfully, Keria helped him. And being the wiseasses they were, April took David's hand and tugged it toward the shore.

"Now it's our turn to go exploring," she said in a facetious manner, only she was serious.

"Good idea," Nathan said.

"We'll be a while. Got a lot of burnt meat to clean." April turned to David, back at the shore. "Come on."

"You chose an isolated beach spot, I see."

"Don't get any ideas, big shot." April sounded a bit off-key.

David kept silent on that subject. "So I've never seen you before, yet Keria knows all about you."

"I used to live here when I was a kid and with Tia when she had a daycare. I was one of the special ones who got left behind. That was an interesting day."

"What do you mean?" David asked.

"All the other kids got picked up when closing hours came, you know. At first, I just thought my parents were running late. But…" She fell silent for a while. "Hours passed, and they still never showed. I knew they were bad parents, but that's so low."

They were walking slowly as April revealed her past to David. He placed his hand on her shoulder. She paused immediately, not expecting what had happened. David removed his hand, thinking she'd say something cruel or she felt awkward.

"I'm sorry," he said.

"No, no. It's okay. I just didn't expect it."

"Are you sure?" he asked.

"Yeah, I am. I wouldn't have asked you to come down here with me if I thought you were a creep."

"So, why did you?"

"I wanted to talk. Keria got her chance. I wanted mine. On that note, have anything to tell me?"

When the food was ready, they ate as the sun sunk in the sky. Activity, like presumed, had spiked when the temperature declined.

"Toss anyone?" David asked.

"Me!" April put her half-empty glass of lemonade beside the icebox.

"Us, too," Nathan said.

They felt like rowdy teenagers again, throwing a yellow Frisbee back and forth, shouting and laughing at one another. The townspeople took notice of the noise but never bothered the rambunctious summer party. The four of them were a fair distance anyway from anyone's home, and who cared? It was Keria and her friends.

The sky was a hazy mix of orange, yellow, and faint violent colors when dusk arrived. David set up a small bonfire by the edge of the hill. It was kept away from the trees for fear David might burn those, too.

The Miles Winery was about the only thing visible in the night, aside from a few dimly lit homes. The winery emanated warm, artificial light that poured onto the concrete. The maze had a few lights of its own, but the fountain outshined them with its bright, lustrous orbs that lay inside the moving water, and the ones that imitated the moon on top took the show.

"April, what was it about that song you mentioned earlier?" Nathan leaned against Keria.

They were all sitting around the bonfire.

"Oh, boy," she murmured.

"Oh, come on! It's the whole reason you carried the thing here! Remember?" Keria reminded her.

"Yeah, that's true."

"Hey, she doesn't have to," David said, smiling, "but she should."

"Hey! All right. Fine."

April got up, grabbed her case from a pile of blankets, and sat back down next to David. The light from the bonfire shimmered off the shiny surface of her violin as she cradled it out of its casing.

"That's the best lookin' violin I've ever seen," David said.

"Thanks. Okay, listen closely. It's the only time I'm playing it."

April slid the black bow through the white strings. She did not have any vocals to this song, though she had quite the singing talent, but rather a beautiful ambient structure morphed the world into a steady beat of pure reconciliation.

Nathan pulled out a folder from a bag that sat nearby and opened it.

"What is that?" Keria asked softy.

He showed her the picture he'd been working on for weeks. "I used to practice drawing in Rotor. I thought I'd attempt it again."

He felt nervous, as the moment was so sweet that he didn't want to taint it with work he'd stopped years ago. Keria gently removed the thick paper from Nathan's slightly trembling hand and smiled.

She stared into it, seeing two figures, a male and a female. The male was colored in icy dark and light blue color and held out his hand. The female was outlined in a warming orange-red color. She also held out her hand. The male and female's hands met each other's, and where the female touched, her warm colors replaced the icy blue, appearing to spread through the rest of the male's body.

"It's really abstract but—"

"I love it!" she said.

Keria stepped into Nathan's home, attached to his waist with her tongue overlapping his. They blindly tumbled over small objects, making their way to the nearest soft surface when Keria said in an intimate, smooth voice, "Wait. Why don't we go upstairs? I need a good washing."

She started removing her shirt and threw it on the railing of the staircase as she made her way up, leaving Nathan bewildered in the living room, wanting more.

He ascended past her peachy shirt and entered the hallway, seeing Keria peek her head through the bathroom's half-open door. The shower was already running by the time Nathan got there. He gently pushed the door aside and saw Keria still merely missing her shirt. Her bra was black. Her skin was a mild tan. She stood there, looking pleasantly needy and defenseless. Her shorts wore unzipped though. That was certainly new.

"Is it hot enough?" she whispered.

He wrapped his hands around her slick, curvy body, as if it were a friendly hug before removing her shorts in one quick pull. They tasted each other in brief collisions, in the motion of a dog licking a human hand. Keria's panties lay on top of her bare feet as the steam escaped the glass door in larger quantities. They both added more force to their embracement when entering the shower and slammed the door shut.

The steamy air smothered the two. Every glass surface had already fogged over. Keria tilted her head back to reveal her tender neck and allowed Nathan to follow up on her demand. The black bra was still covering Keria's breasts. Nathan removed them, tossed it toward the silver nozzle, and began washing their soft, spherical surface with soapy water, feeling all around her waist in a circular pattern.

Soon, Keria felt her moistened flesh hit the glass door behind her. She gasped for cooler air, yet didn't want it. Their bodies cushioned further and deeper. They made love in the shower and twice in bed and talked their way through the night.

Clever Isle was quiet, all except for the clanging of beer steins and murmuring of the usual nightly drinkers. Budweiser soaked the table beside Neil. A yammering fool by the name of William Hopper had just recently passed out in his own puddle of booze. William found himself here every night after his sweet wife divorced him.

"Cindy! We got another sleeper!" hollered Clean.

His appearance was nothing of the sort, unless one saw greasy hair, hole-rotting jeans, and a shirt that depicted a pig on top of a goat as classy. Clean was the guy who called out the messes of the joint.

"Be there, hon!" she hollered back, holding two steins in her hands.

Neil was sitting alone below a smoky light in casual clothing, a thick black shirt and brown shorts. It was all cigarette smoke, the shit he hated most. But anything beat watching Nathan bang his daughter out in the open. But hell, the whole town was going on about Keria.

The Isle was its own town. There was no talk of Keria here. But Neil had heard enough and carried the gossip along with him. Only he could hear it, ringing inside his head.

"Ring me up another one, girly!" Clean shouted. "Line 'em up! Speed it up! We ain't got eternity!"

Neil stood and figured that leaving now would be best for his maturing headache. He patted his back pocket to ensure his keys weren't misplaced and threw a fine tip on the table for Cindy. The pretty brunette had better hurry. Clean was on her like a pig on a goat. He'd follow her right to the tip and snatch it.

Neil walked through the smoky bar, coughing and feeling the two thousand or so chemicals enter his aging body. A lively game of blackjack was taking place to the far right, across from the stained glass entrance that cast an eerie green light onto the wooden planks below, thanks to the lamps outside. When he made it outside, the salty air nearly made him gag.

Neil's 2013 silver Hyundai Genesis sat in the parking lot by a stone wall that separated the lot from a small grassy field and the road out of town. He heard something rustle in the bushes behind the wall.

"Hey, who's back there?" he spoke deeply. "Stop fucking around."

Saying Neil was drunk might be considered harsh, but he wasn't sober, not by three beers and one shot of Bailey's.

The Genesis lit up as Neil unlocked it with a click of a button. The bushes began to jangle with grainy animal sounds.

"The hell..." Neil whispered.

He took an empty soda can from his car, silently made his way around the wall, and stared into the lush bushes before throwing the metal container into where he thought the noises came from. Two raccoons zoomed out into the field.

"Shit!" He stammered, feeling edgy and alarmed.

The road was a wicked black. Clouds above drowned the moon. Streetlights were never placed on Oak Berry Road in hopes of keeping people away from the bar during its night hours, hardly an effective take. The origin of the Sleeping Grizzly was this: make a bar closer to the houses so people could walk home and lights soaked the place 24-7. All that idea did was add another bar to the menu.

Neil spotted a sobbing child wearing a pink robe standing beneath a crisp shard of light that hung above a phone booth. Neil huffed, glancing back at his Hyundai, but stopped himself from leaving. As he neared the little girl, the air-conditioner buzzed louder. *Like the cicadas*, Neil thought, feeling unsure of the situation. *The two could buzz and buzz and buzz and buzz and—*

"I lost my dad." The girl hadn't looked up. She must have heard Neil's heavy footsteps.

He paused. "Where did you last see him?"

"Here somewhere."

"In or outside?"

"In."

"How did you end up out here?"

The little girl finally peeked up, revealing her dark blue eyes and gentle face. She must have been about six years old.

"I can't help you if you don't tell me."

She still didn't say a word. Neil noticed the phone was cut.

"He said to wait for him."

"Did he say where he was going?" Neil was still studying the phone.

"To pay his dues."

Neil turned his head back at the girl, meeting a new shape in the bushes. A man stepped out, grinning madly.

"Is that your—"

"Daddy!"

"Yes?" the man said.

"Did you pay your dues?"

The daddy nodded slowly. His grin was glued in place. He spoke childlike and slightly high-pitched. "Yup, yup. Daddy paid his dues."

Terrified, Neil turned to dart for his car. The grinning man took hold of him and slammed his meat-covered skull into the stone wall beside the air-conditioner. Stunned, Neil swirled around to see the man and his daughter smiling. The moon felt generous tonight, escaping the clouds in just the nick of time to submerse Neil in its glory.

"Sleepy time, Mr. Miles." The little girl held a pipe.

Where she got it, Neil would never know. He didn't die easily. The little blonde girl first shattered Neil's kneecaps. He fell to his crumbled knees, thinking they must look like a collection of white bread crumbs and opened his mouth to scream. The little girl wasn't born yesterday. Oh no, she slammed the pipe into his rounded back to shut him up and, with one smooth thrust, drove it into the side of his head like a golf club hitting a ball at a driving range. She found bone breaking to be quite enjoyable. The final blow jingled his brain and split his head.

Daddy noticed the job was getting messy and finished it, but the girl got her kicks and giggles. They awed his corpse hazily, as if they were half-asleep and half-normal, and left it there to rot.

CHAPTER 7

All Talk, No Show

A flashback hit hard, and though Nathan tried to ignore it and place his full attention to the present event, his mind drifted. Albert Ruiz's funeral took place on a frigid, dry day in February in a busy neighborhood that was once his hometown. It was quiet inside the Rolle's Funeral Home. Outside, the world never looked so occupied and chaotic as it did to the mourners. The world was blissfully unaware of their pain and grief. It didn't help.

Nathan knew the day would come if he weren't to go out of this world first, but this was sudden. Albert was found dead on the beach, lying facedown in cold sand by his fishing boat. Cause of death was exhaustion, supposedly. His body was ice-cold, like he'd been frozen in a block of ice when he was found.

Both Nathan's parents were dead. Albert had been the parent to a degree. Now he was gone, too. He thought of this, remembering how Tia had dragged his sorry ass from the pit of a deranged, gang-infested city. He no longer had a job, being targeted by God knows how many people. He thought of this as he held his hand firmly onto Keria's shoulder as she cried while Tia struggled to place the cloth over her husband's swollen head. He looked nice in the tux, better than the suits he's always worn, despite being so badly bruised. *Poor bastard didn't have to go out like that. Hell, not at all.*

He was only trying to protect his daughter. Nathan only demanded time to show who he was, a man worth accepting. Now that was no longer an option.

Father Casper kept the funeral short, and thank God, he had. Five people left during the viewing. Too many had trembling hands. Worst (and this was during the viewing) a two-year-old boy ran round the home screaming, "Touch it! Touch it!" while pointing at Neil's corpse.

Neil was buried; Albert was cremated. The difference to Nathan was Neil's funeral was a hell of a lot longer. It seemed Keria was holding her own, along with Tia, but he knew they were just good at hiding it.

Neil's death was certainly a shocker, but it was his tombstone Nathan couldn't come to terms with. *That angel.* That weeping angel was real all along, and it was coming in the form of death. It stood there in the howling wind, exactly as Nathan's dream portrayed it. Only now the inscription was clear.

The repast after a funeral always felt wrong to Nathan. It was like celebrating the death of your loved one. As a kid, Nathan learned from such a party that the only way to fight grief was to drink. But Nathan only had a few light beers. Someone had to drive Keria home safely. Though he made the right choice, fate wanted him back under the bottle. Keria fell asleep in Tia's home. So Nathan left alone.

The fact that Nathan's house stayed the way it had since his arrival for this long meant something. However, for the first time since moving to Silverhill or Hollow Heights or whatever the fuck they called this place, Nathan pulled out a table and emptied a full bottle of scotch. It hit him harder than it had in years. It'd been about a month. His tolerance had gone down a little.

He did not dream, but a faint voice buzzed in the back of his mind. "Sing our song." It muttered, "Or pray you're God. Neil is dead. You are free! Or are you sad, and is she gone? Your lovely girl, has she left to hide?"

Nathan leaned into his arms, clenching his fingers together in a fist so tense that his knuckles emitted a red and white color. He sweat, felt his pulse beat against his skin, and nearly hollered into the air, "Shut up! Shut up!"

The voice went silent for the remainder of the night, and he thought to himself, *What happened? What went wrong?*

Only a few days ago, love surrounded him, Keria, David, and April. Now it was death and insanity. It was like a mental plague was now plunging the world—their world—into madness.

Nathan heard the phone ring as he laid his head on the table. He wanted to answer it, but he was unable. He felt the alcohol race through his bloodstream and medicate his every muscle until his arms, legs, and entire body were nothing but lazy tissue that refused to move. He took one last look at the empty bottle and passed out.

Agent Moore of the FBI called Nathan several times on the night of Neil's funeral, all leading to a voice mail. Nathan called him back the following morning.

"Hello, Mr. Moore? This is Nathan Ruiz." Nathan spoke in a jagged voice, feeling hungover. The image of the weeping angel stayed with him all through the night and was currently taunting him.

"Yes, this is Agent Moore."

"You want to talk to me about Neil, don't you?"

"What time will you be available?"

Agent Moore's voice was stiff and dry. It made Nathan's throat ache. And he liked to pause. Yeah, he was one of those guys.

"What time? This afternoon should work. Tia's given everyone the day off."

"Do you have a lawyer?"

Those were the magic words.

"Good question." Nathan thought about Tia and her stash of money. But now wasn't the time to be mooching.

"No."

"Then I'll assign you one. See you at..." There was one of those pauses.

"At one," Nathan said stiffly. "Where exactly am I supposed to meet you?"

"Down in the police station of course."

"Right. Of course."

The FBI agent smiled at the end of the table with his legs crossed. His one hand was half buried into a pocket with the other leaning against the table. His hair was a strange golden yellow mixed with a light brown, and his skin was a fading tan. Also, he was a tiny man. Agent Moore was about to play good cop/bad cop, or at least that was what Nathan assumed.

"Mind?" Agent Moore slightly waved a digital recorder in his right hand.

"Not at all," Nathan replied.

"Excellent. First off—and one of the most important—where were you the day Neil died?"

Nathan glanced at his lawyer, Mickey King, who merely nodded. "On a hill beside the Miles Winery's grapevines. I stayed at Keria's for the night."

"Keria Miles, right, right. You two are seeing each other, correct?"

"Yes."

"No problems in this relationship that deal with Neil?"

This was the headache. Before the unpleasant grouping of lawyer, suspect, and cop, Mickey warned Nathan about properly addressing his conflict with Neil. Agent Moore had no problem jumping right into the topic.

"Suppress all anger. Only tell the truth." Mickey demanded with much emphasis. "And remember they will twist your words. But that's where I come in. Just tell the truth, stay calm, and wait for my nods and waves."

"Well?" Agent Moore asked in a crude tone.

"He wasn't fond of me, especially when it came to dating his daughter. All because I used to live in a city called Rotor."

"Ah, tell me. How did the both of you address this conflict?"

"What do you mean?"

"Fights, arguments—" Agent Moore's eyes were cold and damp, like a mine's interior. He hadn't thrown in a pause since the chat on the telephone, and Nathan got to thinking Agent Moore wanted Nathan to do all the pausing for him in person.

"No fights. Can't say we've ever had much of an argument. I don't believe I've shouted at him before. I can't remember much of what I've said. I usually ignored him. You know, I was trying to avoid any more reasons to be disliked."

"You had secrets you wished not to tell him?"

"No. I felt obligated not to say anything. When I spoke, he'd attempt to make me feel outcast with the Miles family or the whole Hollow Heights township."

"Ah, yes. Silverhill's new name or addition. I understand you left because of having to cope with losses. Your sister Sophia—"

"Sophia," said the voice in the back of his mind. It sounded edgy and distant, yet louder than the night before. It felt more alien.

"Your father Alan, your mother Eve, and your grandfather Albert."

"Yeah? You don't think I know that?"

Mickey waved his meaty hand at Nathan as Agent Moore smirked.

"I ask the questions," Agent Moore said. "What I'm aware of Mr. Ruiz is that several people think you killed Sophia. A man by the name of Jeff Jones personally came up to me this morning to say he had reasons to believe these suspicions of a murder are worth debating."

"Please, tell me," Nathan replied coldly. "What are these suspicions?"

"Again, I ask the questions. Now…" Agent Moore sat up straight, folded his hands on the table, and leaned toward Nathan with his falsely integrated eyes. "I would like to hear your story first of what happened out there."

Looking into the man's pupils was like peering down into the ocean at night. Nathan sighed, realizing he had to go through the horror with a man who would twist his memory around even more than his previous nightmares had.

"I was lying in bed, thinking about my father. We all were, I'm sure, when I noticed Sophia was walking down the hall. I leaped out of bed and asked her where she was going. She told me she was going out to find our dad. With that and being the foolish children we both were, we actually went out into the storm into a boat and traveled out into the Atlantic to search for him. I was old enough to notice she was acting strange, perhaps because our father was missing. She said bizarre things like how she saw our father in the waves. And before I knew it…" Nathan paused. "Before I knew it, the ocean was tugging her under."

"Tell me. Do you think she actually saw him?"

"Of course not."

"No possibilities of knocking her in?"

"No, I wasn't touching her. I was still in that boat."

Uneasiness came over Nathan, along with a new thought. *Had I done it?* For the first time, he dug into that possibility, but no matter how Agent Moore made it seem so, Nathan knew that just wasn't the case. She had fallen into the ocean somehow, and he had nothing to do with that.

"Was Sophia on any medication?"

"No."

"Were you?"

"No."

"Were either one of you supposed to be on any?"

"No."

Agent Moore leaned back in his chair and peered past Nathan at the two-way mirror and then back at Nathan. "Okay," he murmured. "I'll have to double-check, but assuming you are telling the truth, let's move on. Jeff wasn't the only person to question your story. However, Jeff was the only one who came up to me. I'll have to bring him in for questioning. We need to stay in touch. I've heard your voice mail too many times, Mr. Ruiz. When is a good time to call you?"

"I suppose the evening, but my work schedule is unpredictable."

"Right, okay. One last thing. I'm aware you enjoy drinking. Is that an issue?"

"Don't," Mickey said to Nathan.

Nathan remained silent.

"Very well then. You are free to leave."

Nathan walked with Mickey to the front door. "How'd it go?"

"I have to say pretty well. If you didn't commit the murder, there shouldn't be much trouble; however, I need to know something immediately."

"What's that?"

"Who is Jeff Jones?"

Nathan rolled his eyes and told him outside the station. Mickey chuckled.

Lillie was feeling bad, the kind of feeling cheerleaders get when fucking a jockey football player under a set of bleachers. Her row of customers consisted of old-timers and a shitload of coupons, all except for one man.

"Condoms?" she asked as the lean man placed his pack onto the desk.

"Want to test them out?" he asked.

The store was dead of people. Liz was peeking over slyly.

"Sure," Lillie replied.

The lean man was Chris Beagle, a sex toy of Lillie's.

In the storage room, the two engaged in their testing. A child entered the store.

"Can I help you, sir?" Liz asked.

The little boy looked nervous in his casual T-shirt and shorts. "Yeah, I'm looking for a Mr. Moore, the FBI agent. Have you seen him?"

"No, but I'm sure you could find him at the police station. Where are your parents?"

"I'm in a hurry. Can you tell me where to find this station?" the boy hollered.

Liz saw the desperation in the young man's blue eyes, so she ignored her motherly screams to continue the pursuit.

"Up Creek Road, turn left at the intersection of Creek and Joe, and then follow Joe down 'til you see it."

"Thank you."

"Welcome," Liz said cheerily.

The boy was out the door in the blink of an eye. Lillie and Chris came out of the storage room.

"Have fun?" Liz asked.

Chris looked awkward and Lillie disappointed, yet strangely amused.

"This town's slowly going crazy," Liz said. "Some kid just came in all panicky, asking for Agent Moore."

"Maybe he knows something," Lillie said.

"Yeah, maybe. But Neil was clearly murdered. What if one of us ends up killed next?"

"Yikes," Chris said.

"Stay indoors. Hey, I've been meaning to ask you. Are you still going through with...you know...Neil's request?" Lillie asked.

"That's a good question."

Liz dazed out. She fixed her eyes on the window across from the register. She said she would. But now, the man was dead. What to do? Liz wanted a little fun herself, but Keria was already dealing with enough.

"I doubt I'll go through with it," she whispered, pressing her white polished nails against her tender lips. "I just don't know."

***

Keria knew her actions were wrong. Avoiding her lover, ignoring the winery's plead for attention, and sealing the windows and doors to life drained her of what joy there was to experience. Two days after her father's funeral passed, there was little to no progress in healing. A letter lay beneath her door. She bent down to grab it and flipped its rectangular body to read the little note written in purple ink, "Sorry for your loss."

That's the fifth one today. Only "Nathan" was written at the bottom. She felt sick, like a clump of chunky, year-old milk sat at the bottom of her stomach. She opened the letter and pulled out a picture, though far less detailed than the previous art he'd given her on the picnic. It did just the job. It was the four of them again on that hill. Briefly, she relived those moments. She was seeing the interpretation of her boyfriend's need to rescue her. She missed him very much.

Keria unlocked her door. Her eyes were still moist from crying, and Tia rushed over.

"You left." She looked down at the sheet of thick paper in her daughter's hands.

"Yeah," Keria replied weakly.

Tia hugged her forcefully, feeling tears of her own leak from her eyes when she said, "Nathan's been asking for you. Said you just disappeared."

"I know."

"Of all people, he knows grief."

"Honestly, I was mad at him for leaving. I just wanted him back so badly that I let it go. Now, after all this, I understand why he left. He lasted longer than I would have."

Tia released her hold and merely held onto Keria. "Nathan's perfect for you in these troubled times, seeing how he got through his own grief has helped me through my own. You have to go see him. If he has that effect on me, surely it would for you as well."

"I am right now."

"Go." Tia turned around and left for the cellar door. "Where are you going?"

"I'm checking the shipments and barrels. That way, Nathan has more time with you. He'll have the day off tomorrow."

"Okay."

Tia smiled, continued walking for the cellar door, and descended the old wooden steps, feeling the dampness of the underground room crawl over her skin. There was a lot to do. Many bottles of wine shipped last night currently sat unorganized in the back by the stone wall while loafs of bread sat on a table by the staircase.

Keria rushed out, not thinking twice about her father but only to see Nathan's face again. She was concerned about the FBI agent she heard about. Nathan was a suspect, but whether he knew it or not, he was looking fairly clean. Jeff, on the other hand, was being questioned endlessly, so it seemed. That's what she heard from a local newspaper, and her mother had mentioned Nathan's status with the law last night when the shipments were being loaded off the truck.

No way is Nathan guilty. That slimy piece of shit Jones on the other hand, she thought. *It's always the weird ones who do what they're told and hide in the demands of their victims to seem so innocent that they can catch everyone off guard. For when the moment comes, they can get away with their darkest desires.*

Jeff had always wanted to be a manager. It didn't mean he would kill for it though. And Keria knew damn well that Jeff didn't have the balls for such a task. But she didn't want to think of Nathan as a killer, the man responsible for her own father's death. There was nothing to gain. She was his, and there was nothing Neil could have done to break Nathan. He had all he needed. But that left a question up in the air: Who the hell killed Neil Miles?

Comparing Nathan and Jeff side by side, Nathan did seem the more likely to have committed the murder, but what about this Mike Ribbons guy? Keria thought of Mike and April's description of his house. *Why was it so beat up? What happened in that home? Did he really treat it like a summerhouse or like something darker?* It was all up to the big shot FBI agent. For better or for worse, Agent Moore had a higher say than anyone else in Hollow Heights.

The heat was staggering in the interview room, but Jeff experienced such discomfort.

"The air's broken. Didn't ya hear me?" yelled Greg Holler, the head policemen. He was a little heavyset, like most of the policemen here, but he was the only one who had white hair.

"Fucking place," Agent Moore muttered. "Anyone got a freakin' cold Snapple or something?"

"Heat getting to you?" Jeff asked.

"No, people are. Ready for the big old questionnaire?"

Jeff nodded respectfully.

"Good. Sit back. Relax. I've got plenty."

Jeff was getting a lawyer fresh out of law school. He guessed Nathan really did have the luck of a fully realized Buddha statue because his was equipped with one of the better law degree people this shithole supplied, with no help from the great Tia.

"All right," said Greg. "Let's see how Jeff does."

Greg wasn't fond of a hot shot from the FBI. Whenever he asked why Agent Moore came to Hollow Heights, he'd get "official duty…can't spill it." Agent Moore was a wiseass, as round and shit-filled in the mouth as Neil was. Maybe this agent was his long-lost brother.

"This town is something I must say. You take care of it, don't you?"

"I tend to the Miles Winery, sir."

"No community service? You seem like the kind of guy who would commit more."

Kenny Smith, Jeff's lawyer, raised an eyebrow. He was a balding man, but he still had much of his hair, and what he had was a dark brown color. His eyebrows were heavy and thick. He often wondered why the hell that hair refused to trade places.

Agent Moore took notice. "You spend a great deal of time around Neil. Heard you idolized him, too. Though I've gotten the idea that everyone here idolizes the Miles family."

"Most do, sir."

"That's troubling to me. Famous people can make friends all right, but you know what else they're good at, Jones? Making foes. And lots of them."

"Are we asking questions concerning Neil's murder and my client?" Kenny broke out.

"Ah. Mr. Jones, where were you the night Neil died?"

Jeff glanced over at Kenny, who raised his eyebrow yet again and tilted his head at Agent Moore, looking like a dog using its head to roll a ball.

"I was in my house."

"Inside?"

"Yes."

"Okay, doing what?"

"Reading a book."

"Uh-huh. Okay. So you're an indoors kind of guy who works outside. You've told me a lot about Nathan Ruiz. Now I have to know. Why do you know so much about him? He's certainly not a friend."

"No, he isn't. Like you said, I work outside. I hear things."

"Like?"

"What I've told you."

"Really now? I heard a little different during other interviews."

Shit, Jeff thought. He knew what was happening. He could feel it in his bones, and it gave him goose flesh.

"How I do things, Mr. Jones, is this. I engage in my own personal interviews with people. This whole chat in the interview room is show for my most interesting suspects. You and Nathan are the only two I have. Reason you fit into this category is due to the many interviews I had with townsfolk. What you've told me wasn't known to any of them, even the employees of the Miles Winery."

Agent Moore leaned inwards facing Jeff. "What were you and Neil up to?" Agent Moore glared up at Kenny, who fell utterly silent in both speech and gestures. Jeff knew he was on his own.

"I...uh...we..." There was a pause. "We were trying to sort out the issue with Nathan, the him not being a safe date thing."

"A what now?"

"Him not being safe," Jeff stated with sudden fierceness.

"Explain."

Jeff explained the best he could. The poor guy dug himself a deeper hole, yet saved his ass at the same time.

"So by stalking Mr. Ruiz, you discovered these traits, such as his drinking, and wanted...uh...what was her name...Liz. You wanted Liz to know."

"What Neil wanted was for his daughter to know. I wanted Liz to know so she wouldn't bang the asshole. I wanted her. I was sick to death of Ruiz. But still I did what Neil asked."

"You hated him to death, huh?"

"Best not to spill anymore personal feelings." Kenny warned.

"Tell me exactly what you did and what Neil wanted."

"He wanted Keria to discover Nathan's real side. No one knew if there were another side to him, but Neil was convinced. Quite frankly, I believed him and still do. But anyway, we set up an arrangement to have a test, so to speak. Liz would seduce Nathan, and if she succeeded, the truth would be revealed, the one where Nathan was a cheater, drinker, and so on. Neil didn't think otherwise. There was no fault to his idea. He was hell-bent."

"Thanks for the new suspect."

Asshole, Jeff thought, almost muttering aloud.

"Has Neil threatened your job in any way, if, let's say, you never went through with watching Mr. Ruiz through his window during the hours before midnight or whenever you—"

"No, but I figured he'd make me co-manager if I did these things."

"All right."

The heat was turning dire, stressing out Agent Moore. Jeff noticed Agent Moore's discomfort and smiled in a way only his mind's eye could see. With no way of dealing with the heat, Agent Moore would have to close the chat and saddle onto his great almighty horse of justice and ask Liz his next fucking set of bullshit. Agent Moore scanned his mind for any questions and couldn't find any that wouldn't raise Kenney's thick eyebrows.

"You're free to go." Agent Moore turned away.

He left in a hurry. The heat, nerd, and newbie were getting under his skin, as if he could read their thoughts.

⁙⁙⁙

Tia was questioned first. But like the other interviews, Agent Moore hit a brick wall. She had to sweet-talk her way out of trouble. Because her husband died, the cops were all over her.

"Hello, Agent Moore," she said, half-smiling.

"Mrs. Miles, I'm sorry for your loss. However, I presume you understand what happens in these cases." Agent Moore found his seat and sat stiffly.

"No, I never had my husband killed before," she said.

"What I mean is that you're the spouse. This will get personal."

"If it must," she said.

"Great."

Interview rooms always made Tia nervous, along with hospitals. Agent Moore was shuffling paperwork on the table. He had an eye for Tia. She looked appealing in her brightly colored flannel.

"Greg tells me this town was created thanks to your husband's belief that Black Bell, that strangely placed mine, if you don't mind me saying, still had coal inside. And a lot of it, as things turned out. Is this true?"

"Yes. I find it funny, too. We're a port town and a mining town. Doesn't usually happen," Tia said with a weak laugh.

"Yes, I agree."

"Neil had a lot of ideas left, too. We were gonna build a huge playground for the kids and open some new centers, like the one I used to work in, for busy parents, too."

"You used to work at a daycare, correct?"

"Yes, Sun Child."

"Now has Neil known these miners personally?" Agent Moore slid four pictures toward Tia. They depicted the miners.

"No. He looked for a group who would be willing to reopen Black

Bell. He was having difficulty doing so, but we got lucky, and these four came to us."

"All right. From my understanding, they were killed in an accident. Some kind of rock fall?"

"Yes, that's what the police told me."

"What did Neil do about this?"

"Nothing. What could he have done? I mean, we had a ceremony for them. Out of that, it's all police work."

"Neil had it covered. They had signed a warrant, accepting the risks that come with coal mining."

"Um, yes, you asked because—"

"Because I wanted to know what he did for them, Mrs. Miles. Moving on. I'd like to know more about Nathan Ruiz. I tried calling him; however, he has yet to reply. You, on the other hand, have come on this very night. I am thankful, but please tell me. Why has he come back? Why is it that someone dies shortly after he arrives? That's never a good sign, Mrs. Miles."

"No, it doesn't look good on his part, but I know Nathan. He wouldn't do something like this. He's in love with my daughter. That's also the answer to your question. I believe he came back for Keria."

"He came back for her? Or the free house you gave him."

"He did not expect it to be free. In fact, he did not know about that until after he got here."

Agent Moore expressed his disbelief by raising an eyebrow. "Why did you give him a free home?"

"He's not the only one, sir."

"But why? I can't comprehend any of this. I thought when I read it that I was seeing all typos or a crook slipped something into my drink."

"All tax is paid for. So what's the crime? Is it bad to be kind?"

"It's unheard of, Mrs. Miles."

"I believe I did the right thing for him and the others. At the core, Agent. Most still paid. We simply moved from one place to another. Nathan had to cope—and still does—with a terrible tragedy. He left to make a new life for himself. But Keria told me he ended up in poor living conditions. That did not make him any less part of our family here in

Silverhill, Hollow Heights. He finally came back is all. There is nothing abnormal about any of that."

"One last thing. You winery isn't quite a winery, you following? At its core, it sells other brands. You have a few crafted here, but—"

"Yes, Agent. Our winery is more of a brand seller. However, we do, in fact, sell homemade wine. So we are a winery."

Agent Moore fell silent. Tia made her point, and pursuing against it any longer wouldn't end well. More importantly, it would just be another dead end anyway.

He let out a heavy sigh. "Regarding Nathan, he is my prime suspect. Until I can uncover a better candidate, you are my second. Don't go anywhere outside Hollow Heights without my permission. Have a good day, Mrs. Miles."

Tia stood and left the room silently. Agent Moore remained seated. He was thinking perhaps too hard about her relations to Neil. Tia was very fragile looking. Her strengths were in her head, not muscle. But that made her scary to Agent Moore. He thought less about her being the killer but rather her being the next victim. Seeing as the town idolized the Miles family like a majority of Americans did Chuck Norris, it was likely someone would get carried away. Neil was already dead. And though Agent Moore made it clear to Tia that she was in second place on his most wanted list, he knew she was a target. But he had his pet peeves, and Tia happened to be one of them.

Still, at the scene of the crime, Neil's knees were smashed, broken into tiny fragments. And his head was dented in, like a sheet of flesh merged with bone. The town had a crazed killer out there. And an unofficial answer, mind you, Agent Moore thought it was that redneck by the sea, Mr. Wilkerson. But he soon discredited that idea. He had no relations to Sun Child.

It had to be someone from that daycare, he thought. *But who would be murderous enough to commit such a crime as Neil's brutal death?*

Keria didn't stay long. She gave a little chat and a kiss good-bye. She left in a hurry. It was all in the style of a dying relationship. Nathan sat at his table with a glass of scotch and no ice. Like a common cold waiting for the great sneeze, he felt that inner voice sneak in on him again. At first, Nathan thought it was thought, just echoing a little. But it turned alien.

This speech, it was heavy yet light. High-pitched and deep. No, he thought, *it is just me. If I sit here and think of only my thoughts, it won't—*

"Peel," it spoke. "Peel me. Peel me like an onion. Let me tear your eyes so they understand. Peel me like an onion."

Nathan stood up and walked out the door. He left for the Tiki Pier, hearing his thoughts break into the alien voice's. He paused, felt ill, and became goose fleshed at the sight of Mr. Wilkerson and his shitty house. He stood up straight in his blue-collar clothing, wearing a grin and staring directly at him. Nathan gave a worried but controlled stare back.

"Peel."

The children who upset this man before walked up to him, wearing all the same cloths as they had before. They took their stumpy hands, placed them on the man, and began to tear at his skin. Beneath the bloodless sheet of white flakes that made up this Wilkerson fellow was the dark, shadowy surface of the figure from Nathan's dream, tall, lean, and utterly silent. The children all sat around it, and Nathan told himself to wake up. He didn't.

"Is it one of those dreams again?" he asked himself in his mind's voice.

But the alien's came back and said, "You're awake, Nathan. So very awake. Look at the things I show you."

The kids were empty of life. They were husks, empty, little husks being controlled like a puppet.

"Who are they?" Nathan asked himself, truly feeling like he'd gone insane.

"People. Like you, only younger. Except for that tall one. I don't know who that is."

"Why are you telling me this?"

He didn't hear the world stressor but felt it. That tall thing was an illness of some kind. It had to be, and it was.

CHAPTER 8

Growing Trenches

Nathan awoke in his bed, thinking, *Hey, at least I didn't sleepwalk.* But the pain in his chest from the heavy drinking he committed to after his little episode (as he called it) was intense. His body felt torpid as he stood. Once up, he looked into the bathroom mirror, bushed his teeth, and took a warm shower. When finished, he stared into himself again and sighed, unsure of his own well-being.

He shuffled his feet to the sofa and turned on the television, thinking that buzzing would return. It didn't. He sat there, trying to remember when he last fell asleep, but realized there was no concern. He'd fallen asleep drinking. That was it. That sleepwalking fit to the beach was a one-time deal. When Nathan turned his head sideways, he noticed something written in black words on the kitchen wall. All he could see was "FIGH."

"Figh?" He stood up.

He entered the kitchen soft-footed, seeing the words "FIGHT US." The marker was heavy, still carrying that dreaded smell of collected chemicals, ready to burn one's senses or satisfy them. *Someone must have snuck in during the night,* Nathan thought.

But the alien voice had something else to say, murmuring "no" in the back of his thoughts like a lawyer giving hints and advice during questioning.

Sitting on the kitchen table were those creepy little rag dolls. All but one was aligned in a circle. The other was in the center. *So I did sleepwalk after all. I had to have. That's how all this shit happened.* Frustrated, Nathan knocked the dolls off the table in a fit of rage.

His hangover reminded him of those head rushes he had because another one occurred with a tiny, sharp pain. Something really was causing problems. But what illness caused fevers, cold chills, and sleepwalking? He feared it was some kind of brain dysfunction or tumor.

"Nothing paranormal," he told the alien voice, his own voice.

Though the thought of brain tumors made him wish it were, he could not believe the supernatural was at work here. But Howard and that dream questioned it. *That stressor.* Whatever it may be existed, paranormal or not. It was inside him, causing him to do these crazy things. *I never should have went back to that place. Never*, he thought angrily.

Hollow Heights Police Station sat under the beat of the sun's abnormally hot morning blaze, sucking in the brilliance of power so many were harboring in their gardens with solar panels, thinking they'd outmatch the Miles. Two cops, Maya Douglas and Ellis Doyle, were drinking their coffee outside the station, talking about the townsfolk who believed harboring the sun would make them better than the rest.

"I guarantee you," Ellis said, "if I ever went up to anyone owning a solar panel and asked him what makes it so glorious, he'd stutter and say something like, 'I'll figure it out once I have the power. The power you refuse to take.'"

"But don't they have it?" Maya asked.

Ellis shrugged. "They probably use it up for porno marathons. Or that solar panel idea—of I dunno—doesn't actually work!"

Maya chuckled, nearly spilling her hazelnut coffee. Maya drank hers black, only if the coffee were flavored. It didn't matter. She earned respect from the guys, especially the old-time sailors who lived down the road, and, of course, the fishermen. It was the same difference, more or less.

"What do you make of the case?" she asked.

Ellis was dazed, but not showing lazy eyes at Maya's thin, skinny body with a near overall tan. He was watching those annoying people—one of the many, he would add—working on their garden. Over half the police department saw her on the Golden Seashell beach, thinking, *Damn, does she have the body to be out there. The sun's surely her friend until she gets older, dries up like a fucking raisin, and succumbs to skin cancer.*

Maya was gorgeous, but Ellis had a wife. And unlike the others, he felt a need to keep his eyes off Maya in any relation to sexual thoughts, as best he could manage. Also, Ellis had poor self-confidence, often dyeing his hair, which was currently black, because he hated the way it looked.

"It sucks," he said, sipping his black Maxwell House coffee with no sugar. "Hard to believe."

"I mean this stuff doesn't happen often. It's the first recorded murder in Hollow Heights."

"It is, but don't let it get to your head. That's when you fall."

"Fall?"

"Yeah, out of the case, out of life. Just try not to think about it."

Maya giggled. "That's the first life advice I ever heard from you. Wait a second. Was that supposed to be your big catch phrase?'

Ellis only smiled back.

Just as Ellis began walking up to the front entrance, Maya noticed a boy running down the road. "Hey, Ellis."

"Yeah?"

"Look."

The boy was obscured in the distance. The heat rising out of the concrete overcame his image. It was late morning. The clock was nearing eleven o'clock.

Ellis remained on the stairs, still as stone while Maya approached the boy. "What's the matter?" she asked in a gingerly fashion.

"I know what's gonna happen next!" the boy nearly bellowed. His voice was both alarming and convincing, like the murderer had spilled his entire plan into the child's ears just moments ago.

The boy, Dylan Christen, sat in the interview room with a half-eaten lollipop in his hand, swinging his feet up and down below the seat.

"He's six, parents are missing, and he was shaken up, but he seems to be okay now," Maya said.

Agent Moore nodded. "Okay, good work. I'm going to talk to him and try to get more about his parents. I will start gathering a search party. He didn't say what he knew?"

Maya shook her head. "He only wants to tell you."

Agent Moore entered the room, closed the door, and half-smiled at the boy. "Hello, Dylan, I'm Agent Moore."

Dylan looked up at him silently. Agent Moore sat down.

"So what is it you won't tell anyone?"

"The nanny."

"Who is the nanny?"

"The one leading them."

"Them?"

Dylan nodded very slowly, like he was hesitant to do so. It made Agent Moore feel watched.

"My friends," the boy finally said. "They aren't friends anymore."

"Does the nanny have a name?"

"She disowned it. But I know she lives here somewhere."

"All right, listen. You want another lollipop and this bad nanny taken down, right?"

Dylan nodded.

"Then tell me everything. Don't hold anything back. Remember, we are the good guys here. Keeping what you know away from us only gives the bad guys a better chance to win, okay?"

"Okay. I was walking to Kristina's house. She's my bestist friend. We went to the big pier with the weird lights."

The Tiki Pier, Agent Moore thought.

"I was fine, and she was fine. We wanted to watch the sun, but then that scary woman came out. The nanny, she wasn't happy. She yelled at Kristina and pointed at me. We both ran, but she was gone."

"Who was?"

"Kristina was gone!"

Dylan, at the young age of six, was already fighting grief and doing well. His eyes were nursing tears. Sooner or later, he'd learn to let them go. Perhaps he already had on his way here.

"I kept running and running and running until I met my house. I wouldn't have stopped if I heard her scream or anything! She was gone!"

Gone, gone, gone.

"We'll bring her back," Agent Moore stated.

Yeah, we will, alive or wrapped in a body bag. Maybe we can sew her body parts back together if the murderer were kind enough to separate only the main joints and if he didn't burn her body, he thought unwillingly.

"You came here right after this happened?

"No. I asked where you were. My momma told me a FBI man was here. I asked for you at the superstore. Then I came in here. She was the nanny, the ex-babysitter."

"The ex-babysitter?" Agent Moore peered up at the two-way mirror. "Okay. Go in and tell Greg to give you a lollipop. You did outstanding," Agent Moore said with a warming smile, making the kid feel a touch of purpose, satisfaction, and a little hope.

Dylan did not run out of the room in joy, but he appeared to be holding up all right. He was a tough kid. Agent Moore, for the first time in Hollow Heights, got a lead. Suddenly that influence to shape Hollow Heights' first murder case he had on his trip became a very real desire again.

Yes, he knew. They did not. Though Greg had his suspensions or maybe he did know, he just realized spilling it would do no good. Agent Moore also knew that, deep down, this new town needed this. The FBI had to ensure the well-being of American people. So here they were, mostly just Agent Moore himself though, tangled inside a police department that failed to see much action. *Yes, action. Murder,* Agent Moore thought.

It was murder they did not understand, so he had to guide them. He had to end the evil where it bloomed, no, soiled. He must end the evil before its roots grew into places unreachable, like that damned sea. Most of all, Agent Moore couldn't have another dead child—no more wrapped dreams or burned passion. No dislocated hopes. He thought of his most difficult cold case three years ago. *That girl…those girls…not here.*

Agent Moore followed out the kid and ensured Greg gave Dylan a lollipop.

When Dylan left, Agent Moore said, "We got something today."

"Yeah, and I don't like no bit of it."

Agent Moore bit his lip. "How do we go at this? I need some insight here."

"Oh? The FBI agent himself?"

"Yeah."

"Let's talk with the others."

The night screamed party, but nobody felt like it. Cops flooded every intersection in town. Liz bought two six packs of Budweiser and a bottle of Captain Morgan, like the guys asked. Suddenly everyone wanted to stay in his or her houses and lock the doors. Lillie came over though.

"Why are you looking out there? Is someone coming?" Lillie asked. "No, it's just—"

Lillie's phone rang. She answered it in a heartbeat. "Hello?"

"Lillie! Come over. The guys may not want to party, but I'm up for it!" Hanna Solomon shouted.

"Awesome! Where are you?"

"At my house. Bring beer! My boyfriend's upset cuz I don't have any of the good stuff."

"Hope he don't mind Bud and Morgan. I'll be over soon."

"Sounds great! Oh, be careful. Cops are everywhere tonight. Do you know why? Eh, forget it. Just be mindful. See you!"

Hanna was always the fruity go-to party planner. Of course, she was up for it. The problem was that both Liz and Lillie weren't fans of her style.

They made it to Hanna's house safely, not receiving one speeding ticket when Liz realized she made a bad idea long before the party turned sour. Her most profound ex's car was parked across the street.

"Oh, shit, Liz."

"Yeah, I see it. It's him."

Despite this, they left Lillie's silver Ford and walked to the front door. The moonlight made the yard look eerie. On the grass was a swing set, which cast a long, looming shadow on the white picket fence that separated Hanna from her neighbors. A toy car, one of those sit-ins, stood beside the swing set, blanketing the first swing in a shadow. The stone squirrels felt alive, as if taken by the night and now had an urge to chew on their legs.

"Ugh." Liz sighed, hitting the door open in frustration. *Just the sight of that man.*

"Oh, shit. Look, it's the register girls!" Braden shouted.

He wasn't anything special. Hell, no one was here, all except for—

As Liz walked in, she made sure Lillie was by her side. "Don't even think of leaving me alone tonight."

"Understood, girl. I got you."

The house wasn't big, and it wasn't crowded. Hiding wasn't going to happen. Liz eased in when Lillie ran into an old friend and introduced him to her. His name was Daniel Chief. He had long blonde hair. He was lean and five foot seven. He stood out in appearance, wearing torn jeans and a black shirt with a heavy white skull engraved in the center. Also, he wore large black earrings with piercings above them that were only black dots. He was an odd fellow.

"Yeah, I collect all that shit, shrunken heads, voodoo dolls, and whatever else screams old-fashioned horror."

"Monster heads?" Lillie asked.

Liz found herself uncovering a new side to her best friend. "I didn't know you were into this stuff."

Lillie shrugged. "Depends."

"What do you mean 'depends'?" Liz said mockingly.

"I like cheesy old horror movies. Sheesh! It's no big deal or anything. Of course, I prefer newer ones. They're much scarier. Ain't nothing like a good horror movie to speed up a relationship, you know?"

"Should have known." Liz's eyes opened wide. "Ooooo, hold the phone! Is that how you do it?"

"Do what?"

"Sneak around like it's nobody's business."

"Not following." She smirked.

"You know what I'm talking about!"

"A magician never reveals her secrets."

Liz smirked but with mockery.

"Well, girls, I'm gonna grab a beer. Want one?" Daniel asked.

"Sure, the both of us," Lillie said.

"Ah, no. No, I'll skip on that," Liz said rather quickly. "Find me a cola."

"Absolutely," he said.

As Daniel left, Lillie murmured, "A cola. Really?"

"I'm not taking any chances today. I find your friend odd, and shit, you know who—"

"Mike? So what? Honestly, you're the one making a scene, not him. Just relax."

"Yeah."

An hour passed, and the music grew louder as the beer cans piled wherever they were finished. Braden took someone's bra and wore it as a necklace, prancing around like a professional football player after a fully realized touchdown. The woman whose bra he had so kindly borrowed made out with six men, dry humped two, and finally slept with Braden at the end of their gig.

"See, this isn't so bad," Lillie said. "I haven't even seen him. He probably left."

"Worked up over some asshole?" Daniel was sipping his Budweiser. "I'll handle him."

"Best you don't and stay here."

"Ah? All right." Daniel raised his hands. "I'd rather stay with you anyway."

Maybe it was the way Daniel said those words that made Liz feel attracted to the guy, that or the alcohol. Either way, she just started easing in. This wasn't so bad. And that bastard Mike wasn't even here.

Hanna planned this day for weeks, and she made it clear that Jeff Jones wanted in on it. *But where was he? Probably messing with his computer,* Liz thought. She really did feel bad for the guy. He was a hard worker. *And as a woman grows older,* she thought, *the wild men like Daniel got less desirable.* Nathan was what Liz dreamed of, a guy who knew how to stay calm yet wasn't dorky and worked hard. *Or does he work hard?*

Electronic music played, and the strobe lights flickered without pattern. Hanna's house smelled like booze and sex. Like a dingy strip club, dirty dancers overcrowded the house. It was odd. Liz didn't want to be here. *Has something clicked?* she thought. *Or am I just getting old?*

Suddenly, the whole party felt like it held her down and gave her free food and drink but demanded she stay under its rules. It was the rules of a rave girl, a stripper, or late-night prostitute sitting behind a K-mart parking lot. *No. I'm no K-mart slut! I'm a decent woman, just with flaws I have to fix…like anyone else.*

Liz studied the party. She was seeing these people differently. Yes, they were her friends, good friends she would say defensively if asked. *But why did they look so different tonight? There was Hanna with her makeup. She was always with it. How often do I wear makeup?*

Daniel was drinking away his awareness, stumbling through the crowd. Lillie looked upset. *Had he done something wrong? Did he say something mean, or was it just because he wouldn't stop chugging? How often do I chug?*

"But Daniel has daddy problems," Liz said to herself.

His daddy hated him. She remembered how Daniel wanted to live with his best friend Dom because his father would come home from the Clever Isle every night and bother everyone. It showed all right. He was creeping out of every bottle and party like bubbles overflowing from a bathtub. *I don't have daddy issues.*

The music filtered through more robotic music. To Liz's surprise, no neighbors had complained yet. "Yet" was the key word. *When had they not filed public disturbance claims?* Surely some green-masked bitch was dialing on her phone now, spitting into the speaker and listing her stern dislikes to the fat man at the calling desk about how Hanna was throwing another wild carousal.

"But stop. Come on. Really. Just party," Liz told herself. "So what if they're a little carried away? What's so bad about it? A woman needs her fun. That green-masked hag should know that. Did something crack in her head? Has that knowledge spilled through her mind like a leaky pipe over the years? We're just having fun."

Was that happening to me now? Was my mind cracking with age? After all,

I'm the one most sober, sitting alone on the couch. Fun was like a boyfriend. I needed it to get by the days. Without fun, what else was there?

She had control with her needs. She wasn't overdosed with love, carrying children from place to place, from one daddy to another, because she couldn't withhold her need for love. *And look! I'm not wasted now, unable to control my need for fun. But that is the sick truth. We have no control. You need a relationship, miss? Three months later, married. Six months later, divorced,* Liz thought, thinking of her mother. *Mommy problems.*

Liz grabbed a beer, snapped it open, and chugged it. Hanna had two kids with two different fathers. She might have a bun in the oven now, too. She mentioned pregnancy dreams all the time. *What was it, teeth falling out or something?* She popped open another can and chugged it. *Hey, hey! Slow down!* Liz felt like she was convincing a non-Catholic he'd go to hell if he didn't convert. *Yes, that green-masked hag is calling us in. She's cracked. But not me. I'm just carried away, taken by the storm.*

Maya played with her hair and supported her elbow with her jittery hand, and after pacing around twice, she finally asked the question everyone wanted to know. "What are we doing?"

"Keeping an eye out for the killer, Miss Douglas," Agent Moore said sternly. "We got leads here by the Tiki Pier. If that boy is correct, we may catch this nanny."

Again, Maya felt distant with the FBI agent. He appeared confident and surly, but his confidence was no more than a gimmick to the human psyche, a wishful thought of one's being, one that always implied disaster for those who took it past its purpose. This son of a bitch from New York City waltzed into Hollow Heights with a pompous grin on his face, wearing some shiny badge that here, distant from any city or large township, did little for any case.

What did he want access to? The winery? A bookstore? Hell, Mr. Moore, why don't you take the special potty painted gold? Go ahead. You have the badge, Greg thought.

Greg was in charge until Agent Moore showed up. How was he

feeling? Maya wanted to know. She looked around and saw him leaning on a boat. His uniform caught her eye first.

"I think the salty air got to him," Maya said as she approached Greg.

He shook his head, sighed, and almost mumbled, "I still don't know why he's here."

"I do," Maya said in an instant.

Greg raised an eyebrow.

"The FBI has had their eyes on us since we built the town. We're new. They want dibs on our first murder case."

"I dunno, Maya."

"Think about it. What other reason could there be?"

"See now. The FBI keeps that quiet. How could we know? If you want my honest opinion, I think it has to do with Neil's business."

"You mean the Miles Winery?"

"Yes. How'd they get so much money? They own half the land that makes up our town."

"Meh, it's Black Bell, remember? Neil paid a few retired miners to check it out. They found gold and—"

"You really believe that?"

Maya glared at the water's edge.

"I heard the same damn thing countless times. I'll give 'em credit where it's due. Hearing the same story repeated in a small town with little change is imposing, but I ain't convinced. I'm sure it's nothing big, but Mr. Miles probably has secrets against his wife and daughter that made their fortune a reality. Hiring retired miners? Old men working in an unstable mine? That's quiet the plot hole."

"If you say so," Maya replied doubtfully, "so you suspect something went wrong with him? Somebody came back to finish a deal Neil didn't go through with?"

"Hell if I know. Neil's dead. That's safe to say. But this whole thing's got me concerned for Tia and Keria's well-being."

"Same."

The air turned a little colder. Aside from the clashing waves, the world sounded like a nest of cicadas. A steady breeze lurked in from the Atlantic's darkness, and the sound of seagulls came when everyone least expected it. Two hours passed since the search started, and all anyone managed to find were more questions for the FBI agent.

Agent Moore's feet got mangled in beach grass. Everyone watched him try to untangle with side vision at first. Soon, everyone smirked, not realizing he or she was doing it while watching Agent Moore with full eye-on-eye contact.

"Find this funny?" he said flustered. "Pay attention to the pier. Do your goddamn jobs."

"We would if there were anything to find," Gina Harris exclaimed. "We've been watching it for hours." Gina was a lazy cop. Most called her the whiny bitch. But everyone was happy to hear her voice. "You think the killer will show up to a place where every cop in town is?"

"We are looking for any possible evidence, Miss Harris. Did you not pay attention?"

Gina rolled her big blue eyes and huffed.

"Now get to work."

A half hour passed. There was still nothing. Agent Moore told over half the crew to return to the station and call it a night. They shuffled home, all thinking the same thing. *What a waste of our time, pieces of our lives we won't be getting back.*

An hour later, Hanna Solomon's party turned ugly. No amount of alcohol could remove the sights given to the partiers by Mike Ribbons himself and the one who the children often referred to as "the nanny."

"Did you hear that?" Maya reacted to the screaming of young adults that vaguely vibrated the street.

"Move out. Down the street. Now!" Agent Moore began sprinting.

The rest followed.

———

Keria lay on her bed, staring at her phone that lay on the table beside her television. Nathan had called her twice and left four text messages. One was long-winded, and the others were short. She wanted to call him back but couldn't move. *What's this feeling? Am I dreaming? I feel so, so numb.*

Her body had the sensation one's arm feels when the blood circulation is cut off after sleeping on it. She literally had trouble moving until, without warning, her body collected itself and the numbness moved to her brain like a rush of wild water. She couldn't fathom what was happening. Each time she felt the nightly breeze hit her bare skin, the numbness grew twice as fast, like it fed the feeling. Its influence was greater than any wine she had ever drunken, greater than any lie that ever affected her. It was even stronger than Nathan's loving motivation, or so it seemed. She couldn't fight it. When the feeling advanced further during its takeover, memories became hazy.

She got up to dial 911 but forgot the number and reason to call it, as if this illness purposely took that knowledge away at that very moment to ensure full control became a reality.

Her memories weren't so much taken as they were blocked. Back in high school, Keria remembered hating the torture of forgetting books just after repeating the words, "Major homework assignment! Don't forget your math book!" at lunch, art class, and gym. She would forget a phone number or name, all these things and remembered and forgotten. The very forgetfulness, on a normal occasion, would cause a minor to semi-minor issue. It was nothing serious. *Right?*

Whatever one would call this blocked-more-than-minor memories, Keria suddenly remembered nothing more than the life she spent before Nathan's return to Silverhill. And then, in a time span of about two minutes, she forgot everyone's name except her parents, David's, Liz's, and Lillie's. They were her old friends and the young version of Nathan who fled without telling. She remembered David staring at her breasts at the age of eighteen and when he said at nineteen, "Forget Nathan. He's not coming back. Let me be how you move on." But he never said that. David never said that. So why was she thinking it? Remembering it?

Without the knowledge of Nathan's return to remind her, Keria felt a desire to shed her bra, stuff David's face in between her breasts, and have him journey freely down her waist. It was the kind of lust a person felt after a ruthless breakup. She lost her anchor. Truth was momentarily blinded.

Noreen. That name escaped the numbing void that plagued her thoughts. *I'm too young for that! I can't be getting Alzheimer's already! Just can't! It doesn't do this! I don't remember—*

What Keria's memory was left with by the end of the strange event was about up to the year before Nathan came back, a whole 450 days if one wants to get technical. She felt no sexual desire to be with anyone and remembered so little of people that being on her own felt safer. Keria shuffled back to bed, rubbed her body across the sheets lazily until her head met her pillow, and fell into a deep sleep.

Nathan had a similar sensation, a little pitch in the brain and some memory loss, however minor. His body turned things cold, yet his body was also a victim. Nathan was no warmer than his depiction of the man he had given Keria during the picnic. And where was his warming muse? He felt her going cold, too, with no call back and no texts again.

"Just stop," said the voice. "Stop."

It sounded so dry…so so close. It was more alien than ever. Nathan chose to ignore it.

Thinking back to a late-night program on TV he had seen in Rotor, Nathan remembered a therapist talking about voices and how they at first sound like echoes of your own thoughts and then slowly—or promptly—become that of another's, or so the hearer claims. Nathan tried to convince himself that his mind was playing a game. All the losses he'd suffered and the sudden change in his new pleasurable lifestyle in Hollow Heights called for insanity. He just had to stay in control.

But the voice had its own restraint, speaking in mumbles and whispers every moment Nathan had to think. *Got to move that damn table*, he thought.

"Move it."

This channel sucks.

"Change it."

What the hell?

"All hell."

Need to get something to eat.

"Feed."

I need to…uh…need to—

"Running away can't work no more."

His phone rang. Nathan threw himself up in an instant and answered it. "Hello?"

"Nathan? It's Tia. Something's wrong with Keria."

"I'll be right over."

He could hear an ambulance in the background and people talking in a rushed fashion. It was chaos mixed with distorted phrases. Nathan spent no time trying to make out one word after Tia spoke. He rushed to his Audi and left for the Miles Winery, only to notice that the chaos was up by Keria's home. He couldn't get there fast enough.

It was hard seeing her on a hospital bed, so blind to the world. Keria looked healthy fast asleep. The longest two hours of his life passed after the doctor said to wait for her tests to be finished. When the white-cloaked man stepped out, Nathan and Tia shot up from their seats like rockets. His hair was blonde and messy. He had a tan that completed the look he seemed to be going for, a beachgoer. *Another beach goer.*

"She's in shock, but should be okay. We just have to wait it out," he said calmly with no traits of doubt boiled in his eyes. That was what Nathan always searched for first, what was in the eyes.

"What a relief," Tia said.

"We'll know for sure when she wakes up." Nathan showed a great deal of skepticism.

Again, the doctor spoke, "Of course, but I wouldn't lose all hours of sleep over it. She's suffered a loss. Everyone knows. Poor girl just needs to come to terms. This may be her way."

"Yeah," Nathan muttered. He walked away.

"Nathan!" Tia hollered.

He ignored her and continued down the bustling hallway. Tia let out a heavy sigh and felt like a hot air balloon popped in her throat.

"He's just worried. When she wakes up, he'll be fine," the doctor said and turned away.

Tia allowed her eyes to wander toward Keria's room briefly. Looking around the hall, Tia met that unfortunate juncture where the world looked careless. She smirked at their ignorance. It beat bursting into tears, right?

The bottle of Highland Park flew into the wall and shattered, and its seductive stock stained wherever it touched. Nathan hollered, releasing all his frustration into the air. The place was a drunken gringo's dream. Booze stained the walls. Painkillers Nathan had saved were now shed of their private preservation, and there was no work tomorrow. *Why hadn't I been there?*

"Remember, she denied you, Nathan," said the voice in its mixture of high- and low-pitched vocals. "I called her so many times and sent her messages like I was a fucking mailman!"

"You were utterly denied."

Nathan plopped onto his recliner, regretting not falling onto the couch. He fell silent, wanting to hear the voice speak on its own terms instead of whenever he did, just to feel less crazy. Instead, all he heard was the wind outside his window, hitting the lose glass regularly. It howled, and it whispered. There were points when the wind sounded like the alien voice's mumbling. Nathan glared up at the ceiling, tilting his head back against the cushion of the chair, and saw a stain that defined a dark, inky face of the figure from his dreams. Then he passed out.

CHAPTER 9

Play Things

The town was beautiful, at peace with its former self, the graveyard town on the other side of the Miles trademark, which everyone now referred to as Silverhill. There were fancy homes and great thinkers. People with dreams and the motivation to acquire them prospered. There was a tiny beach around every corner, and one of the world's most creative wineries swallowed more than half the land with its sour grapes and fancy attention-grabbers. Nathan had come to know this.

It was easy to appreciate the landscape, crafted by hard-core believers of the American dream, but often overlooked was the sunrises and sunsets. They highlighted Mother Nature's salty bathtub, or fish tank as the fisherman called it, with starburst coloring and a new day's mysteries, a dying day's failures and successes.

Mr. Hawkins, the mailman who feared no rain, understood the sunrises and mysteries that came with them. He delivered the mail lethargically, knowing what lay beneath the faultless skin of Hollow Heights and imagining the town as a supermodel with liver damage, ashy lungs, clogged arteries, and a mind hell-bent on revenge.

Often, Mr. Hawkins saw the skin and nothing more. During days of bad weather, he would see the innards, pulsing and pumping and screeching and halting. It was satisfying to know many of the townsfolk had solar panels nesting by their gardens. What wasn't known to anyone other than the owners of at least fifteen gardens (and Mr. Hawkins) was that the power harbored by these panels was used to support hidden pot gardens.

The town was beautiful, filled with life and inspired people. As the sun hovered above Hollow Heights in the afternoon, kids were out playing ball by the many beaches, awing Spangle and calling it by that name. Mr. Wilkerson gazed out his window with lazy eyes at the children, bees left people alone as they were too busy populating flowers up on the surrounding hilltops, and the fisherman were committing to heavy labor out at sea.

Mothers cleaned their amiable-themed homes and baked pies and home-cooked meals while their husbands were out. Basements held wine and most of it from the Miles Winery. And let's make sure we all know community service was respected!

One of the coziest homes in Hollow Heights was Mr. and Mrs. Smith's. They were generally the second-most idolized people in town, the third to a good few. They were in the public's eye, the perfect American family. The couple had two children, one ten-year-old boy and one seven-year-old girl. The Smiths held hands when the world was watching. They had one Ford minivan and a typical silver Nissan Altima in their glorious driveway, one of the smoothest in town. Flourishing flowers aligned with the cobblestone walkway. (This made up for the garden they did not have.) And two stone turtles sat beneath a red maple tree. Also, the lawn was always freshly cut. Got to appreciate that nice crisp, grassy smell!

Mrs. Smith's OCD kept her in line, and if that didn't work, Mr. Smith would punch her in the gut and say something fitting like, "Clean your act and the house. Are you stupid? They are watching. We can't look like the others. If I see you sitting around one more time, I swear I'll throw you out that door."

Miss Donor was the mailwoman. She knew but ignored. So she could be thrown into the denial category. (She didn't quite fit into the knowing as she drugged herself every night and forgot most of the shit.) What she did remember was something no amount of drugs could erase, but that had nothing to do with Hollow Heights.

At night, delightful lights lit the walkways to each road and house, every beach, and the path to the docks. An eerie black light lit Mike's room. Mike was currently and always thinking of a way around Mr. Wilkerson's yard when playing soccer. Him and the other kids preferred manhunt though. One might get the impression of a suburban community, but remember, everything here rusted and died when the storms came in. The town was a big salt treatment, but then again, any port town was.

A corpse of a forty-year-old male lay beneath the docks. By now, his eye sockets were tunnels of flesh worms housed in. Was this the first real murder case? Maybe. There was another body somewhere under Oak Berry Road, but no one would ever know until a hurricane swept the docks, and even then, the guy was so well buried. And both were.

But yes, the town was beautiful.

Liz let down her guard. Could one blame her? The booze had simmered everyone's energy to a screaming halt, and the party favors were gone. There was a six-pack of cola nobody wanted, the cheap shit that rolled over. If Daniel hadn't passed out, he'd likely throw the cans onto the front lawn and make a scene, thinking they were toy rockets or fireworks.

This was top class. Everyone was stylishly wasted and spread across the floor like beached whales. The only ones awake were Mike Ribbons and his comrade, the girl in the pink robe. Her eyes were cold like snow and appeared dilated. She stood completely still, waiting for Ribbons to remind her he was indeed her father.

"Find Liz," he said.

The girl nodded and walked around the partiers without bumping into anyone until she spotted Liz. The girl glanced over her shoulder. Ribbons gestured for her to come back. The kid was slick, much more graceful than Ribbons.

"What do we do, Dad?"

"We clear the problem."

A shadow stretched over the drunken partiers and the beer-soaked carpet as Ribbons revealed his trusty revolver from his back pocket, which was tucked deep inside his heavy black robe.

"Daughter, when you get an ex—and I guarantee you—you will. Remember this day."

And with one clean shot, Liz was dead, and the rest were screaming.

The town was active in a new way, one that was less concealed to the underground but rather spreading to the streets. When the cops made it to Hanna's house, everyone alive was tripping over one another.

"I'm Agent Moore! I need everyone to calm down!"

Nobody listened to the fool because they knew the nanny wasn't finished, and certainly no smug-faced agent would stop her killing spree. The nanny wanted the girl out first, so she walked onto the house's stone path. The cops studied her for a weapon but soon had her shuffle across the road.

"Who's in there?" Agent Moore asked.

"The nanny's bad man," the girl said in a weird, playful tone.

The child was terrified. *Poor thing.* Agent Moore knew what he had to do. This was personal, outside of the FBI. He didn't know anyone here, but he made a promise, and no crazed daycare bitch was going to tamper his word.

In the darkness of the bloody living room, Mike and the nanny stood in.

The old woman said, "Okay, go. Show them your way. Your power. Don't confine yourself just to Sun Child."

He left the building from the back and hopped into the bushes behind Hanna's picket fence. The cops had no idea. They never got around (quite literally) to what house harbored the chaos until after Mike was tugged away. He used his own two feet, seeming to carry on their own will as he ran deep into the woods. The nanny waited inside Hanna's house with the little girl in the pink robe. Both their eyes were empty of emotion.

142

The nanny stood in the doorway wearing a blue and white spotted nightgown one would see an old farmer's wife wear. She was holding a newborn baby between her flabby arms.

"Oh my God," Maya said softly.

"Yes, isn't God wonderful for giving us this child?" the nanny spoke.

No one believed the old lady could hear Maya from where she cradled the newborn, but somehow Maya's quiet words had reached her.

"No one needs to get hurt, ma'am. You are standing in a crime scene. Please place the baby down and come here with your hands up," Agent Moore said.

"Place the child on the ground? Now why would I do such a thing? Hand me a bed, and I'll do what you ask. Think of the child. Are you not good people of justice?"

Agent Moore's face went pale as the nanny peered down at the baby's eyes with a smirk less appealing than a clown grinning at a corpse.

Agent Moore turned his attention to Maya without adjusting his stance and said, "Go find a baby bed or something. Quick."

Maya hesitantly lowered her pistol, unable to really catch up with the event, and started jogging down the road. People were outside left and right. How hard could it be to find one? A young woman in her early twenties had a tiny, pod-like bed. The woman pushing the baby pod lifted her child, disturbing him from his sleep, and allowed Maya to take it to the nanny.

"Ma'am, we are getting one." Agent Moore suddenly remembered a series of crude memories of his sister as a newborn and toddler.

Agent Moore was only four, still surprised he remembered, but maybe we always remember things we've seen even as old as a day. Only these memories, these terrifying first glimpses of life, stay in the darkest corners of our mind and are the dreams we never remember having. Agent Moore felt like his promise was about to be broken, and infant fear haunted him once more.

It was the way his sister was handled and tossed on the sofa like a tiny beanbag. But any real damages would likely be the result of the TV he watched. People spilling rounds of ammunition at one another, cursing and raping each other. It was the History Channel. His father would always watch it while spending "quality time" with his children. *Boom! Boom! Oh no! Now he's sleeping. Now he's oozing red paint all over the ground. Someone better clean that up*, Agent Moore thought.

"Don't be picky," Agent Moore said.

"No need to be. The baby only needs a safe place to sleep." The nanny assured him.

The little girl in the pink robe eagerly stepped behind Agent Moore and whispered, "She's the mean one."

Oh thank God, Agent Moore thought as his eye caught Maya running down the road with a baby pod.

"We have a bed. Maya will place it near you. I want you to slowly approach the pod and gently place the baby inside. Then step back and hold up your hands."

Agent Moore nodded at the space between the nanny and him. Maya forced herself to where she thought was a decent place to put the pod-like bed.

When at a fair distance, the nanny said, grinning, "It's red. Quite all right."

"Slow and steady, Granny." Agent Moore demanded.

Her grin grew, and her eyes developed shadows below the lids of her eyes as she hummed the nursery rhyme "The Little Old Lady Who Lived in a Shoe." After placing the baby in the dark red cushion, the little girl in pink shoved Agent Moore down, and all the cops turned to her, leaving the nanny free to escape. But that wouldn't happen. She no longer carried the infant in her ugly arms. Greg noticed the nanny begin to run and hastily shot at her when he saw her face the house. *You're old? I don't give a damn*, he thought.

She released a grizzly howl from her saggy throat, and a loud, steady wheeze lingered as she laid face-first into the ground. The baby wailed, and the little girl beat on Agent Moore's chest as he lifted her up.

"Where the hell is the other guy?" Agent Moore hollered.

"No! No! No! No!" screamed the girl, throwing her arms wildly. "You can't have my daddy!"

"I have men all over looking for him," Greg said calmly.

"Good work, Holler. We'll catch him. Drag that freak to your car and take her to cell B. I'm sure your drunken friend is housing A."

Greg smiled, but only a little.

Mike Ribbons loved a scary story. He and his best friends, Deland and Macro, did, too. That was why they loved camping and owned this cabin in the woods in Maine near Silverhill. This was long before Mike's Hollow Heights move. He loved it, so much so he didn't mind the idea of dying inside its lovely interior.

Mike had no idea where he was. As he ran forward, deeper into the black forest, he saw a blanket of light leach out across a lawn. He felt wet, thinking he'd fallen into the ocean. But once close enough to his cabin, he saw that fresh blood covered his entire robe. But he felt relief. He was here of all places.

His pulse felt bitter, like it'd been beating for hours. He removed the robe, revealing a normal green shirt and blue jeans, and stuffed it into a set of bushes showcased by the moon's gleam. He ran into the cabin, happy to find it was unlocked.

He hollered in his mind, "What did I do?"

It was fruitless. The answer remained hidden from memory. Slamming the front door open in a fit of panic, Mike scanned the living room. With the lights on, Mike prepared to meet the fools who took his home. But he was crafty and, above all, knew this place's heart and soul, the ins and outs. So far, the living room remained the same. It looked old, but really the cabin was not so. *No differences, as there should not be.*

Mike and his two goofy friends never sold the cabin, but it appeared someone decided to break in. *Was I drugged by this same person or people? If so, what did they make me do?* He slithered among the furniture in one quick, steady motion, peeking around every corner.

The first floor was clear. Mike entered the kitchen, looking for a steak knife. He heard lingering footsteps above, slightly rattling the dangling ceiling light above an old table. Seeing a chief's knife sitting by the sink, Mike snatched it and entered the basement stairway, closing the door, only leaving it cracked open, eye width. The footsteps paused and suddenly beat against the floor. Whoever was up there started running. *Sounds like one person. I can take him or her. That son of a bitch will pay for this.*

The intruder descended to the first floor. And after that, there were no more footsteps, as if the person stood below the staircase, perhaps listening for Mike to make the first move. But he wouldn't. *Oh no, not by any means.* He was the crafty one.

In this unnerving silence, Mike tried to recall what happened. But his mind felt fuzzy. *Like white noise on an old television.* Nothing was changed down here. *But what about upstairs? Are there bodies up there? No. The house would reek of the rotting dead. But the blood on my robe was fresh. What if… what if there were fresh bodies up there?*

Several footsteps traveled through the house, and with them, a memory surfaced. It was Mike putting on that robe, and he remembered why. Someone did not want him to appear normal. The reason was too vague. It was just because until the footsteps could be heard again, as if whoever were walking drew nearer, knowingly and slowly. With each step, the stranger made the night's events return, piece by piece.

What was the reason? He was the fall guy. People had to take notice of him, and they did. He remembered being pointed at, talked about, and eyed by the townsfolk. *But no cops. I don't remember there being any cops.* There were more footsteps. *I felt drugged, unable to control my own movements. Something about the sun. I always heard the word "sun." Shit, that old woman. She did it! She told me to leave after some child was—*

The intruder entered the kitchen. Mike tried to swallow his fear, stuffing it down so it wouldn't burst out in a scream. He managed, but it felt like a jagged rock scraping its way through his throat. His palms sweat against the knife he held, afraid it may slip and fall, giving away his position and rendering him defenseless. The person inched by, wearing a hood. Mike could recall everything now.

He must have been drugged because he was visiting his Hollow Heights home, preparing it for rent. It was his cabin here. He wanted to stay in. But somehow, his veins went icy cold, and he got dizzy. Shivering, he told his girl Shelly he had the chills again.

"Take some Advil!" she shouted from the other room.

Advil? For chills? No, he would eat, if his numbing arms would allow it. In the home, he heard movement, thumping and tapping. Shelly was a noisy woman. She didn't know how to be crafty. *Not like me.*

He thought about his high sugar level and the shakes he often experienced if he did not eat. He felt that now, all these same feelings inside the cabin. No draft was creeping up from the cellar behind him. It was just those shakes and sudden chills. *These chills are coming from the kitchen.* The air-conditioning was freezing in there.

The hooded person continued his search. It sounded to Mike like the kitchen was empty once more. A scent of flowers invoked a tender sense of safety. Maybe this asshole was settling in, spraying the cabin with air freshener. *Hell no. Not my cabin.*

Mike pushed open the door, braving his fear. The footsteps stopped in the living room, and Mike ran into it, shouting. But no one was in there. The footsteps weren't coming from the living room.

"Who's here? Huh?" he finally hollered. "This is my home!"

The Hollow Heights home got like this, too. Shelly was nowhere to be found. He asked where the cooking spray was.

Notta damn thing, he thought. *Was it happening again, only in the cabin this time? What happened after the silence?* The memory of the robe's fitting and origin was impossible to remember. Nothing seemed to exist after Shelly disappeared. *Maybe it was S—*

He heard a click. Stiff as cold iron, Mike felt the scream build up in his throat like vomit. He held it in, shallow as a three-inch grave. His dignity was on the line. The muzzle hovered nearer. He could feel its presence. Then its cold metal met his skin, and his flesh felt an electric shock of fear, like lighting meeting water, and he screamed, begging the killer for mercy. He couldn't see who it was because he was too afraid to meet the eyes behind the madness.

"Shelly, you bitch."

"Oh?" The woman kept her voice in a whisper.

The gun was fired, the bullet nudged deeply into Mike's brain, and his body dropped distastefully to the floor. And the killer stepped out the front door.

Like solving cases on *CSI* or some other crime TV show, cops would laugh and say it doesn't work like that. It usually took months to years to solve a crime. The paperwork piled high, as expected, but much sooner. It turned out the townsfolk in Hollow Heights were correct on their feelings about "CSI reality" the following morning when Agent Moore announced the finding of Mike's corpse. They wanted him gone because, if that FBI agent dug any deeper into this town, he'd solve more than just the nanny case. He'd uncover a whole new world.

But it was nice to know the killers were found and stopped. Some looked up the case results online. Others refused to know the details. They weren't pretty, and things were fucked up enough with what the news reported about Mike's body on the TV. In the case of Mike, his death was announced as a suicide.

"Results," Agent Moore said. All the cops of Hollow Heights were seated in the meeting room. Agent Moore had to give his presentation. "With the killers identified, I was able to contact Mr. Graves, my trusty lab partner, for background information. Let's begin with the child." Agent Moore clicked a button on a tiny remote to show a new slide on the wall, a picture of the little girl in the pink robe, only she was wearing a Disney Princess shirt and pink pants in this photo, holding a stuffed rabbit.

"Kailey White. A nature lover whose parents were killed by a truck driver when she was three years old. The nanny, as children have been calling her, babysat her daily except on weekends. The nanny's actual name is Mary Qualey. She had it illegally changed. Strange enough, her birth name is unknown. She's taken over Tia Miles' previous job as a daycare babysitter before the Miles Winery was founded. What you, the law enforcement of this new town, may find disturbing is that this nanny, as she made herself out to be, taught cult-like beliefs to her customer's children during their time in the Sun Child Daycare. As it sets by what you call Silverhill, I would like to talk to, um, current residents of your old port town. Perhaps learn Mary's birth name. As for the case in itself, no more is permitted."

"Good work," Greg said. He was standing by the left wall, Agent Moore's right side.

Agent Moore nodded respectfully, not exactly happy with the sheriff's outburst. He said in a colder tone, "It turned out that Mary was beating these children, and Mike Ribbons found this out. Kailey is Mike's adopted daughter. What we got from Kailey was believable. She and Mike wanted to have Miss Qualey killed. The newborn Mary carried was a baby left at the daycare for the night hours, a new set of hours opened only five months ago starting from nine at night and ending at one in the morning. Mike kept quiet about his distaste for what Mary had done to Kailey and set her up at Hanna Solomon's house. Why Kailey called Mike 'the nanny's bad man' is a likely result of her teachings at the daycare. It's disturbing, but it appears Kailey played Mike for the fool, and as a result, he shot himself in his cabin.

"There's room for a possible third adult involved. We found fingerprints all over Mike's doorknob with no match to a resident of Hollow Heights. Let us know immediately if something comes up." Agent Moore gave a quick stare at the others before looking back down at his report. "Likely this other person was designed as a decoy to lure us away from Mr. Ribbons."

Several pictures appeared on the wall, but it wasn't necessary. Agent Moore explained enough. The findings hit them all pretty hard. A crazy child abuser? A man and his adopted child killing? A cult teaching taking place in the daycare? The world felt like it flipped overnight, and all the disaster reports were just now flooding in.

Agent Moore sighed. "As for Neil Miles, his death was a failed attempt at involving Nathan Ruiz into the killing of Mary. How that would have helped them is unknown. Any further questions?"

Agent Moore studied the room. The only one not looking satisfied was Greg, the man who had just said he did good work. This spiked Agent Moore's interest.

"Okay. You are all dismissed. Greg, may I speak with you?"

As everyone left the room, Greg approached Agent Moore. "Anything you want to tell me?"

"Yeah. I'm not likin' the gap on Neil's death." Greg scratched his scruffy chin with two fingers. "It's discouraging. Why—"

"Neil wasn't the boss of the Miles Winery. His murderer put Hollow

Heights into fear. That's all it takes. Nathan was close to Keria, so I've heard. My guess is they thought the two of them would go to Clever Isle."

"Mr. Moore. We know things. It's a small town. We all know Nathan only came here because of Keria."

"You don't know that."

"Aye, I do. And what we also know is that boy goes to the Sleeping Grizzly. Surely Ribbons had known this?"

"I leave that to you, Mr. Holler. As of now, the nanny case is solved in my book. If you'd like to pursue something else, like that gap, fine. But the little mind-the-gap play is not in the interest of the FBI. Believe me. I know. Cases like these have decoys. I know one when I see one."

Greg looked displeased. "Visit Mary's cell, Mr. Holler. She's all yours."

For once, Jeff was fond of his fear. On the news, the death count for Hanna's party was listed quite frequently. Liz was the suspected target. Aside from her, four others were shot and killed.

"To think I would have been there," he said aloud.

He was cozy at home, watching Hollow Heights shift into something darker he never saw coming with the help of Fox News. But it felt great for a time. He was done. There was no more sneaking around Nathan's house, no more of Neil's bullshit plots, and especially no more fantasies of Liz.

He watched the full report and read all the headlines. The event was water that never soaked. He, by the end of the following day the murders took place, disbelieved everything. He never shed one tear. The way his mind worked was this: the pain lingered forever in the form of disbelief, a gentle but unforgiven sheet of blockage that allowed Jeff to see the truth but ensured it remained untouchable, sealed in plain sight. He knew she was dead but often forgot because his mind never touched the idea.

An attractive news anchor shook her head in response to someone's outrage about Sun Child.

"Our children are not even safe here!" an overweight mother hollered into the microphone.

They didn't show much of her. It was just her face, spitting into the microphone, and that was relatable to Jeff. He was there, and then he wasn't. He was involved but now a shadow of his former self, polishing the higher power's pretty little gimmicks. He was simply there, tending to a trademark, someone else's trademark.

"Not even." He reminded.

The fountain was child's play. Only the kids saw the thing.

"Seems Tia never should have quit her old job," the news anchor said.

Jeff agreed. He felt sick-minded about the Miles. He got to thinking how horrible his intentions were to become Neil's boss and possibly overthrow the winery because he felt most small there. Working for the big shots made him hateful. But he was damn lucky to work there.

Done. He wasn't done with his job, of course, but he was done with anyone outside of work. *You want a favor? Tough shit. I'm not helping,* he thought most certainly.

It was just him in a dark room, watching the TV. There were no worries and no more new pain. Computer parts lay beside his recliner. He got to thinking, *Now that Liz is gone, maybe my mind would focus more on my hobby and less on getting laid.* Those lonely parts could easily be assembled, like a collection of Legos that a child had just unearthed from a hole in the couch or back of his closet. *That's all they really are, lost pieces of old Legos.*

But Lillie was still alive. She was Liz's closest friend. Maybe she had a little oomph in her, the same kind Liz had. She was hyper and tainted, dirty desire. He refused to believe Lillie would so much as lay a finger on his hand. The night she drank, waiting for Neil to arrive was her constant red flag. Liz seemed more professional that night.

Who knew? He thought that Liz wasn't the most openly goofy, non-sober bitch in Hollow Heights. *And wasn't Liz the one who talked to me? Lillie would never have come to see me at work.* Jeff popped open another Budweiser, his third one. And he intended to drink much more. Liz loved Budweiser. For whatever reason, he remembered it was all she ever bought.

What if I'd been there? Would it all be the same as it is now? Could it have been me who'd been killed instead? I wish it'd be that way. This is just— He cringed at the sight of an image of the nanny that appeared on the screen. He rolled over, stared at his computer parts like he discovered a gaping hole, and closed his eyes.

Anger was more a pleasure to Jeff than this. What exactly was this anyway? It was sheer failure. Not only did Jeff avoid Liz for what felt like the hundredth time, she was stone-cold dead now.

"Shit happens," he said. "Just deal with it. Not like I thought anything would change."

But it did. People died.

"Hollow Heights sucks," Jeff muttered. "It sucks so bad."

The door opened in the cell room. Discarded and left to rot, the only permanent prisoner was Mary. But she wouldn't stay for long. Agent Moore was leaving soon, and Mary would go with him.

Greg closed the door behind him. Already, William Hopper, the top-class town drunk, began asking for an estimate for his release.

"I ready told you, Mr. Hopper. You ain't leaving 'til the end of the week, you hear?"

"I can't help it. It's not my fault the roads are so dark. I had to ask for rides. Everyone said no. I had to keep buggin' 'em! What else was I to do? They oughta do something about that, you know what I'm saying? Huh?"

Greg passed him, keeping his firm walking posture from making even the slightest turn toward William. One of the fluorescent lights flickered above, near Mary's cell. Greg tuned out William, trying to find Mary's strange humming. Everyone, including Agent Moore, claimed she'd continue. Her cell bars were sleek but strong. Her shadow was cast on the portion of the wall Greg could only see until he stood side by side with cell B.

"Mary?" he asked in a frail whimper.

She sat slanted on the left side, looking paler than she had before. Her cell held a bitter chill that glissaded through the bars like radio waves. Greg felt it hit his skin. Mary peered up at him.

"Just you and me know, see?"

She nodded. "And this stays between us, hear? I want to know your motivation. What convinced you to act the way you did?"

"Convinced?" she asked. "Hardly the correct term."

"What do you mean?"

Mary smiled, but it wasn't menacing. The smile was quick, daunting, and hopeless. "I can't really answer because I don't remember. I woke up in my bedroom feeling sickly, thinking I'd been attacked. A nightmare more or less. Then as if it escaped my mind, I saw something."

Greg raised an eyebrow. "It was looming around my eye. Then I was overcome with dizziness, and I passed out. After that, I was here."

"You mean to tell me you were unaware of your crime?"

"What crime?" she asked with a feeble chuckle. She shook her head, as if feeling dizzy again. "I'm here so it must have been bad...whatever it was."

"This feeling of dizziness, has it happened before?"

"Oh, yes. But I never woke up in another place. When I passed out before, I always awoke where I'd slept. I don't recall ever sleepwalking, but I do remember waking up after the first time I'd passed out like this."

Mary took a heavy breath. Her old voice box needed a little recovery. "It was raining very heavily outside. And I heard someone walking outside my house. I have a wooden porch. Someone was pacing on it. Slow footsteps, not heavy like the rain. But my walls are thin. I often used them to hear if someone were coming to the door. But whoever that was never stayed in one place. And finally, when the pacing footsteps went away, I got up and peeked out my bedroom window. I saw someone off in the distance looking back at me."

"I'm assuming you couldn't see the person's features because of the rain?"

"Precisely. I tried, too. Believe me. I was terrified, already shaken up by my passing out and achy body. And then here this person was, pacing around my home. Watching from afar."

"You should have reported this to the station."

"Yes and no. Yes, since there was a guy lingering around my home, and no, because he up and vanished. You fellows are trying to stop crime, but your system is flawed. If I were to approach your station, Mr. Holler, I'd be ridiculed, laughed at, and sent to the funny farm."

"What did you see?"

Mary showed no restraint, only anger. She thought she was wasting her breath. "I saw the man or woman outside, too far away to see his or her features. I stared at this person and heard something fall beside me. I peered over, afraid somebody else was stalking me, too, but my bedroom was empty. I looked back out my window, and the person was closer. Another noise came from behind. I ignored it. The strangest thing, Sheriff...I should have been able to tell the gender of this person. Maybe it was my age, but whatever my reason, I tried to see..."

Mary went quiet. Greg was about to open his mouth when Mary opened hers. "I saw shadows branch and orbit this figure. I was frozen in fear. I woke up just moments ago, maybe still hanging from a dream. I closed my eyes and told myself it wasn't there. And what happened when I reopened them?"

"The figure was gone."

"Correct."

"I'll file for insanity, miss. That way you won't be imprisoned."

"Not in jail anyway," she said.

"Instead of stickin' to my original proposal of keeping this chat to ourselves, I'm givin' you the choice of accepting my claim."

"What are you claiming?"

"That you have some kind of mental illness."

Mary was offended but knew Greg was on to something. Still, did she really want to be in the loony bin? Sure, if it might, she could eventually leave.

"Sure, Mr. Holler. What have I got to lose?"

Greg had some more questions. Now that he broke the ice, he wanted to know how she felt about Neil's murder. "Before I go, mind if I ask you somthin'?"

Mary looked up at him silently.

"What was the real reason behind Neil's death? Go ahead. Just tell me. I won't go against my word."

"Sheriff, how could I know? I told you my part in the manner. It's all I can tell you."

"Did you not know Mike Ribbons?"

"I watched his daughter. I know nothing more."

"The FBI agent says you abused her and taught kids a cult belief about gods and demons, leaking through to our world through energies and people's passings. Is this true?"

"I said one day, a day I should have never brought up my bizarre encounter with that shadow person, which I wondered where it came from. I said random, but what I thought possibly could have linked that being to me once and only once. But I'm going to guess this. The source you heard about…what did you call it…cult-like beliefs or something? This came from Lora, the mother who picked up Katy that day when I talked about it. Your fellow comrades must have listened to her mouth. Unwise. She's a gossiper, that one."

Greg was puzzled and frustrated. Again, he felt convinced the case was unsolved. But he knew he couldn't pursue possibilities like this, demons and shadow people. It was like what Mary said. His job was flawed. Greg thought of it as close-minded and limited.

He hit a new kind of brick wall, the first time in his entire career. He'd have to make do with it, and maybe that would be enough. But now Greg felt a new fear, one of the supernatural. Would he wake up to see a shadow? *Overthinking this,* he thought. *Simply overthinking.*

He knew he should have moved a long time ago before the mine reopened, before he got suckered into moving to the new town of Hollow Heights. He was the outcast. His home wasn't anything special. In fact, it was worse than his previous. And God forbid he ever stepped out of line or the cops would accuse him of murder.

Mr. Wilkerson packed his bags. He felt used, washed up, and, above all else, foolish. His parents were right that he didn't belong here. This was for the upper-class people of the world, not some hillbilly. Had he even made one friend? No. Did he ever lay eyes on a woman who didn't look away? Absolutely, but she didn't notice he was there until after she met his eyes or him for that matter.

His parents misjudged Mr. Wilkerson. And after the whole children being scared of the nanny bullshit, he knew fingers would be pointed at him by the parents whose children smashed in his windows. *Come on now. If I never yelled, they would continue to break them. Now they break them accidentally while playing a ballgame.* Mr. Hawkins knew more, but poor old John Wilkerson was caught up in crude affairs. It was pure ridicule. *They made me angry and hateful from the start.*

Something clawed at his door. *Goddamn those kids! Now what?* The door shook, like a cat was pushing it, trying to get its owner to refill its bowl.

"Back off, you hear! I'm leaving! I'm done!" John hollered.

The door stopped shaking.

He felt relieved to return to his hometown. If anyone were foolish, it was his parents for moving here in the first place. What was his real reason for staying? He didn't like being defeated. Yeah, that was it. He could not expect that. It was do or die. So, he presumed he died.

The clawing at the door returned. It was louder this time. John stomped his feet to the door and opened it with his mouth open, ready to scream at whoever dared bother him. But the doorway was empty. It was impossible for someone to leave that quickly. The clawing was carrying on as he opened the door. How—

It was an omen. His mother always warned him of those. He gently closed the door and went back to his bed to stuff in the last few shirts. This place always made him feel watched in so many different ways. But this omen was new. It hardly mattered as this was his final hour in Maine or two, depending on traffic.

It was time to stop rewatching *Tucker and Dale VS. Evil* and take action for his own life. He closed the bag and picked it up off the bed. He was eager to get the hell out when the window above his bed shattered. He yelped and stood by the door, more like a frightened kitten than a meaty bull. Why was a messenger bothering him? *I'm leaving! What's to tell?*

"This home ain't held anything for me. Good riddance! Go ahead and trash the place!" he bellowed.

Four days after Mike's death, there was the final dream.

The Tiki Pier had become something of a tradition to go to when under the weather for some locals. For Nathan, it was his house or the Sleeping Grizzly. Tonight, it was standing across Black Bell. Four men stood on the surrounding rocks that bulged out of the cliff around the mine's entrance.

They were staring intensely, just shadows holding pickaxes from afar. The wind was energetic, twisting and swirling through the trees and clouds high above. The water had that pulsing movement again, and empty boats were floating in the sea.

I'm standing in Silverhill, Nathan thought. *Over there is Hollow Heights or where it should be. It was missing. And there way over there is Spangle and Black Bell. Has that changed, too, somehow?*

Here the inner voice was quiet, and a strange presence felt in control. Nathan's dreams were its worlds now. But at least he could think here. The four figures stood vaguely off in the distance as if signaling him to come over. *Sure, send one of those ghost boats, and I'll be there. Take me on another goddamn tour.*

It didn't quite work like that. The boats were doing their own thing. Nathan peered back down at the water and oddly placed two fingers on his pulse. The beat matched the water's pulsation. He slowly released his hand and studied his surroundings. Cold, diligent clouds, dark water, and chilly winds were present. Everywhere was dark and cold. There was no other choice to make. Nathan had to go to Silverhill. Up that hill were lit homes. A storm was coming, and from the looks of the sky and feel of the salty wind, his best bet was to take shelter in a home.

Nathan fought the wind as he walked up to the old town. Perhaps one of the strangest occurrences taking place was that Hollow Heights was missing. Only the original Silverhill existed. *Stuck in the past. Same pulse as my own. All the feelings of dread and grief fly freely in a storm.*

Every house and building was locked. Nathan was about to give up and cope with the storm back by a better view of the lighthouse when he spotted the morgue's door was open. It was basement level. He nearly missed it. The place wasn't welcoming, but as soon as he decided to walk toward the mine, the wind picked up, and the air dropped twenty degrees. He'd have to settle for the morgue.

It wasn't pretty, but it beat dying in a dream. The cold chill should have woken him up, but it didn't. This nightmare was like the one after the trip to Howard's house. Beneath damaged fluorescent lights, there were freezers on both sides, and in the middle, there was nothing but the old, rusty, white tiled floor. A locked door stood straight ahead, the knob strangled by chains, held in place by one large, rusty lock. The entrance was still open. No unknown forces had slammed it shut behind him. The wind tunneled down the stone stairs with a horrid whimper and jingled loose chains that hung off some of the freezers.

Within the whimpering wind, a faint voice close by said "Hollow Heights" in a speedy tone. It sounded female.

"Hello?" Nathan asked.

The wind's whimper settled to a moan, and the chains continued to rattle. Nathan's cloths felt damp. Down here, the air was foul, like someone had left a bucket of fruit that expired a month ago.

"We understand your struggles," said another voice. Both sounded familiar.

"No, you don't. You don't know me."

"We do," said the female.

"Yes, honey, we do," said a new voice, another familiar one that froze Nathan's body in place. Suddenly, all the freezer doors slid open, and up sat the bodies of Nathan's past. His mother said, "We know because we are them."

Their eyes were empty of emotion, hidden behind cloth. Skin and all were icy cold.

"You have to fight us, Nathan. You choose not to, but you can't avoid," Sophia spoke.

"Fight us, Nathan," they all said at once. "Fight us. Fight us. Fight us, or you can't save her."

Nathan stepped back toward the entrance, shaking his head in disbelief. He was about to burst into tears.

"Kill us off," they said before going silent.

They kept their sitting posture, deathlike in their little freezer beds. The entrance was still open, but Nathan didn't leave. The locked door was his next destination, and he knew he couldn't avoid it any longer. It was to be his advancement, whether into insanity or understanding. It didn't matter because both, it was safe to say, lived in the same hand. Whether one was greater than the other was, the two were always at war. Even the tiniest, glossed-over concepts held the potential to rise.

Keep doing it, even if it doesn't work and you know the new thing is likely to work but you just don't care. You want what you can't have, Nathan thought. *Insanity!*

"Where's the goddamn key?" he shouted. There was no movement. Nathan turned to his mother. "Mom?"

Eve smirked. "Don't you understand, Nathan? You are the key. We are in you. You are us. The lock is you."

The feeling of compassion that came with Eve's words was a lie. Eve wasn't really there. She was an illusion cast by whatever made up these nightmares. "Yeah, you're right. None of you should be here. I'm ridding you all, starting with this place."

Nathan approached the door and took hold of the lock. The chains fell off, and shortly after, every freezer slammed shut. Nathan glanced back and then down at the lock. It felt like foam. He made a fist with his hand, and the lock crumbled to dust. He stood wide-eyed in his plaid shirt, thinking about what possible madness laid beyond the door. He closed his eyes as he turned the knob and pushed it open.

Nathan opened his eyes to see Keria lying on a table, occupied by a figure that towered over her head. It was a human shadow, yet its height reached eight feet, five inches.

"Keria…"

"Yes, a husk," said a deep voice.

Nathan shook his head. "Enough of the bullshit. Who are you?"

"Not the one responsible for the voices in your head?" it asked.

"No? You look the same as it, only taller."

"Peer down at the empty basket. Think. This isn't the present, but rather the future. The one you will bring to her."

"No. No no. Oh God, Keria! What's happening?" Nathan fell to his knees and started to cry.

She was dead. Dream or not, the woman he loved lay coldly in front of him in some rusty old morgue that existed in a nightmarish world. Behind him, the others were soiled.

"Keria, talk to me! Why can the others talk and not you? Talk to me!"

"Empty tissue, Nathan. You must deal. It's expected of nature, of energies to twain into their proper happenings. Keria and death, forming you and grief. You, not I, dealt the fates to do so. Nothing can change your fate. She will be dead, and you will be left to mourn. It's the calling from the fates."

Nathan stood up. His vision was blurry. Keria looked like an angel sleeping on a demon's bed. The figure stood silently. "How is it me? I didn't do a damn thing to her or anyone!"

There was silence. The next thing Nathan saw was a teary vision of his bedroom and the sight of the words "Fight us" written across every wall. It was midday. Tia gave Nathan extra shifts for the past two days. Of course, there was no comparison to the energy taken by that nightmare. He felt his mind was strained the most. He'd have to gather his real mind-set so he could fight what he thought to be insanity climbing its way up to his logic and prepare for another attack.

What could he do? Keria was still sleeping in a hospital bed, and the doctors hadn't the slightest clue why. They stuck with the idea of Keria going into shock because of Neil's death, but it'd been a little long for that now. No one believed shock was the correct term anymore.

Nathan was sitting in the back of the Sleeping Grizzly drinking scotch. The noise was moderate. Ryan Adams' "Halloween Head" was playing in the background. Two very attractive women were singing along while Joe poured mixed drinks to the "fancy" and whiskey to the "simple."

"Thought I'd find you here," said David, holding a folder in his right hand.

"Shit, don't pop up like that," Nathan replied.

"Normally I wouldn't, but I'd thought you'd like to see this." David showed the folder with emphasis and tossed it onto the table. "I've had this sitting in a drawer for years and just remembered. I'd stay and chat, but April hasn't talked to me all day. I plan on visiting her."

"Thanks."

"Don't drink too much. Keria needs you sober when she wakes up."

"I know. You're right."

David nodded. "I'll see you later."

Nathan didn't bother opening the folder until David left the bar. But when he did, he wished David had uncovered it sooner. "Black Pollen" was scribbled on the folder's sticky.

ENTRY #1

Let me start by saying that I did not ask for this. It came to me. Loneliness can change a man, but I had family. I never needed a partner to make my life worth living, and I certainly never wanted the supernatural to show its dark side to me. I was happy enough with my life. I had my answers.

After two years of fishing with my grandson Nathan, I began noticing differences in the water. Fish were floating on the surface and dead in my net (once on a hook, believe it). I blamed the fishermen for the externality. God only knew what they were doing.

I wasn't some environmentalist, but I had complained many times. Fishing was Nathan's getaway from nonsense, my own, too. Soon, the news got involved, but not because of me. Sea creatures were often found washed up on the shore. I thought, "Great! Now they'll listen to me," but no, they had not. So I did my own research for a time and got nowhere with it until one day when a storm hit Silverhill hard. I noticed a pattern to the beached sea creatures. Every wild thunderstorm that rolled over our town resulted in minor or major wash-ups of dead sea life.

I'm not talking about common thunderstorms, but the ones that made the air thirty or so degrees cooler. I asked around, but people assumed it was normal. Everyone thought I was the goofy one to begin with, so I kept my mouth shut and began ignoring the storms myself and the voices that whispered to my thoughts, especially those.

Beneath the first entry were two aging photos of clouds from a thunderstorm. But the strange part was a set of lower clouds. Its shape was like a current underwater, leaving behind an eerie wisp. The coloring of this lengthy cloud was utterly black. Not rain cloud black, but shadow black. Both pictures captured it.

ENTRY #2

A month later, I experienced my first ever sleepwalk during one of those storms. I remembered going to bed and waking up to see Black Bell's entrance. How could I see it in the middle of a stormy night? Four glowing figures stood beside it. Well, one stood on a rock above and one below. I couldn't make out any details, having left my glasses behind. This trip wasn't exactly planned.

The nightmare I had was unforgiving and stayed with me more vividly than the four figures. My wife was with her boyfriend, they were joyful, she was pregnant with his child, and he was engaged to her. She accepted quicker than she had with me. Black dots swam above the event. I thought nothing of it at the time as I was so taken by the horrible images and sounds of the woman I once loved—and still do—enjoy life as I sat in cold, silent darkness. I had no money, which was shown to me, too. The engagement ring was enriched in diamonds. Mine had nothing of the sort.

I found myself experiencing vivid, emotionally draining nightmares just like that frequently. I couldn't take it anymore. I started moving in my dreams instead of watching them. That's when I began noticing the black dots and referring to them as "black pollen." Why? I don't know. They looked like floating seeds from those ugly white puffs that grow all over our lawns during the spring. The phrase just fit.

Lucid dreaming became a habit. I followed those dots that (up high) lead to nowhere. A select few flew into Black Bell with an anxiousness that didn't belong to a cloud. I followed, this being a dream, I didn't think death could reach me, you know? I had no light with me, and luckily, I did not need it.

Hovering inside the mine's first tunnel were small sheets of green mist. They had no definite shape, but I could see a pattern in their movements. At this time, I realized I was in the heart of it, utterly unprepared. Just a dream, right? Yes, but this entry was written after my experience. For you see, I was sleepwalking. Those bastards led me right into the physical nest. I often wondered what would have happened if I didn't run out of there and swim my way back to shore.

ENTRY #3

I made it home. But I woke up sicker the following morning than I had since the nightmares began. It hit me then that this problem had to be dealt with, only not by me. I'm not as dumb as people think. A week after my trip to the mine, I was too sick to move. I lay in bed, thinking of the source. I closed my eyes for the final dream, chained to my bed for the purpose of writing my discoveries in case I wouldn't make it back.

Here's what I found. A five-foot figure stood in the Atlantic, peering back at me. It was skinny, moving as if it were struggling out of a hole. It was oddly silent. I said, "What are you?" Of course, I got no response. The figure buried its long hand into the water and pulled out a fishing net, one that overflowed with fish of all kinds. I looked closer and saw that each fish was bleeding from its peachy eyes. "What do you want from me?" I hollered. "What do you want from me?"

The figure, still holding the nest of fish, pointed to the empty landscape on the other side. I looked, seeing nothing but open land, and said, "What?" The being slowly dropped its hand and placed the net back under water. It also submerged.

The four figures I saw by the mine appeared again in more detail. They were miners. "Dead miners" came a thought. "Dead miners who uncovered the secret." It was clear to me then that this dream was given to me, that these thoughts were not my own exactly. The creatures harbored the mine. They used it to hide from our world. That black pollen in the air is tiny entities leaking into our plane. Our universe is empty to them, so they hide in the mine and wait for a host. Only then could they mature and feed on your body. They are not so complicated, as they act like a virus. A weak mind is no greater a home than a smart one. It merely depends on the space of their brain. And currently one sucks the life from you. It's feeding on your energy. Thus, you are weak, cold, and with us.

The miners spoke to my head. It was a dream so they managed well. "Do not think these parasites need a host to feed. They travel only in storms, looking for new hosts. If it's a failed trip, some nest in Black Bell. Most leave. Sea life falls victim more commonly than us. But we are far greater hosts. You have to kill it off before it reaches stage two."

My parasite lurked inside me with more knowledge of myself than I knew. And with that, it could control me enough. So I guess I fit stage two. It wanted me to feel like I was crazy so I wouldn't fight it. It did not want me to think it was real. If I were to fight the entity, I had to go to the mine. But my body was too weak. The last thing told to me by the miners was to never allow the parasite to bring you into the mine, this meant by sleepwalking. I had to go there awake. But I couldn't, and I wasn't gonna live like this anymore.

ENTRY #4

I expect the worst to happen; however, I can feel the entity show itself to others in vague ways. It also tugged at them. I'm not letting this creature mature further and, above all else, not allow it to lead more of its kind to anyone else. I unhooked the chains. Yes, I'm gonna fall asleep unfastened. It was the only way to get to Black Bell. My only regret is leaving Nathan. But if I don't, he'll be just like me. I'm ignoring the fact that it doesn't matter, that these things just keep coming. My only hope is that these papers reach him in time to fight back and not be taken. It's not the fact of being controlled that bothers me. It's how this thing can affect others around me. Maybe I'll make it back, but in case not, I'm leaving my papers organized on my table.

I would tell him in person or over a phone call, but any contact gives my matured entity a chance at him. It was edgy for the opportunity for my grandson. It's scary to think Nathan might have what they need. This must get to him.

Nathan sat back in the seat, awed. He also disbelieved. Albert's handwriting was chicken scratches, and Nathan's head wasn't clear. Maybe he misread the contents. He skimmed through the entries twice after reading and started thinking less about whether he was crazy and more on how perfectly timed this was given to him.

"David," Nathan said angrily, "you son of a bitch."

CHAPTER 10

Dream Logic

When one lives a life hidden in the dark, concepts and memories can mingle and join forces. Aside from David's sudden remembrance of Albert's entries, all concepts had lived in a set of dreams. Now, there was something outside of such logic, written by another hand and experienced by another soul. No inner voices, illusions, or dream people were telling him the secrets. Wherever David stood in this scenario didn't change that fact. Someone or something was pulling strings in that mine. Black Bell always harbored a bad vibe. Now Nathan wanted to see that feeling manifest and destroy every ounce of its being.

The deaths of loved ones and the growing urge to drink kept him clanged to the shadows, but it also demanded for a change. Nathan threw on casual clothing and walked out the front door with a shade of confidence, directly after his return from the bar. *If I'm gonna die, I'm gonna die trying.*

"What are you looking for?" asked the voice.

"Nothing that concerns you, pal."

The sky was overcast as the clock hit twelve after seven. The sun looked cold behind the icy clouds. No black dots traveled through them, as far as the human eye could tell. For a hot summer evening, the temperature sure dropped. No storm was actually brewing. A woman stood beside the entrance of the mine. Nathan could see her, but the distance erased her features.

Nathan carried two knives in his back pockets and a flashlight in his front. Once he made it to Silverhill, he took one last look at Hollow Heights and slid down the dry hill to the water's foamy edge.

"Maybe what I'm looking for is beyond just saving Keria," he said aloud.

"Oh?" said the voice deeply, now at loss with its former high-pitched mix.

"Maybe this is what I needed all along. Some kind of redemption for running away."

The seagulls replied with unrelated chatter.

The Atlantic wasn't cold, but it sure wasn't a Jacuzzi either. The briny water often filled Nathan's mouth, and though he swallowed little, a single gulp was enough for him to gag and delay a breath of fresh air. He struggled through the rippling waves, trying to reach the undesirable rocks that awaited him, and he often felt his body stiffen and quiet. But Spangle towered over the sea, and it kept him going, a memory and a concept working as one.

Stepping foot onto a sandy surface would be nice, but it was all sharp, jagged rocks from here on up to the mine. They were mossy and seaweed-coated, and slippery bubbles bulged from the uneven ground. He gripped each rock tightly, hearing a faint sobbing. It sent his nerves to hell. Nathan's arms were feeling like liquid-filled pouches halfway to the landing. His heart beat savagely.

Just above where the walkway lay, soft footsteps overlapped the wind, exactly where the sobbing derived from. Nathan couldn't bring himself to advance any farther. He kept still on a set of somewhat even rocks. He kept his eyes toward Black Bell and saw the weeping angel statue (now green and peeling) stumble into the mine with its hands over its eyes. The isolation on the cliff was eerie enough. Now the statue joined in.

Nathan was no rock climber, but he managed okay. The landscape looked alien from the eyes of the mine. Peering out at the old and new from the unknown felt like he had just crash-landed on the moon and was now seeing the earth float in space. He dug out his flashlight, took out a knife, and finally turned to meet the mine in person. The wind was loud, fishing boats rang their bells alongside the buoy, and a group of gulls circled the lighthouse above.

His clothes were dirty from the climb and would only get earthier on the way to answers. But the darkness beyond the entrance acted as a wall. Of course, he could walk through it, but until Nathan pierced the dark with his flashlight, he did not dare enter the mine.

Hardly inside, the world's ambience became distant, and the stories about the lost miners and the ringing bell became all too real. He listened past the dripping water for the little bell of death, feeling his way through the first tunnel of the tiny mine. He caught glimpses of the angel and green mist off the edge of his eye, but they quickly jerked away into the darkness harmlessly, as if they were small animals or false visions of a damaged mind.

The heavy-duty flashlight revealed a strange door on the ceiling. It led to a narrow tunnel. It was locked with the same chains and rust as the morgue's door had been, only there would be no simple way in this round.

The air was frigid and damp and smelled like tainted rain. Large puddles of water sat everywhere on the rocky floor, and the sounds of boats and the wind softy echoed by in a ghostly manner. A noise, other than dripping water and echoes from outside, came from behind a wooden door on the left wall. It sounded like whispering. Nathan pressed his ear on the aging wood against his better judgment and tuned in.

He heard fragments of words until a voice directly beyond the wood said, "Don't listen to me."

Nathan flung himself back, stepping over empty cans of Busch, and nearly fell on his ass.

The mountain-sized hill sat a quarter mile away from the lighthouse, and that was where the end to this tunnel lay with a sign warning of unstable wood and apparently the start to a series of veins that had contained gold not long ago. The question that needed answering was: How deep did the parasites nest descend? It was easy to get lost in a mine. It wasn't like Nathan had a fucking tour guide.

He paused and shined light through the dusty air, hoping to see the big wall. Something reflected the light back.

"Finally!" Nathan said, imagining the sign.

He jogged for the wall and soon realized that reflecting surface wasn't the waning sign. Aiming the beam a second time reflected nothing.

"Playing mind games, huh?" Nathan asked aloud. He sighed heavily and released a sarcastic chuckle from his galling throat. "What am I even doing?" he murmured. "What am I even doing?"

The wall curved like a growing wave. Two tunnels stood beside it, one on the left and one on the right. Healthy moss and other plant life grew inside cracks, and water was more common. There were still no paranormal entities.

"Where are you?" Nathan hollered.

The echo ran all through the mine. He slid down the curve of the wall and let himself fall onto the hard ground, just missing a deep puddle of brown, murky water. He buried his head in his hands.

For half a minute, he felt utterly stupid for coming in here. He was soaked with seawater, his skin was covered in gooseflesh, and Keria remained on a hospital bed unchanged. The best he had to go on were beer cans, and shit, some group of teenagers probably came in one night asking for a haunting chant and dropped them all over.

"Crazy man," said the voice. "Why come in here? To see water and stone? More visions of insanity? You can be home. Drinking. Why be here and afraid? There's no veracity to be found anywhere, especially in an old, cold, abandoned mine such as this. Do you wish to see Keria? Go to her and see her before she dies. In her final moments of life, you choose to venture through an empty mine instead of visiting her? She's better off dead than with you."

Nathan felt a cobweb scamper through his body with a sound that imitated bare feet running across wet stone. He dropped his hands, quickly grabbed his flashlight, and shined it toward the left tunnel. A nude, skinny, wet, scaly body with no arms or head ran deeper into the tunnel. Nathan felt this heart beat faster than his train of thought could process, and without thinking, he began running after it.

With eager eyes, Nathan followed the being. He lost sight of it for a while before coming face-to-face with another wall. *I'm inside the mountain now.* The miners dug horizontal up to the very top of the mountain. The emergency escape ladder, which was a mile climb from this level, stood just to the left of the cut. Nathan was on the second level. If one were to enter Black Bell through the mountain (Mt. Elder Wood), one would be on the first level.

To the right, Nathan could see the cut that led to the bottom. He felt off balance, now fully aware of how dangerous the mine was to a uniformed visitor. He peered down, trying to see the bottom level and thinking the miners should have coiled a fence in case idiots like him decided it was okay to wander the mine. Watching one's step would be wise, a real lifesaver.

Just as Nathan decided to turn his attention back to the tunnel, his flashlight's beam hit a key on a string, nailed into the wet stone on the left side. It was in reach, but it would require a gutsy move. With nothing else to go on, Nathan placed the flashlight down and blindly reached out for the key, feeling like an astronaut fixing a lose wire on the space station.

"Gotcha," he said aloud, feeling the key's wet surface pierce his skin with a cold brevity of gelidity.

The scaly body shivered beside Nathan in the darkness when he stepped back, holding the key tightly in his hands. Nathan never screamed so loud in his life. He fell back, thinking he was about to fall to the bottom of the mine and spatter like the legendary Humpty Dumpty, but he promptly shot up onto his feet and ran for the curved wall, hearing snapping bones come from all angles.

Nathan hit a wall with his flashlight's shaft of light and saw Sophia crawling on the wall violently after him, keeping up with his running pace precisely. She stared at him with black, emotionless eyes. *The green mist is manifesting. And it's coming for me, from every creak and every hole. From above and below because the layout is to their advantage and always would be.*

"No matter where you go," said the voice. "In here, they can always reach you."

Nathan couldn't see what was chasing him as he ran, but all the people from the morgue dream were crawling around him, including the tunnel's rigid ceiling. Nathan tripped on a large stone and fell to his knees.

He turned around to face all his dead loved ones—bloody, pale, and wet and growing scales just like the armless-headless body. They didn't attack him because they couldn't. They were images with matter and weight, but they could do no greater harm than a forty mile per hour wind gust. Nathan ran down the tunnel.

Waves of emotions hit him, feeling the displeasure of rejection, a failure to succeed in a career, and the act of watching someone die or having killed someone he loved by mistake. The worst of emotions stabbed him. It didn't matter how little these feelings fit his actual life. They were there, and reason had no power over them.

He was invited to stop by a group of people he knew. Above hung Eve. She was clapping. On the left and right sides stood Alan, Albert, April, Neil, Jeff, Sophia, Liz, and Lillie. They were both clapping and whistling. Nathan stood in the crowd, trying to catch his breath. He was being cheered, pat on the back with supportive noises and gestures. He felt embarrassed.

"Congratulations, Nathan!" shouted Eve. "You ran so far, far away from—"

"Oh hush! Can't tell him, Mrs. Ruiz!" April interrupted.

Nathan turned to meet her dark eyes. Her body looked paper-thin. But so did everyone else's.

"Think of how happy Keria would be if she knew how you ran amuck in this mine as she lay dying. I'm her best friend! I can tell you."

"Oh, hush yourself," said Alan. "You're just as bad as my stupid bitch of a wife!"

Bam! The sound of a gunshot echoed throughout the mine, starting from above Nathan's head. Eve was now missing.

Jeff said, "You people are far too noisy."

"I wouldn't talk," said Neil.

"Hush, babies, everything's all right," said Tia. She wasn't present. Only her voice popped out of the darkness.

"This is supposed to be a celebration for Nathan!" Liz hollered.

"Oh really?" Neil replied.

Lillie said, "Shut up, old geezer!" and faded in the dark, alongside Liz.

Sophia's skin had a blue tint. Shadows overcome her eyes.

"Lost in the dark," the voice said in his mind.

He couldn't take it anymore. He hollered, "Get away from her!"

He was about to run for her, wanting, no, needing to touch her again. He wanted to pick her up, hug her, and tell her how sorry he was for what happened. He needed to vent about how much her passing kept him awake at night. But no. He couldn't, and he stopped himself from getting any closer to the entity.

"You're not anyone. None of you are anything more than a paper-thin copy of my mind."

"Stop lying!" Sophia shouted. "Can't you see that you're lying?"

Nathan turned away, feeling all those negative feelings claw into his soul again. He closed his eyes, thoughts, and even the voice of his personal entity. A dry, painful pulse beat in his throat as the air beat on his body and ate at his skin like it were submerged in below-freezing water. When the air lifted its heavy cold fog, he opened his eyes and turned back around to see nothing but the darkness. Fearing they'd return, Nathan kept his flashlight focused on the wall closest to him and continued forward, nearing the ceiling door.

The only sounds audible to the human ear were falling stones and dripping water as the dead watched Nathan stare back like a cornered rat. Nathan was unaware of the talking that carried on around him. Replays of life went through his head but only the negatives: deaths, guilt, heartbreak, and understanding of how powerless he was to stop it all from happening again. This meant Keria was next to die. All the dead smiled and crawled away into the dark.

With a sob, Nathan cried, "Get back here! Come back! You can't take her!"

There was green mist all around now, weaving in and out of creaks and holes. The entities stopped hiding to torment Nathan until he gave up and left the mine. He stood up for what felt like the fifth time and examined the area. The mist overlapped the dust. *I still have a key. But where...that door...*

Blue mist lingered down the first tunnel but quickly faded.

"There," he said softly.

He brisk-walked to the ceiling door, and a pain that felt like the hangover of a vivid nightmare blinded him with blue fuzz, wild images, and sounds. They were echoes of the mine's past, not at all related to the parasites that now coated its foundation.

Michal Tomes, Alger Truffle, Eger Deland, and Bill Griffin were the four miners. Their nicknames were in the same order: Shuffle, Brown Bottom, Slow Blow, and Hell Bell.

"Mike, why you drag your feet like that?" came a voice.

"Alger, why you always slip, you like bathin' in tat water?"

"Come on, Eger. Hurry up. She's gonna blow!"

"Bill, there ain't no fuckin' bell!"

Each one of their voices echoed madly. This mine wasn't just tainted by the other side's envious creatures, but also carried memories of the people who worked here back in the coal days and the gold. But why only four souls? Why was it always those four miners who reached out? The memories went further than nicknames, carrying flashbacks and feelings along with them.

> We were treated like abused Chinese miners out in Oregon, so when we got the job at a brand-new mine, Black Bell, we climbed on a plane in a heartbeat. Me, Brown Bottom, Slow Blow, and Hell Bell, well, at the time, we called Bill "Crow." The boy liked to feed the birds. We took the job to get away from Stanley, the tight-suited fuck who owned old Deer Creek Mine. We were the only four miners who ever worked in Black Bell until the new gold vein was uncovered, the one we tried to hide. You don't understand. That mine isn't worth the trouble. Going in there stirs things up, whatever they be. They ain't tommy-knockers. You might know more than I do. We died long before they got to us. How? Come on, Nathan. Think back. Right, of course, you can't. We were secretly murdered. Funny, ain't it? We were better off working with Stanley.

Violent images flashed, turning Michal's ghostly words into visions. The four miners marched through the second level after igniting the dynamite. Slow Bow held a caged canary in his right hand. After leaving and waiting two minutes outside the mine, the fuse proved faulty, and an unnerving trip had to be made.

"No, not happenin'," said Brown Bottom.

"Well, someone's gotta go in theres," said Hell Bell.

"You're holding the bird," Brown Bottom responded.

"Yeah, and I'm the slowest. I'm not gonna go in there."

I went in cuz no one else would. Much like you, I heard and saw things. Somebody climbed up the hatch that stood above before we got to workin' here. I swore it still to this day. I called to the boys and said some intruder was in the mine. They heard me and came in. "An intruder?" Brown Bottom had asked me. "Yes, up the ceiling door," I replied. "I know who it is. Fuck her!" hollered Brown Bottom. He forcefully opened the door and screamed, "Get out here, Christina!" I asked, "Did you take your pills?" He said, "Ain't no way they work. That bitch is up there fuckin' with us. I know it!" He kept telling us Christina was following him during our nightly bonfires. He took responsibility and got a prescription for his illness. It got worse, like the pills had no effect after a month of taking them. Every time somethin' went wrong, he'd blame her for it, even when on the pills. Sometimes, I swore I'd seen her myself. "Goddamn it, Christina! I said get the fuck down here!" The fool didn't listen and threw his body back, not thinkin' twice about the fall, like you, Nathan, when he saw somethin' lurch from the room above. He cried like a baby. He hadn't really wanted to see his ex, but she appeared in that mist, let me tell ya. She showed and glowed. Only Brown Bottom saw her, but we understood. "Get up, Bottom. We gotta go," I says to him. He just don't listen. I told old Slow to bring him outside, but Bottom insisted we all went, saying, if that fuse should go off in this place, we'd all go together. On our way down, we heard murmurings of our pasts. None of us spoke, thinking we'd been makin' it up. After the fuse took us, we knew this place was evil. Yea, once we got there, a gust of wind triggered the spark somehow. We went out in one wild blaze of glory. Reason for tellin' ya all this is to make it clear. Find the source, and kill it off. That means burnin' down this fuckin' mine. Do it now before they get ya like they got us. We tried to get ya here sooner, but it's not easy from where we are. That key opens the hatch Brown Bottom saw Christina in. Something may be hiding in the door where we were blown apart. It's carrying whisperers of memories we don't recognize. Your choice. But somethin' to think about: Who would bother locking the hatch and placing the key in an open cut?

The blue, head-rushing fuzz followed after the insightful vision. He was close to both the whispering door and ceiling hatch. It made little sense picking the whispers over a thought-out locked door. Michal made that clear.

From the wavy wall by the splitting tunnels, the cry of children riddled boorishly. And a voice, one that sounded much like Neil's, howled in pain. Nathan shined the flashlight toward the noise, revealing a horde of grey, skeletal children running at him.

"Shit," he said, turning for the ceiling door.

These images were higher up in charge, overly energized by the evil entities. Nathan held the key and unlocked the hatch. A ladder came tumbling down, nearly ending the journey in a less satisfying outcome. The children got to him, clinging onto his body in frail hugs. *These entities are newborns and will stay newborns until they too find a host.*

But strength was in their numbers and emotional attacks. They had undefinable, aberrant faces that would make Picasso's art look prevalent in the seventeenth century. The sounds released from their tightened throats sounded like an old woman gagging and whining. A few managed to tear into Nathan's suit but were pushed away easy enough. *Just keep them eyes closed. Peek only a little.*

Their touches felt like rubber rubbing skin. With two long reaches, Nathan grabbed hold of the ladder and pulled his body closer through the sea of unearthly beings. Once he was leaning into the ladder, he pulled himself up, using every ounce of strength he had and broke free. This heightened the energy of the children, who were all now desperately surrounding the ladder. Nathan slammed the door shut when he made it above the opening and turned to meet his enemy, miffed and out of breath.

CHAPTER 11

Divide

David stood in pure moonlight toward the right of the room, his face hidden from sight. A large ceiling window displayed the edge of the cliff the lighthouse sat on. David gave no response to Nathan's arrival at first.

Shelly, the woman Nathan spotted before trucking across a piece of the Atlantic Ocean, stood nearby. Her appearance was clearly pampered, giving off a vibe of obsessive behavior with every adjustment she made to her dirty blonde-colored hair. Other than fine-tuning, her movements were placid in the pasty haze given off by the moonlight. Her face appeared dull with eye shadows. Nathan noticed the crazies had a similar trait now. It was becoming undeniable. But he still had no idea as to who Shelly was.

Across from David and Shelly stood a metal cage-like room. Inside it were two people, Tia and April. April looked weak, sitting on the hard ground with her head against the wall, but she was alive. Tia was in bad shape, covered in cuts and seawater. It must have burned a whole lot, but she seemed to be handling it okay, for what the odds were anyway.

"I called a therapist to Silverhill." David was grinning. "Thought it'd be a worthwhile deed for the ill." David also wasn't moving much.

He acted as a stiff body with a moving mouth and set of eyes, which had uncanny eye shadows.

The dusty room was poorly lit, done so on promise by the designer of the lighthouse. It was to be a secret cellar to house-boxed supplies, a majority of it just lightbulbs and other bits for repairs. But the past might have had darker purposes for this room. Like the cage, it wasn't possible to carry it into the room. It was built as a part of its main construction.

"What are you doing?" Nathan asked.

David turned to meet Nathan eye to eye. Like Mike's and Mary's eyes, his were also dilated.

"Nathan..." Tia said weakly. "Just hold on. I'm getting you out of there."

"And what will you do? Carry them out?" David stood statically, only adjusting his grin to a long, unwanted smile. "Well, what are ya gonna do? You came all this way, buddy, and I don't just mean to Black Bell. You came to Hollow Heights because you had to. You don't give two shits about Keria, and if you did, you never would have left. If that weren't enough, listen to this. You would have taken Keria's job offer on the spot. But you didn't, did you?"

"You don't under—"

David approached Nathan hastily, paused a foot away, and said, "If you cared for her, you would be by her side in death instead of playing in a fucking mine. Isn't that right, warehouse boy?"

"What about you, Mike and Mary? What the fuck is wrong with this town? It's all you, isn't it? You're responsible for everything."

Like words only revealed on paper under artificial light, with every question Nathan asked, he felt like the answer veiled itself in David's responses. But he thought it was just a feeling.

"I know I'm going crazy, but you're here, and so is Tia, April, and whoever that is over there. I'll take it all as real. And David, you just happen to be in my way the most."

"Why live a life you're not sure is real if it's so gloomy?" Shelly asked. "What if you returned home and Keria was waiting for you alive and well?" She smiled. "Might as well live in that, right? And it makes more sense than us really being here. Why would this room even exist? Where are you really?"

Nathan grabbed his knife and flung it at David, who dodged it without looking.

"I can read you. The question that's aching you is how. It's one of two things, both you can't admit. You're making this up, or we have complete power over you. Which would you rather cope with?"

The lighting in the room was making Nathan nervous. There was darkness in every corner, and David could move quickly. Nathan held a defensive position, waiting for a reply.

"Such talk is offensive. I'm your best friend."

"It appears my best friend died a long time ago," Nathan said morbidly. "Why do you have it out for the Miles? Why kill Neil, imprison Tia, and set up a way to get to me and April?"

Tia's face posture matched David's now neutral expression.

"I could say anything to bleed into your questions. We could talk 'til sunrise."

Nathan suddenly wondered how long he'd been in the mine. "How long was this planned out? You could at least tell me that."

Shelly stepped forward. "He can, but he won't. David's been through enough, or have you forgotten his miserable fishermen lifestyle?"

"He doesn't hate his life!" Nathan shouted.

"Oh, I don't? I knew you didn't pay attention very well, but this is unacceptable. Have you not heard my complaints?"

Nathan stood still, waiting for David to continue his rant. But he fell quiet. "That's it?" Nathan asked. "We all complain."

David didn't look sure of himself. Shelly quickly took over. "You think he was a happy man because of that girl April? Of course not! We both met her at the same time, long after my return." The flare in Shelly's eyes dwindled to a null quality. Now they were both silent, as if waiting to remember something.

"It's true I had other reasons for coming here, and it's true—no, likely—I'm making all this up. But I already stated I'm going through with this. Let Tia and April go."

Shelly ambled to the cage and pulled out a silver key from her pocket. She turned her head to ensure Nathan saw her pale expression and unlocked the door without looking away from him. "Drop your knives."

Nathan dropped them with a look of distrust. After the knives clanged onto the ground, Shelly grinned, turned her head, and walked into the cage.

"Let's test your mind." She picked up April with unbelievable ease and tapped April's head with her index finger. "Every detail of April's body is correct, right? You need to know."

"Yeah."

"Have you ever heard her scream before?"

David's steady stance jolted. Shelly pulled out a revolver and put its muzzle to April's forehead with eerie stillness. April's eyes closed. She expected the worst. What was Nathan going to do to stop the bullet? How could he possibly be fast enough to stop Shelly's finger from making one tiny, easy move that would end her life in a flash?

April choked under her breath, trying to be the brave young woman she made herself out to be over her life as Shelly said, "Oh, she'll scream and cave into the pressure of certain death. The thin line, Nathan, is always there in our daily lives. That city Rotor carried this feeling in a lesser weight every day. Don't kid yourself. You chose this. It's your reality! Your—"

The fire of a gunshot ended Shelly's words before she could finish, and her body came tumbling down on top of April, who shoved it aside. It was a dicey decision that could have caused Shelly to flinch in a natural reaction to pull her own weapon's trigger, but luck paid out, or Shelly wasn't quite herself. *David would know*, Nathan thought.

"April!" David hollered, beginning to run to her.

Nathan ran to Shelly's corpse, took the gun, and aimed it at David, who instantly flung his arms up. David remained silent.

"I don't know what's happening, but I can't just let you near her. I'm sure you know something. Explain."

"I feel like I know too little. It's all theory," he replied. "Just tell me."

"I found handwritten journals your grandfather wrote. After you came back empty-handed, I went to visit Howard myself. He never answered the door so I decided to visit a few places. I figured I'd do something while I was there. I went to Albert's house and saw a folder and—"

"Yeah, I know. You gave them to me at the bar, don't you remember?"

David said nothing.

"Well?"

"No, Nathan, I don't. I don't even remember coming here. In fact, where the hell are we? April was nearly killed! I want answers! You know more than I do. I only glanced at the papers. I thought your grandfather went nuts!"

Nathan noticed David's face was pale. Before, his eyes were dilated and shadowy below the lids. Now they were normal, and fear remained intact, never leaving the slightest unlike his previous anger.

"Keep talking."

"About what? The papers? I planned on giving them to you, but something caught my eye. A shadow by the front door, as if it popped up from the ground. It looked a lot like you. Honest to God."

Nathan lowered his pistol and dropped his eyes to the ground. David rushed to April shortly after.

He kneeled down, straightened April's hair, and asked, "Are you okay?"

She looked up at him, into his eyes. "Yeah, but what happened to you?"

Nathan walked a few feet away, rubbing a palm on his forehead. Tia kept to herself inside the cage. David approached her, asked if she were okay, and returned to April. Everyone assumed Tia felt safer inside the cage.

"I wish I knew. Who did I shoot?"

"That was Mike Ribbons' girl. Not sure if they were dating or married. She was the one who kidnapped me."

"Well, it's a good thing Nathan didn't shoot me. With a comeback like mine, I'm not sure I'd trust me either."

"Nathan?" April asked.

"Yeah?"

"It was Keria, wasn't it? That brought you here?" Nathan kept quiet. "I know you did. I think this whole thing is beating around her somehow. Can you think of a reason why?"

After some thinking, the answer was yes. There were pieces he could snap together. "Well, it started with Neil, who's her father. Then Mike Ribbons and the nanny. What was her name?"

"Mary," David said.

"The FBI claimed an attack on the winery was an attempt to involve me into the case. If that's true, than targeting Keria would be even better, right?"

"Wrong," said the voice.

"Shelly must have been the last culprit," David said. "She probably drugged me and kidnapped April."

"Seems believable," Nathan said.

"But you're still not convinced," April muttered as David helped her onto her feet.

Tia's head turned to meet Nathan.

"Who else? I feel the same way. How could this Mike guy or Shelly know about your grandfather?" David brushed the edges of April's dusty hairlines.

"I'm thinking." Nathan's eyes went cold. Both April and David noticed.

"What?" David felt a hit of adrenaline.

A long, wheezy, horse-like sigh came from the cage. The air dropped twenty degrees in seconds, and a rough wind picked up outside and beat the glass window. Once Tia finished, she rose up onto her feet against her body's well-being. Her leg bones cracked as her leg muscles twitched, nearly caving in on themselves.

"You should sit down," someone would have said. "But that wheeze…"

"You've dug deep, much more than you should have. It took you this long?" Tia chuckled. "Of all the people here, you had the answers. But again like everything else in your life, you buried the truth deep inside and forgot all about it or any possibility it ever existed."

Unnatural shadows surrounded Tia's body. The interior of the cage darkened mysteriously, as if a storm were forging by the matter of the growing darkness.

"Aw, don't look so surprised. It's not as complicated as you think, and I'll even explain. You're a drunk, so your lack of understanding is excused. Let me start by asking the same question that must have crossed your mind. How in hell did I get so powerful here in Hollow Heights? It started with the lighthouse keeper, Gray Wish. Another drunk he was. I asked him about his secret in a seductive manner after he'd had enough to drink, and he told me everything. Oh, it was something all right. Tia was long gone by this little chat. Gray told me about the veins of gold the previous miners discovered before they left. They sealed the tunnel, making it appear like a dead end at the very end of the mountain. Without Neil knowing, I contacted desperate miners from Oregon, who I had come over online, and had the four privately investigate. The discovery of the previous miners had closed this mine because of its original intention of holding hostages. Its purpose was never to guide boats! It was created to guide us!"

"Nathan, what is she talking about?" David asked.

"Parasites. My grandfather talked about them in those journals you found. It matched my experiences since I visited Howard. And this mine, when coming here, what about the whispering door?"

"The miners' deaths? That wasn't by my hand. As you know, there are many others in the mine, waiting for people to prey upon. I caught Tia like the one who got you. During a storm. Not many are so easily prone, like Keria. It took years of attempts to throw her into the coma she's in today. Yes, Nathan, as long as I am around, she's as good as dead. And don't think stopping me will save her either. When it matures inside of you, she's as good as gone." Tia started laughing, a kind of guffaw that sounded like dying baby animal's mixed with human vocals.

"The nanny and Mike had played their parts only because I knew them long enough. They were an outstanding distraction. I had all the time in the world to web their heads in my influence. Neil, on the other hand, was impossible. Stupidity and ignorance was his blessing for a time. For me, it helped working at a daycare, and Mike had some serious karma issues. Cheating on his girl. But above all, we got you. Without you, there'd be one less of us today. And this little cage, time after time has opened the doors for us as well. Ever since the lighthouse was built, we've been housing in flesh."

"Who the hell made this place?" Nathan asked.

"A very skilled leader, one who far surpassed any of us. He's idea was genius, to create a trap for us to use."

"So everything involving Mike, Shelly, and Mary was a trick to mislead us?"

"Like I said, that daycare became useful. What better way to stir a situation than to involve children? The justice system goes goo-goo over such things."

"But you drew attention to yourself by having them kill Neil."

"Only momentarily, Nathan. Come on. You can't tell me and be serious that I haven't been under the radar all this time. It may be hard for you because, in a sense, I've been all there ever was to you. Even Keria left you by the end of your return before she fell ill!"

"That was all your fault!"

The shades of darkness that stood out from the lighter shadows around the cage expanded. They were alive, the veins of the entity that harbored Tia's body. Nathan thought he was a fool, but he wouldn't be misled to believe he caused Keria's pain. He had before by leaving. But not this.

The air felt heavy. April fell to the floor, unable to support her weight in the ever-changing magnetic fields. Green mist slithered through the door hatch below, glissading through its cracks.

"April can't stay here. David, help her out."

"What about you?" David hollered.

Tia grinned.

"Just go! I came here to find the truth and whatever came after it. You getting killed won't help anything. She used you to distract me. It would be a good idea to leave the lighthouse." Nathan tried to make it seem like a joke, but David took it for what it was, picked April up, and began carrying her to the hatch.

Nathan expected Tia to fly out of the cage in a horrid hurdle after David and April in their most defenseless moment. But she kept still. Tia looked past Nathan at the two as they escaped down the hatch. Once they were gone, she fixed her undivided attention back to Nathan.

They made it below the lighthouse. David scanned the tunnels for the pulsating green glow of the parasites.

"Do you think he'll be okay?" April whispered. She felt glued onto David like burned flesh on a hot stove. "I'm more worried about us. Nathan was drenched."

"So?"

"That means he must have swum here. You're in no condition for that."

As they reached the mine's entrance, they felt the passing of entities. At times, they saw them maneuver by in wispy flutters. The entities couldn't care less about the two of them because Nathan was the threat. David thought of how long it must have taken one of these things to grow so strong but was baffled by how something as thin as a tiny cloud could drain a person in the first place.

"I think I can handle the walk through the woods," April said.

"That's a long trip."

"Yeah, but treading through the ocean isn't going to happen."

A narrow but negotiable path lay out behind the lighthouse. It was night. A chilly breeze aired along the cliff side. David and April saw Hollow Heights off in the distance.

"Holy shit, that's far," April muttered. But she smiled.

"Why are you—"

"Because, David, I've been wanting to talk to you about something since the picnic. And now I have the time to."

There was a tugging feeling, like they felt the need to go back because Nathan was still there, talking to that thing that claimed to be Tia. It was changing. They all knew it. To what though? Something devilish? Hollow Heights didn't look the same. The incident begged the question: Was this town designed by the entities in the mine?

Howard had a good reason to stay behind, if this idea is true, David thought. If it is, then Silverhill must be the ideal place to go. He would take April and Keria when (or if) she wakes up and move back or, hell, someplace entirely different. *Yeah,* David thought, *it doesn't matter. Hollow Heights or Silverhill. Those entities are always around, watching from Black Bell.*

"Are you okay?" April asked.

David snapped out of his train of thought. "Yeah, I think so. You?"

"The same."

"When Nathan gets out of there and when Keria wakes up, we're leaving," David said.

"To where?"

"A new state. Any suggestions?"

"Um, how about the moon? I'm sure we don't have to worry about people there."

David chuckled. "Very funny. I was thinking maybe we could live in the Poconos."

"Hell no! That's in the middle of nowhere!" April half-shouted. She began to cough.

"Don't push yourself too much. Try to relax. I wasn't really planning on it. Would be nice though."

"You're something else, you know that?" April muttered.

David and April fell silent, listening to the night's wind and insects. The night had a peaceful vibe. All the negative feelings came from their minds, and they both knew it. If they could somehow forget what just happened and release themselves from thoughts of the creeping dread that stalked Nathan, maybe it would go away and subside into the cold, damp rocks and sleep. Tia would wither, and Nathan could escape, too.

The darkness in the woods was different from the mine's. It felt empty, just the absence of light, nothing more. It didn't move, shift forms, or quiver when touched. Though both April and David thought they heard whispers in the wind, they didn't realize ghosts were talking to them, unable to be heard because David and April's ears could not pick up their vocals. What were they trying to say? Something important for their survival?

"Think anyone would believe us?" April asked.

"No, and we're not going to mention anything."

"I just hope Nathan fixes this. I want to talk to Keria again."

"I hope so, too. He handled the ungodly city of Rotor. I'm sure he can handle a restless sprit from a tiny port town," David said.

"Not sure. I know what a city's like. And it's nothing like this." April insisted.

"I know one thing for sure."

"What's that?" April asked.

David peered back at the lighthouse. He couldn't see Black Bell because it was on the other side, facing the rusty town of Silverhill, out toward the depths of the ocean's open waters.

"I'm not living anywhere near an ocean."

It was like watching a freak show, only much darker (literally). Tia stood cocky in the cage, cracking her bones and twitching violently. And while Nathan did not know, the other entities were gathering enough energy to inflict harm on him, surrounding the general area from below, in the depths of the mine. The airy mist was harmless for the time being. It lingered, as if watching Nathan's every move, listening to his every thought.

"Turning back is still possible," the voice whispered.

"It's right, you know. You can turn back," Tia said.

"I'd rather not fight today or ever for that manner. I rather enjoy that winery and having you work alongside me. Hate to say, but I doubt things would be the same, regardless if I walked away."

Tia placed her hands on the left and right sides of the entrance and used it for support. She looked in control, but that didn't matter, not to Nathan. He felt breaths of hot air hit his neck and heard an occasional whisper from the things that hid in the mine. The ones below were waiting, hoping the ones talking could psych Nathan to leave. Like Tia, these entities wanted to leave a host alone, as it was already being controlled. These otherworldly beings were not hostile toward one another. They were all brothers, though with their own goals. They didn't steal, if it were avoidable, the host's living soul before it was the right time.

"We don't want to kill you. Turn back." Tia's voice was beginning to lose its feminine charm.

Was there a notable reason for this? Nathan wondered.

"I'm not that dumb. I'd be killed off in the end anyway."

Tia didn't like that response. Her smile died, and she spoke in a sterner tone, "You don't know that, Nathan. It doesn't have to be complicated, even after all this. If I wanted to live a chaotic life, the winery wouldn't be as it is."

"Honestly, it's a bit more chaotic here than I remember back in my childhood."

"Business can have that effect. You know this. Look, Keria can be well. In the afterlife, perhaps. But she's a plague in our world. We can't have her smooching her way through the secrets like your grandfather had. He was more modest, and he wasn't spared."

"What are you talking about?"

"Why, you don't know? Keria wasn't that innocent little lady you made her out to be. I can't put the full blame on you. This town makes her look like an angel. They put that rep onto me, too, remember? And we both know that's a complete myth."

Nathan didn't say a word. He had to think. He'd heard this before from Neil. Both Keria's parents, whether one was human or not, said something similar. *Why?* Nathan thought. *Why both?*

"Truth tends to hurt," the voice said.

"What is she really like?" Nathan asked.

"Like anyone else. Come on!" Tia sounded like the woman Nathan thought she was before things went to hell. "No one is actually that dedicated. They wouldn't wait that long to bring someone back. That's the reality, Nathan. I understand. Believe me. You sat alone in your pitiful apartment room with gunshots outside, carrying on along with the daily traffic. Of this you buried yourself in false vanity, a sheer fantasy that can only exist in an optimistic mind!"

Nathan chuckled. "Do you really think I'm an optimistic person?"

"Of course not! Did I say you made up that fantasy? Not from scrap! You conjured from another mind and used it to deny what you saw as the truth. Sitting alone and not truly socializing or seeing much new, you fell in that state of mind for years. When Keria finally felt like she wanted to bang you, she called you. But you merely chatted on the phone. I, Nathan, wanted you to come here most, so I set up a job opportunity. See, I knew you'd be a perfect host. So weak and so powerless. As you sat there, drunk or sober, did you not feel that way? That you could do more? Were more than some man in a shitty city? More than a drunk warehouse worker? I got you a job at a renowned winery. Not Keria. She was continuously leeching onto David. Has Neil not said anything about this? I expected him to because it was so obvious. And being the way he is, I expect he would use that as a way to relieve you of her infected hole, the one she bears between her legs. She's trash, Nathan. Dirty trash! I can say this with ease, not even with the tiniest lie because she isn't my daughter.

But if Tia were still around, Keria would have fucked everyone in town! You're not the only person I've warned."

Nathan kept quiet. He felt the air add weight and the warm puffs of breath touch his skin with stronger gusts. It was nonsense. It had to be. *But what Tia's entity said made sense.* And it was hard to argue with that. He felt like she was right in the mind, but at heart, she was wrong. Which organ carried the correct answer? *It wasn't the time for this decision.*

"But it is. Your sacrifice was for Keria, and if she's really so ugly, were you thought she was all inspiring, why kill yourself to save a pile of garbage, hmm?" asked the voice.

"Nathan, still around?" Tia asked.

"Yeah, wish I wasn't."

"Don't talk like that now. Usually where there's doubt, you gotta cut it out. I'm sure plenty existed before the fantasy took over. Otherwise, you never would have left Silverhill. You would have dealt with the grief to be with her. He would have been your source of light. If that person you saw her as truly existed, you would have thought she was worth fighting for."

"Enough!" Nathan bellowed. "You mentioned my grandfather, Albert. What else do you know about my family?"

Tia dropped her hands and leaned on her right side. The shadows around her continued to move with unnatural beats. "They were so challenged. Especially your father. Alan was an asshole, and your mother was a punching bag with feelings. The two made a great American family," she said sarcastically.

"What?"

"Oh, stop. Listen."

A spine-gnawing sound echoed from behind Nathan. After a single snap, he heard all he needed to hear. Beside him, the face of his mother held stiffly on to a thin representation of her body. A noose, wrapped firmly around her pale neck, caught the corner of Nathan's eye.

She whispered, "Eve's been a bad girl. Gave into temptation."

"Get away!" Nathan flung his revolver into the image. It discharged into wavy lines of mist and fled into the darkness to recharge.

"Sometimes it's required to see these things to better understand them. Especially for people like you."

"I saw all I needed to see in the mine! I'm done with these mirages!"

"But yet you still need answers. How do you intend on achieving your desire without my help? What are you going to do? Ask that voice in your head? It couldn't care less about your mental well-being. Fun fact, the less control a human has, the more jurisdiction we gain."

Nathan had one last set of questions he needed answering to, and seeing as Tia was the only one who'd supply the answers, he had to ask her. "One thing, since you know so much," Nathan said mockingly.

Tia rose an eyebrow.

"What really happened to my father, Maria, and Sophia?"

"Good questions. I've been waiting to tell you ever since you came back. As you know, Mommy was busy entertaining Daddy, willingly or not, leaving you and Sophia alone for a good portion of the day, or am I wrong?"

"Keep going," Nathan said.

"Alan and Howard were tight, two alcoholics who knew how to fish and occasionally gamble. Like two peas in a pod. So that day when one of those storms rolled by, Howard got his karma."

"Maria."

"Yes, Howard's wife was out at sea during the natural phenomenon of a high-winded, rainy storm. Only we had a slight influence. In our prodigious manifestation, the temperature dropped, and lightning and thunder heightened above the average expectancy. We didn't intend to kill her. She was caught in the storm is all, and as Alan was attached to Howard, he fell into the same scenario. Howard got through and experienced the loss of a friend. It turns out you were next. Have I mentioned children are easy targets? Sophia was discovered long before the storm. In that heightened energy, she was dragged away."

"But why would her parasite kill her? It doesn't make any sense."

"Some hosts are better than others. For whatever reason, the being inside of Sophia was not comfortable with her. So she was disposed. But don't put the blame on yourself. Such things are out of your power."

Nathan felt exploited. For too many years, these questions haunted him, and here were the answers coming from a bizarre source. *Now what? Fight back or give into the odds?*

Nathan fell into a bad habit of checking around Tia instead of paying attention to her. He knew the others were much weaker, but they showed him terror he wished he could gouge from his mind. He auto-focused toward the dark.

"So what will it be? Stay and get diseases from that whore, or let her die and live a peaceful life in the Miles Winery? Think it over. I know it's difficult."

"I'll take my chances fighting. David broke free of your trance. Maybe Keria can do the same if I can't kill you. Besides, she'll stay in that coma whether I die or not, right?"

"I knew from the start that your noble behavior would be trouble."

"And your job was too good to be true. All that kindness doesn't make up from harming Keria. And threatening me like this? Fuck you."

"We travel in the air too long. I hate killing a host prematurely, but you're giving me no other option."

"Do I look like I care?" Nathan held his revolver firmly, studying both Tia and the shadows. They were becoming one in the same.

He caught glimpses of eyes flaring orange and white until these beings finally revealed themselves, as steady and hesitant as he was before returning from Rotor. *They knew they were weak*, Nathan thought.

And Tia didn't care. She commanded the others to help her. She was the most powerful. Or was she? Nathan had a better hold on flesh, and while proven that these otherworldly creatures could inflict harm in their airy form, he had the advantage. But then there was the thing in Tia.

"Last chance," she said.

Nathan returned a gesture that inflamed her. He got tired of repeating himself.

Tia rose her hands up and said, "You wanted this." And in a sudden gush of alien pressure, Tia's body was removed from view like a hurricane stealing a bedsheet off a drying line outside.

The creatures that revealed themselves appeared childlike, but were anything but a young human. Some had orange eyes, and others were grey, but they all glistened with their own light in the dark. *The manifestation of a deranged nanny*, Nathan thought. *The way these entities work is they take imagery from the human mind, like they couldn't come up with their own, as if where they lived was dull, plain, or utterly black.*

Or maybe they wanted to psych Nathan out. Whatever the reason, they inched closer and closer. He had to think fast. He shot a creature twice. The bullet went through, which merely distorted the childlike figure momentarily. The one on the left leaped into the air and landed on Nathan with unnerving motion. Nathan went to grab it, but his hands leaked through its body. But he felt the weight of a tiny balloon lean against his chest where the creature attached itself. He was there.

Soon, all five were on him, but they had little effect in pushing him down. *They were the weight of a party balloon.* But his first acceptance of the creatures was wrong. They weren't trying to weigh him down. With every passing second, he felt his energy diminish. They were sucking it dry.

"Get off me!" he shouted, but the things were glued on him like feathers on static-charged fabric.

By the time they detached themselves from Nathan's body, he felt more ill than tired. They managed to drain him, but not nearly enough to stop him. However, though the five in the room left to recharge, there were countless others below, now ready to flood into the room. And the five would come back once ready.

Nathan wasted no time. The shadows carrying Tia fled along with her. There were only two places she could go to. There were limits of travel, a boundary of flesh he could take advantage of. *Tia was inside the lighthouse now*, Nathan thought, hoping to God her little devils drained him. *If I could just—*

"Wrong," said the voice.

Tia pounced from the darkness and held Nathan down by handling both his hands, keeping them nailed to the floor like magnets on a fridge.

"How long do you think your disguise could last, huh? You've killed too many!"

"Oh, please. Such horse shit." Tia mocked. "I own this town's sense of judgment."

"The FBI will come back once they hear of another murder this soon!"

"Nathan, shut up. They won't." Tia smiled and eased her grip. "They won't because Sun Child is now a place of freaks. Once a freak, always a freak. And when another murder is displayed proudly, in what the media would say is a cult-like manner, Sun Child will once again be the cause."

"You don't know that. And even if you're right, what about David and April? They'll turn the attention to you before you get the chance to fiddle with my or Shelly's corpse."

"My, you are a morbid fellow. I don't know about you but—" Tia tightened her grip. "I'm not concerned."

Tia's head drew near Nathan's, as if she were about to chew his face off. Her eyes captured his, and he drifted far away like he had on his self-created dream boat. Nathan realized Tia's eyes weren't dilated like David's and Shelly's were when they were under her influence. He guessed she was an exception to that side effect. A host's eyes were deemed normal, but not the ones he manipulated.

"Only once in a while," whispered the voice, "does the host's eyes turn dark and dreary. Like a collapse or sudden misstep by the eye muscles, giving way to the true colors of the one wearing them, human or inhuman. Yours were always dreary. Never once did they even try to fight me. Only in sleep have they dilated."

Nathan felt the collapse. Tia's eyes weren't fighting anymore. As they relaxed, her pupils slowly consumed the white portions of her eyes. He expected the darkness to stop at the eyes, but it carried out past the lids and spread across her face like webby strings. She was morphing into something else now. Though Tia was long gone, he felt like she was still inside her body, just being controlled by whatever these things truly were. But she wasn't anywhere in the lighthouse, the mine, or the earth. Hell, she wasn't present on this plane of time. And neither would Keria if he didn't fight back.

The webby dark that manifested wasn't a simple illusion like the others portrayed. It was an alien-like method used to connect skin and soul. Only in this case, the parasite was using its soul. Instead of connecting thoughts, it was all flesh and bone. This creature was more than a spider sucking in the blood of its food. It didn't feed off Tia's body, but rather stole its controls.

"I'll admit you're right. If I let April and David go, they'll fuck everything up. So I won't have the winery anymore. I'll have to play dead. But I still have what I came here for, a collection of flesh and bone. By changing, I'll look disfigured, but to hell with the quiet life. I can fix this new bodily figure another day, someplace else where people like you don't sniff around."

"Yeah, good luck with that," Nathan said.

"Rotor sounds nifty. Imagine what we could do in such a deprived place and who we could control."

"I'd rather not."

Tia no longer sounded like Tia, and her face was without detail. It was empty of eyes, a mouth, and nose. It caved in on itself, looking like a pink pothole. Where was her voice coming from? Who knew? As for the blackness that tainted her face just moments ago, it wavered aside to conjure its needs from the remains of Tia Miles' body. Nathan broke free of her nearly weightless hands and rolled away, stood up, and aimed at the grizzly transformation that, even though he disbelieved, was taking place before his eyes, his undiluted, cold, disheartened, and not (most certainly) dilated eyes.

Where the webby darkness skulked, the skin would cave in, just as her face had. The jerky shadows were draining all aspects of the body it could use. Soon, Tia's body was a feathery bundle of pink, ugly, weathered collection of loose, flag-like skin that blew in the drafts, giving off as an excise effect of the paranormal entities.

The one responsible for the nightmarish transformation rose up in its new form and shoved Tia's useless body aside. It made a soft thump on the ground as if a cat landed after jumping off a table. Odors were released from the process, smelling like rotten eggs mixed with old cheese with a hint of mothballs. Nathan's eyes went bloodshot. His senses were suffering from the odors, an allergic reaction.

The flesh of the creature was smooth and slick, using the color of white so pale that it could be mistaken for a ghost. Its head appeared disfigured, like it had been smashed in with a shovel repeatedly. Its eyes were sockets of shade with a cut for a nose and a mouth that slanted downward and looked unmovable, locked in place by misplaced muscle.

"You're an abomination, you know that?" Nathan said.

It couldn't speak, not with the way its mouth formed. It turned out that it did need it to speak. It jolted away from sight. And Nathan felt the pressure and dread of uncertainty. He heard snapping bones, ones crudely assembled and less thought out or understood by the entity. For years, it harbored the body, yet even still, it didn't know every piece enough for a proper redesign.

Childlike figures crept out of the dark, trying to distract Nathan from the real threat. They attached themselves to his feet, again feeling rubbery, but they were too light to pose much of a threat. He followed the chilling sounds of a working nightmare until they fell silent.

The hatch to the mine was moving. The others were now soaking through its wooden surface to reach the room's higher level. He had to end this now or be overwhelmed. But how? He searched the area and found six flares taped together, sitting half-cloaked in moonlight.

Despite having the tiny figures latching onto his legs, Nathan made it to the aging stock of supplies and grabbed the flares. He still needed a match to ignite them. He blindly searched with his hand, pulling out of box he felt. Oddly, he felt cold skin touch him on his fourth try. He quickly pulled his hand back as the pale face of the fleshy parasite revealed itself, entering the gleam. Nathan took his knife and stabbed it in the cheek. It wheezed and jolted away again, taking the knife with it.

"Shit!" Nathan flung his hand back in the dark and pulled out another box. This time, it was matches.

"Doesn't matter," said the voice. "What little this can do."

The creature launched its wavy arms at Nathan, tossing him around like a rag doll, intending to throw him into dangerous objects. It managed several times, slamming him into the side of the stairway. The impacts felt worse than the goddamn burning inflicted by the salty water from the ocean that entered his open cuts. Nathan caught one of its hands before his lungs were crushed and jammed his knife deeper into its odd flesh. With a grim whimper, the creature went into hiding. After lighting a flare, the creature finally went up into the lighthouse.

Spangle had eerie noises at night, but not like this. Instead of hearing swaying chains and creaking metal, howling wind, and what sounded like the sea moving, bones cracked, and an anonymous muffled vocal vibrated the walls.

"Where are you?" Nathan shouted. "You got me here. What are you waiting for?"

The entire bottom floor of the lighthouse had a cobweb of shadowy diamonds as the light from the lantern room above pierced through the black gridded stairway. Nathan tossed flares in each corner, turning the moonlight-struck bottom of the lighthouse bright red. The being was attached to the wall above, peering down with empty eyes and veins and whatever else it could make work inside its structure. It hurled away up to the nearest dark spot.

Nathan grabbed four more flares that lay beside the second hatch to the cage room and, one by one, lit them on his way up to the top, killing off any darkness the being nested in. The ghostly creature scurried away with every new flare. *It wasn't so tough*, Nathan thought.

Looking down, the red smoke was beginning to fade on the bottom. There was no time to waste. The other things had to be manifesting. He was out of flares, and the monster was up with Spangle's beam. But up here, Tia wasn't hiding outside. She was standing beside the light, squeezed inside the glass room.

Nathan watched in horror as the creature reassembled its mouth. Once finished, it said in a mellow, unheard of tone, "Such a solemn expression for a hopeful man whose dreams have come true overnight, only to lose them to a thing like me. Do you not care?"

"If I did not care, then why am I here?"

"You show no sorrow. After all, you've seen in Black Bell, here in this lonely old cone. What does it take for you to mourn?"

"I've mourned enough. Let me introduce you to how the real human condition works. Not that you deserve to be shown. Something like you doesn't belong in our world."

"Your efforts are all in vain. She will die by you if not by me. Tell me, Mr. Love, how are you saving her?"

Nathan peered toward the lantern and closed his eyes every time its light swung by. He raised his revolver and shot the glass, intending to pierce the lantern's flow of oil until his clip was empty. This took the creature's full attention.

And the voice in Nathan's head hollered, "No!"

The ghostly parasite launched itself at Nathan, but he still had a knife left. He took it out and stabbed it in its forehead. The knife dealt fatal damage, which didn't kill the creature but fazed it enough to give Nathan enough time. He heard echoes of high-pitched screams and muttering below. *They manifested*, Nathan thought. *They'll all here for the show.*

He lit two matches and tossed them where the oil leaked. He leaped toward the figure and knocked it off the top of the lighthouse. The creature wrapped its tentacle-like arms around Nathan's waist and chest, but the heat from the flames nearby dried their undernourished flesh enough to curl them, rendering their hold weak. They fell like comets toward the angry water as the flames ignited into an explosion. It wasn't movie worthy but would have scorched any living thing to its bones.

The being was dead weight, and its real shadowy form fled away into the night. It gave up, leaving its ugly creation behind. Nathan soon felt the water's impact hit him hard in the back of his head. The creature had managed one last fatal attack on his chest. He faced upward at the wavy surface, through both the top and murky space between it. Nathan could see a glimpse of the lighthouse, which burned like a torch. Soon, the bottom of the cliff was all he could manage to see.

The nightmare where Keria lay dead and empty flooded his every thought, as the water did his lungs. And he realized that they lost. Keria wasn't going to be that empty husk. There was nothing keeping her down. Not even the thing inside him could reach her now. He heard echoes of unearthly vibrations from beneath him. Entities were in the water. But it didn't matter. He could face whatever lay next. Keria was safe in his reality, sane or not. In his mind, he spent the last moments of his life the best he could. So he submitted to the eerie, airless darkness. It was time to reclaim the soul of his love and his own, and he left that task to the sea.

EPILOGUE

Keria awoke with a feminine gasp. Her eyes were wide open as she shot up into sitting position in her hospital bed. Nurse Becky Mills was in the room, caring to the desk for any possible misplaced needles and such when she heard her.

"Miss Miles!" she exclaimed.

Keria was home that night, and she gazed out her bedroom window, watching dark clouds move hastily across the late evening sky.

"Nathan, what happened to everyone?" she said softy, placing her gentle hand on the window. "Where are you?"

Inside Howard's dark home, someone was scribbling, madly and eagerly. It was the therapist sent by Tia, and he was murmuring as he kept a smile across his face, peering down at a sheet of paper with dilated eyes. He muttered repeatedly in a high, childlike whisper, "Nope, nope, no crazy here. Nope."

Howard approached him with a harrowing grin. He and others alike were missing.

Missing but not empty.

ABOUT THE AUTHOR

Inspired by his love of horror, Bob Koob started writing his own stories in high school. He later finished Tales of Wetherfield, a collection of intertwining short stories. A native of Philadelphia, he now lives in Warminster, Pennsylvania.